# Roya

## Elnaz Moghangard

*To the feelers, wanderers, and dreamers,*
*this is for you.*

## Acknowledgements

I want to begin by thanking my teachers and professors for motivating me to live out my potential. You were my superheroes.

Thank you to one special teacher, mentor, and friend, K.B. You inspired my enthusiasm for writing in your 10th grade class. A decade later, you were the first to read my book. It was your voice of encouragement that made me believe I could complete this story.

Thank you to the most talented artist I know, my aunt Shila Vasseghi. Having you design my cover has meant the world to me. I am deeply and forever grateful for the time you invested in supporting my dreams. We are a team.

Thank you to my aunt Shiva for inspiring confidence, my family for exemplifying resilience, and my parents, Mahmood and Shahrzad, for giving me the gift of this life. To my sister Sanaz, my brother Iden, and my cousins, I am grateful we have each other. I love you.

Thank you to my grandma, my first storyteller.

Thank you to my friends, the families we choose. You are my soul tribe.

Thank you to my American and Iranian roots. I am proud to be both.

And thank you to everyone who has touched my life and crossed my path. I am who I am because of you.

"Energy cannot be created or destroyed, it can only be changed from one form to another."

-- Albert Einstein

∞

If love is energy, then love itself cannot be created or destroyed. It has always existed. It will continue to exist.

It simply changes form.

# SHADOWS

# CHAPTER 1

She looks into his eyes and sees a glare so piercing that it strikes through her heart. She doesn't know what hurts more, that he no longer recognizes her or that she no longer recognizes him. Just after the eruption of heavy words carelessly thrown, she feels the weight push against her lungs. Even breathing feels dangerous when he is her air.

In that moment, time stands still. People say such things, and she never understood until now —knowing that it was over, but unable to move. She tries to find a glimpse of who he was to her, but he is nowhere to be found. What she is really looking for is a sight of herself. All she finds is a reflection of pain.

"Roya, you're over exaggerating. It's not a big deal. You are being crazy! What the hell."

"Oh, I am being crazy? You do whatever the hell you want, but when I confront you about it, I am being crazy? You lied to me. I trusted you. How could you do that?"

"Whatever, Roya. I'm not dealing with this right now." He starts to turn his back away from her, but pauses not knowing what else to do. There are no magic words that can erase the mistakes.

"I'm not even surprised anymore. You never want to talk about it. You just want to run away. You're not the guy I knew anymore."

"Well, maybe I'm not! What do you want from me? I'm done talking about this." He's breathing heavily now and presses his fingers to his temples.

"Nothing, Cyrus. I don't want anything from you." She can feel the heat rising from the pit of her belly, through her heart, and into her throat. "I hate you."

The words spill before she can swallow them back. She regrets it as soon as the sentence begins, but it is too late. The stillness in the air becomes almost unbearable.

"Yeah, yeah, YEAH?!" His voice begins to rise. She can tell his sadness is being translated as anger ––the only emotion she has seen him lose control of. As his voice crescendos, her heartbeat begins its own surround sound madness. Then, there is a silence more piercing than even their banter.

*No. No, I don't hate you. I hate that we're fighting. I hate that you can't understand. I hate that we are so close, yet everything feels so distant. I hate that I have allowed myself to be consumed by emotions that I have yet to understand. I hate that I love you so much, and you don't even see it. I hate that you will never see it. But, no, I do not hate you. I don't think it's possible to hate someone you love.*

The cascade of thoughts consumes her mind, yet she holds back.

"Yeah." Once again, her words fall into the dry summer air. He catches them with both ears as if he was anticipating her reaction. From the look in his eyes, she can tell he tastes the bitterness.

She knows she should move, but she can't. She knows she should have responded more rationally, but there is nothing rational about how she feels. She feels betrayed. She feels crazed, wrapped in a cycle of desire, pain, nostalgia, and numbness. The decision has been made already. She saw this coming before the moment arrived, yet her feet remain glued to the wetness of the damp grass underneath her.

She can tell he is hesitant too. A part of him knows the end has already arrived. This is their prolonged goodbye ––like a grand finale with no encore.

"Well, I hate you too. You're dead to me." The words fly like bullets.

More silence ensues. The moment is so fragile that nothing but the sound of them breathing can fill the empty space between them.

When she finally musters the courage to turn away, time fast-forwards so quickly as if it was making up for the motionless seconds wasted. With her back turned, one foot taking the lead of the other forward, that's when she allows herself to release a single tear. Even then, the emotion is foreign to her. She knows she is losing two people today. She is losing him and herself —a bittersweet mixture of sorrow and ecstasy. Life is sure to change. So, she bends down gently, cups her hand, and picks up her heart from the muddy earth.

# CHAPTER 2

"Roya, why are you so quiet today?" Her mother asks as she reaches for the platter of *tahdig* and *ghormeh sabzi*.

She stares at the dirt green stew. How can something pretty ugly taste so damn delicious she wonders. Since childhood, it has been a favorite of hers. Power walking from the bus stop to the poignant scent tingling her nose, her first reaction was to lift the lid of the steaming pot. She would watch with wide eyes as the condensed liquid dripped onto her little hands when she peered inside. She had so much energy then. Always running, always dancing ––fascinated with the boiling process of stew.

"Roya, I am talking to you."

She snaps out of her thoughts as she reaches for the plate her mom has filled to the brim.

"I'm fine mom. I'm just tired." She hopes this answer will be enough.

"Tired? What do you mean tired? What did you do today besides sleep?"

*No, of course it isn't enough.* She sighs to herself. *I always have to explain myself.*

"It's nothing mom. I just don't feel good." She runs her fork in circles as the green juice colors the white basmati rice. She can hear her stomach speaking, but can't eat with the lump stuck in her throat.

"You don't feel good? What's wrong? Do you want me to make you some chai with mint?"

Roya slips a disgruntled giggle at the idea of chai and mint --the cure all for almost everything but a broken heart. Not even vodka could wash down the aftertaste of separation.

"No, it's okay. *Merci,* but not right now. Maybe later." She replies and excuses herself from the table.

****

The night feels so surreal --the sky is a foggy hue of navy and gray. Through the window, she can see the moon peeking at her from between the scattered clouds. Its dim light briefly passes through the room before hiding behind the clouds once again and leaving her in the still darkness. She turns her back to the window and faces the wall. Doesn't really matter which way she turns, she can't see anything but the sparkling tricks her eyes are playing.

She tries to hold them back, but the tears begin against her will.

*I can't even control my own tears. I can't control anything.*

The tears start softly as if comforting her as she begins to gasp heavily for air. These spurts of anxiety always sneak up on her when she is alone. Curling like a child with her knees tucked to her chest, she wraps her arms around herself. Being back in her childhood home makes her feel like she is twelve rather than twenty-two.

Memories walk through her mind like travelers in an unknown place --guided by careful, yet curious steps. Her thoughts drift to how her mother would hold her when she was young. The way she would run her soft hands through her hair and hum the tunes of Andy as little Roya fell asleep. This was the same tune she would hum as she prepared lunch --waving the spatula in the air like a composer. The same tune she would hum in the rare moments a bewildered Roya would witness her release a single tear and wipe it away.

The murmur of the air conditioning disrupts the silence as Roya lies there thinking of her mother's strength and fragility, like broken shards of glass constructed together to make a mosaic. She wishes she could enter her room now and rest beside her again      —hoping the pain in her own chest would fade away. But, the years have paved a bridge between them. She is close, yet feels so far. And an embarrassed Roya does not have the courage to show her how weak she has become.

She tosses around as the moonlight's shadow passes over her room once more. Pulling the blanket to her chin, she closes her eyes and continues to cry. She tries to hum her mother's tune and lull herself to a brief slumber. For some reason, it doesn't feel the same when she sings her song.

****

The sound of rippled knocks against her pastel blue double doors awakens her in the morning.

"Royaaaa." Her grandmother's tickled voice sings from outside.

Peeling the covers gently, she stretches like a stray Persian cat would after sleeping through a rainy night in some alley. Staring at her toes, she lifts her prickly legs up into the air. Just then, her grandma barges through the door and throws herself on the corner of the bed. Roya fumbles to throw the covers over her bare body still tucked in cheek hugging underwear.

"What are you doing up here *dokhtaram*? Come. Let's go downstairs and have some chai. It's almost noon."

"Okay. Let me change."

"Okay."

"Mamani, I need to change."

"Okay, so get up! I used to wash you when you were a baby. There's nothing I haven't seen. Now, get up. Let's go. You can't hide up here. Put on some—"

"Okay."

She finally leaves. Roya musters the strength to jump out of bed, slip on a pair of jeans, and throw on her favorite navy hoodie.

Mamani is singing Googoosh oldies from below the railway now —

a song Roya recognizes from her younger years but cannot recall the name. Gliding her fingers against the wooden rail, she follows the scent of Mamani's Chanel 5 perfume into the kitchen.

"Bah, bah. There is my Roya. How are you feeling?"

"I'm fine. I slept so much, but I'm still so tired."

"Well, of course." She laughs through her grin.

"Roya jaan, let's go for a walk. We can go by the park. Remember when you were younger? We would count all the birds we saw and give them names? Those were lovely days, you and I."

"Mamani, that was forever ago. Anyway, I don't really feel like leaving the house today. I have a loyal friend waiting for me named Netflix."

"Netflix, chexmix. *Pshh!* Forget that today."

Roya's lips curl at the way her grandmother's thick accent distorts the syllables and makes them her own. "Uhhh, I really don't feel like––"

"Look, you are a young lady now, but you will always be my little *maymoon* first. Come! Let's go together."

Her 2002 Mercedes sedan smells like childhood summers ––the blended aroma of aged leather and sunscreen. Seats textured with memories of having crammed the wet little bodies of Roya and her younger sister Azadeh after a long day of playing at the pool. Today, the combination rushes through her nostrils. For a split second, she remembers what it feels like to be a child intoxicated with the endless possibilities the future promises.

Roya can feel the tires ride over the gravel road as she slides down in her seat and rests her head on the edge of the window. The summer heat is consuming. The dry air slowly wraps around her. As the car carries on, the moving images blend into one. Tree after tree, she watches as they disappear.

Her head feels light, but her heart is heavy. She can't seem to erase the image of him standing before her one last time. The way he looked at her as though she had trespassed into his life. The way his shoulders bent with tension, and his body language screamed *do not leave, but get away from me.*

Just as she had gotten comfortable in her thoughts, she feels the car come to a stop, reverse, drive forward, and stop again as her grandmother adjusts the parking.

"Ah, we have arrived, Roya jaan. What a beautiful day. Can you smell natuuure calling us?" Her singing voice rings with artificial optimism.

"It kind of smells like geese poo and salt."

"Exactly. Wonderful. Let's go enjoy it all! This, THIS is what life is all about. These moments together."

They walk past the brick entrance leading into the open space of the park, sprinkled with benches lining the lake in the middle. The canopy of trees shields some of the sunlight and provides momentary relief from the heat. One Nike clad foot after another, they follow the cement trail until Roya feels her throat clog and her stomach gut itself.

"Mamani, let's turn around. NOW, please."

"Eh, why? What's wrong?"

"I, I, I feel sick."

Her heart feels heavy again, but this time her head is spinning laps around itself. She sees him walking towards them from the distance with two of his friends. He is smiling and waving his hands around as he speaks. She wonders if he has seen them yet.

Just then Mamani follows the look of fear in Roya's eyes to its source.

"Is that—"

"Cyrus. Yes, that is him. I'm so not ready for this right now. Can we please turn around?"

Tugging at her grandmother's arms, she ushers her towards the benches near the lake. Beads of sweat decorate her skin. She finds the seat farthest from the trail, so she is hidden from his view. It has been weeks since she last saw him. Her reaction unsettles her.

*What the hell is wrong with me? Why did I just do that? Why can't I just say hi like a normal person? It's not a big deal, right? Little pieces of people shatter every day, right?*

She sits on the wooden bench as her grandmother stares across the lake's rippled waters.

"Roya jaan." She calls without turning.

No answer.

"Roya."

"Yes, Mamani?" Roya replies half present. Her mind is still racing ––taming the intrusive emotions she had tried so hard to suppress in the previous days.

"Roya, why did you run like that? Away from him?" Mamani gently asks with her back still turned facing the water.

"I don't know." She gulps a clot of saliva stuck in her throat. "I, I just wasn't expecting that. Not today. Not right now. I just––"

She feels the uncomfortable, yet familiar rush begin. Her dark brown eyes soften as the sun reveals the tints of soft caramel in her pupils. Soon, water has gathered in her eyes. She tilts her head down feeling defeated. Ashamed once more to be seen like this in front of her grandmother, but unable to contain herself. She sobs and sobs. Finally, she manages to utter a few words.

"I just love him. Am I stupid for being this way? I feel so stupid. This is not who I used to be."

A few geese splash down into the water. Mamani watches as a lone goose floats just behind its family. She stands tall ––planted firmly in her wisdom and years of experience. Before facing Roya, she quickly wipes a tear from her eye. Her life has been riddled with hardships, but watching Roya ache is something she cannot bear. As soon as she turns around, she stretches her red lips into a smile and walks with grace towards her granddaughter. She sits down and places her hand on Roya's shoulder.

"You are not stupid. What is stupid about having loved? What is stupid about having taken a chance? You are brave. So many people cannot give their hearts the way you do."

Roya looks up at her Mamani. The sobbing has turned to slow tears leaving a stain of mascara on her rosy cheeks. She looks at her grandmother with her puffy eyelids and scoots closer so that Mamani can wrap her arms around her.

"Well, I just feel so stupid. He looked so...so okay."

Mamani squeezes her tightly and gives her a kiss on top of her head as Roya's thick, black hair falls in her face. She takes a tissue from her purse and wipes the black smudge from her cheeks.

"We don't know people's inner pains. You don't know whether or not he is okay. Either way, I can tell you one thing. Sometimes life seems like a string of broken fairytales, but that does not mean the dream is broken. This whole life, *dokhtaram*, is one grand dream."

"I appreciate you wanting to help. But, this feels more like a nightmare than a dream right now."

Mamani chuckles. "One day, my love, you will come to understand that even pain can be beautiful. So beautiful and comfortable that we choose to never leave it. But, I want you to promise me one thing."

"Sure."

"I'm serious. Look at me for a moment."

Roya lifts her head and unravels herself from Mamani's embracing arms.

"The moment that pain becomes beautiful, you must turn it into art and then move on." Mamani stares through her granddaughter's pupils with a fierce gentleness. "Do not stay in pain, Roya jaan. It is the drug of all poetic souls."

Roya listens closely as her tears dry and again leave wet stains on her cheeks. She feels the wind --just for a moment-- brush through her hair and send a wave of coolness behind her neck. She takes a deep breath and then leans into her grandmother without speaking a word. Mamani understands. Sometimes even a single word can disrupt the beauty of a shared stillness. She wraps her arms around her granddaughter and rests her chin on top of her head.

They watch the river carry fallen branches in its current. The geese continue to move together in small flocks. There is an energy in the air that Roya can sense deeply as if it were moving through her. She wants to express it to Mamani, but can't seem to find the words. It isn't a feeling the human language has words for. As soon as the sensation had arrived, it leaves. Roya still sits trying to understand its meaning.

"Mamani?" Roya finally speaks.

"Yes?"

"There are five of them."

"Five what?"

"Five geese."

Mamani smiles. "Oh, so you're not too old to play our game after all?"

"I guess not!" Deep down Roya knows she can never tire of her grandmother's games. They are the last bits of her childhood she feels she can hold onto. "And that one there —that white one in the back with the patches of gray and tint of blue on the head— I think we should call her Naya."

"Naya, lovely. And why Naya?"

"I don't know. I just like it. Sounds graceful."

"I believe in Arabic the name means *renewal*."

"Oh, it does? That seems nice, to start over. To feel new."

"Mamani gives Roya a tight squeeze. "Roya jaan, if only you knew what I know."

"What is that?"

"That you are already on your way. You see, we die many times in one life. We get lost and found and then lost again. Each time we arrive one step closer to the person we are meant to become. Do not fear becoming lost. Worry about the day when you believe there is nothing new to discover. That is the day you become a fool."

"What if I can't? What if I just stay stuck like this? What happens then?"

"Tell me this. Would you like to move on? Would you actually like to find yourself? You must decide, because real growth is messy."

"Yes. I just don't know how. Maybe I can't. There was a time I could envision my future so clearly, but everything I thought would happen didn't. Everything I wanted seems to have slipped away. I don't even know what I want anymore."

"You must make a choice if you want to step forward."

"What step forward? There are no steps, Mamani! I don't even know what you are talking about anymore. Everything you say sounds so easy to hear, but that's not life. The dots don't perfectly connect. Things don't just work out."

Mamani is patient and calm. She takes a long, deep breath and feels the air travel down her lungs. Her chest rises and falls as she releases the breath through her nostrils. "All that matters is that you decide you want to. That is all for now, my dear." She smiles at her granddaughter with eyes that speak of refuge. "Now, speaking of steps, let's get some walking in!"

Roya licks her index fingers and tries to rub the remainder of mascara from under her eyelids. They step  onto the trail and head towards the wishing fountain near the playground in the middle of the park. This was Roya's favorite spot. As a kid, she used to sit on the edge of the fountain, run her hands in the water, and then giggle when Mamani would chase her off.

*"Roya! That water is dirty! Stop!"*

She'd then wipe Roya's hands with a napkin. She always had a napkin in her purse. And pennies too. She would hand Roya and Azadeh one each time and tell them to make a wish.

*"Not just any wish, kids. Your dreams...think of your dreams!"*

They'd hold their breath, make their wish, and toss the penny into the fountain with their eyes closed.

*"What did you dream, Roya?"* Azadeh would beg her sister as she tugged on her arm.

*"Well, I can't tell you! Or else, it won't come true. You have to keep it to yourself!"*

*"Pleaaase, Roya. I won't tell."*

*"I know, I know."* She'd say with a smile but never give it away.

As they near the fountain just around the loop, Roya's childlike excitement returns. She puts her hair up in a ponytail, takes it down after a few seconds, and settles on a loose braid. They complete the loop, but the fountain is dry and covered in heaps of dirt.

Mamani points to the sign. "It's under construction."

"Oh, okay. Well, let's just complete the loop and go home then. It's too hot anyway."

Mamani pulls out a penny from her wallet full of coins. "What about your wish? It's tradition."

"There's no fountain?"

"So?"

"So, it kind of defeats the point of tradition."

"Tradition is what we give meaning to. Today, we make a new one!" She extends her hand to Roya.

She takes it from her grandmother as she closes her eyes. A few moments pass, and she opens her eyes. "Okay, done! Where should I put it?"

"Look around. Wherever you want."

Roya scans her surroundings. At first, she considers the neatly trimmed bushes decorated with peonies. She then turns her attention to a tall palm tree bending slightly to the side. She looks down and notices a peony laying on the ground, picks it up, and walks over to the "Under Construction" sign. She places the penny in the dirt with the peony on top.

"Ready!"

"Why that spot?"

"Why not?"

Mamani shrugs, and the two of them continue down the path side-by-side.

****

The smell of *zereshk polo* and onions invites Mamani and Roya in as they enter the living room. Roya runs upstairs to rinse off and change into something comfortable before lunch. On the way, she peeks her head into Azadeh's room and stands there with one hand on the doorway and the other on her hip.

"Heeey, watchya doing?" Roya says with a goofy inflection.

"Nothing. Just sitting here. How was the walk with Mamani?"

"It was...hot. Too hot, but nice."

"Well, that's good then."

"Yeah, it is. So... I saw Cyrus."

"Oh, really? How did that go?"

"Fine, I guess. I didn't talk to him. He didn't see me."

"Why didn't you say hi?"

"I don't know. I just froze. I mean, there's nothing really to say anyway. I think we already said enough. I don't even care."

"Mhm, right." Azadeh responds without looking up from her screen.

"What the hell is that supposed to mean?" Roya senses herself growing agitated by her sister's nonchalance.

"Nothing."

"It didn't sound like nothing."

"Well, what did you want me to say?"

"I don't know. Something else, anything else. What is a *mhm* supposed to mean?" Roya now stands tall in the center of the doorway and takes a step forward into the room.

"All I'm saying is that you obviously do care. Why are you getting so defensive?"

"Because you're just sitting on your laptop and barely looking at me. This is kind of a big deal."

"Right. So, you just admitted it's a big deal to you?" Azadeh's tone is neutral and aloof —the way a voice sounds when someone is typing while speaking the words to themselves out loud.

"Alright, Azadeh. Well, how was your day?"

"Fine, I guess. Just school. Nothing special happened."

"Nice."

"Oh and heads up! Mom and Dad want to talk to you about your school stuff today. I heard them talking. Thought you'd want to know, so you're ready."

Roya's nerves jolt her awake. *Why today. Why of all days, today. This is not what I need right now.*

"Great. Guess I better brace myself. Thanks for the heads up."

"Yeah, no problem. Just try not to get into it with them tonight. Okay? Just let them say what they need to, and try to stay quiet. Kinda don't want any drama tonight."

"I'll be fine. Thanks though. I got this. See you in a bit."

Roya leaves her sister's room feeling dissatisfied. Carefully, she steps into the shower and turns on the water —gradually adjusting the temperature. She turns her neck in a circle and stretches. The smell of lavender body gel combined with water running down her back is soothing. She begins to hum to herself as she often does when she is alone. These moments of solitude give her mind the freedom to wander —daydreaming of all the things she longs to create, of other lives and stories, of human nature and its many contradictions. These days her mind runs through images of her deepest wishes. There is the one of her basking in a standing ovation as her performance ends with the last string of the violin still reverberating in the air. Then, there is the dream of her staring into these eyes —eyes so deep as though they reflect her own soul like an infinity mirror. There's the one of her laughing with her family, and they are happy. The real kind of happy. The kind of happiness that makes the belly feel full and the mind light —like a balloon having slipped from gripping hands into the sky full of air. Then, there is the image of Cyrus. But, the images of intertwined hands, late-night conversations, and dancing lips have now been replaced with the same scene on repeat.

*"Roya,"* he had said that day. But, this time his voice was not full of admiration. Instead, it was tense and flat.

*"You're dead to me,"* he had said. As if on auto command, a piece of Roya took its last breath.

*"Wait...I didn't mean to say that,"* he had tried to apologize.

The exchange loops in her mind. Each time, it hurts to think about. But, no matter how long she stands in the shower, she can't wash away her own regret. *Why did I say I hate him? Why didn't I just tell him I felt hurt? Why did I just leave like that?*

All of a sudden, Roya finds it difficult to hum. Her chest is heavy. Her lungs feel like someone is slowly closing the valve on her oxygen supply. She starts to take quick, short breaths. Then, the panic sets in.

"Azadeh!" Roya yells as she cries loudly and uncontrollably. She knows she is the only one close enough to hear. "Azadeh, come here! Something is wrong with me!"

Azadeh barges through the bathroom door. Confused and worried, she watches her sister lean against the shower wall.

"I can't breathe. I feel like the walls are caving in. I need air, Azadeh. Can you help me get out of the shower? I'm freaking out."

"Roya, what happened?" She turns off the faucet and holds her sister's arm as she steps out of the shower. "Are you okay? I think you just had an anxiety attack or something."

"I don't know. I just need to sit."

"Let me go get Mom and Dad."

"No! Please don't."

"Mamani? She will know what to do."

"No."

"Maybe some water?"

"Yes, please. Just don't say anything to anyone downstairs. I don't want them thinking there is something wrong with me."

"Okay. If that's what you want." Azadeh leaves the room and returns moments later with a tall glass of cold water.

"I think Mamani might have heard you."

"Oh, great."

"You weren't exactly whispering for help."

"I know." Roya says disappointed in herself. "I know."

"Food's ready by the way. We should go down."

"I'll be down in a minute. You go ahead."

Roya puts on a pair of loose joggers and slips on a bra and tank top. As she applies moisturizer, she stares at herself in the mirror and takes a long breath. She barely recognizes herself. Her cheeks are still pink from the steam of the hot shower, but her heartbeat is starting to slow down to its normal pace. *Get it together, Roya. Don't be so weak. Pull yourself together.*

****

The sound of spoons and forks clinking and clanking against the plates is extra loud this evening. Silence sits in the air as they pass around dishes mounted with food. Azadeh looks at Roya and then glances at their parents. They quietly adjust the napkins on their laps and pour food.

Mamani brings the last batch of spaghetti *tahdig* from the kitchen. She places the platter closest to Roya and Azadeh and whispers softly to them. "I know this is your favorite. Eat up! Eat up!"

Roya smiles. Spaghetti *tahdig* really is one of their childhood favorites, but she still has no appetite. The knot in her stomach always worsens just before a meal. This afternoon the energy is extra tense.

Finally, her father breaks the silence. "*Dokhtaraye golam*, how was your day?" He looks to Roya and Azadeh with tender eyes.

"It was good! I went to school. Pretty much it. Oh, we got our math exams back today!"

"Very nice. How did you do?"

"Better than I thought, really. A-, maybe I did get some of Roya's brains after all." Azadeh looks at her sister.

Roya knows her sister is trying to buy her time before their parents turn their attention to her.

"Don't say such things. Both of my daughters are brilliant. Azadeh, I am proud of you." Their mother smiles and takes a sip of water. "Education is the most important thing in life."

"So... how was your day? Any crazy stories about your college students? I know Dad had that one guy last semester who legit never turned in a paper. And then he caught him smoking pot in the library. I mean, the library? I'd go somewhere with some fresh air at least!" Azadeh laughs at her own comment and looks over to Mamani now for support in distracting her parents.

"Good memory, Azadeh!" Baba says encouragingly.

"My day was stressful. Very busy grading papers. But, it was nice. Thank you for asking, my love." Their mother replies patiently knowing what Azadeh is trying to do. "And you, Roya? How was your day? Mamani said you two went for a walk?"

"Yeah, it was good. We had some nice quality time." She looks over to her grandmother and smiles.

"I'm happy to hear that. Have you started your application for med schools yet?"

"Umm, kind of. I have a list of schools I want to apply to. I'm working on it."

"How about your MCAT studies? How are they coming along? If you need any help, I have a student who can help tutor you in--"

"I'm good, mom. I have all the materials to start prepping. But, thank you." Roya separates the rice from the stew on her plate to keep herself occupied.

"Very well then." Her mom looks down at her plate and then back up as if an idea jumped into her mind. "And how about the recommendations from your professors? Did you take care of that?"

"Yes." Roya now pushes the separated halves to the edges of the plate. They look like two half-moons facing one another.

"Good, good! It's all coming together. Aren't you excited? You're one step closer!"

"Excited?"

"Have you written any songs lately? I haven't heard you humming around in a while. That's all I ever used to hear around this house!" Roya's father tries to change the subject. He intertwines his hands and adjusts his body language to face Roya.

"No. Guess I haven't been inspired lately. Doesn't matter anymore anyway."

"Well, whenever you do, I'd love to hear one sometime." Roya's mother eases back into her seat and relaxes her shoulder.

"How come all of a sudden you want to hear a song? You never wanted to before." Roya snaps.

"That's not true."

"Yes, it is." She turns to Azadeh for support, but Azadeh gives her the *I really should stay out of this* look. "You don't remember when I wanted to show you my portfolio for USC? I worked so hard on that. You didn't want to hear any of it." Roya continues staring at her plate.

"Roya jaan, I didn't want to get you excited about applying only for you to be disappointed when you couldn't go. You knew the plan was med school. We agreed on this."

"Get me excited? Who doesn't want their kid to be excited about something that matters to them? You didn't even come to my final performance! Everyone else's parents were there. You didn't even re-member the date."

"We were working. What don't you understand? Mamani and Aza-deh were there. Weren't they?"

"Yes, and that meant a lot to me. But, Mamani and Azadeh are not you and dad. You two have never seen any of my work. Do you know how that makes me feel?"

"You're not a kid anymore, Roya. One day, maybe you will under-stand what we have sacrificed for you. And look now, the way you are talking to us. Music is a great hobby, but it is not a career."

"A hobby? How can you say that? Your own brother made a life and a career out of music. Why don't you believe in me? All you do is doubt me."

"Yes, your *dayee* did. And where did that get him? He lost everything when he had to leave Iran. Do you want to suffer like that? I am not raising my daughters to live in la la land, Roya. I am raising you and your sister so that you know how to survive. So you can build something that will last you."

"I understand. But, is that all that matters? To survive? What's the point of life then? You go to school your whole life. You obey instructions. You get some job. And you just survive? God, they don't even let you think for yourself these days! I don't want to be stuck doing the same thing every day until the day I die. Some people are fine with that. And for some, being a doctor is their passion. It's just not mine."

"Watch your tone." Her father motions with his hands for Roya to ease her volume.

"Roya, you will never know what your father and I have been through. We have worked extremely hard to give you this life. Where is your gratitude?"

"Maman, I am grateful. I've never done anything to disappoint you two. I've worked so hard in school. I have done everything I can to not burden you. And you're right, I don't understand what you have been through. But, you also don't understand what I'm trying to say. There has to be more to life than just existing. Why don't you want more for us? You talk like you've never had a dream before!"

"I don't believe in dreams. I believe in goals. Goals that make sense for your future." Roya's mother sits up straight in her chair now. Her shoulders are tense again. "And you're not doing us a favor by behaving well. Should we expect anything less? What you choose to do is for your own well-being! That's all we want for you."

Mamani has been quiet this entire time with her forehead resting on her clasped hands. "Delband. Roya. I think that's enough for right now." She says gently. "The food is getting cold, and you've both barely eaten."

"Yes, I think that's a great idea. These types of discussions should not be had while eating. Let's just enjoy our meal for now." Roya's father insists as he places his hand on top of his wife's.

Azadeh squeezes her sister's arm underneath the table to comfort her. Roya's cheeks are red, but she is resisting the impulse to cry at the table. She eyes her divided plate and watches as the broth from the stew slowly trickles back into the rice.

****

*Meeting someone new is like traveling to a foreign land. Falling in love with someone is like learning a culture and making it your own. The way they speak your name becomes a new language. How they hold you, like a new tradition. How they look at you, like a holiday that only you two celebrate. When it's over, that identity is stripped away from you. You are left exposed and misplaced. That's the risk when you turn people into homes. You become like an expat in your own body when they're gone.*

Roya jots her thoughts and closes her journal. The sun has set, but she has yet to turn on the lights. She doesn't mind. She feels comforted by the dark space, as if it were a blanket. The faint moonlight coming through the windows is just enough for her to write. But now, her growling stomach distracts her since she barely touched her lunch earlier. She rolls out of bed and starts making her way to the kitchen. She stops when she hears her parents' back-and-forth chatter. Sitting quietly at the bottom of the stairs, she listens to what they are saying in Farsi.

"Delband, it might be good for her to go. I'm worried about her. She's like a ghost these days."

"Kaveh, absolutely not. I can't believe you are agreeing with my mom. It is too dangerous. Not without me there."

"Dangerous? She will be with your mother and both of our families. You are worrying too much. This is her chance to go before she's busy with med school, and it might help her to get over that boy too."

"You've become so liberal these days, I see. Why can't she do that here? One of us needs to go with her."

"I suppose after all these years the American way has had an effect on me." He smiles with a shrug of the shoulders. "Sometimes, we need to leave what we know in order to find who we are. Roya's not doing well. We both can see that. Her mind is all over the place. I haven't seen her smile in so long. She's become so quiet. This is not our daughter."

"I know." Delband looks around the room conflicted. "I know, but I just want her to be safe. I don't know what has gotten into her. It's like any minute, she's going to shatter."

"Just think about it. It may be a good idea, and you know your mother. If you are the hawk, she is the leader of the flock, eh? She will make sure everyone there has an eye on her. *Mashallah.* That woman raised you and your brothers without knowing the language or customs of a new land. If she can do that, she can do anything."

*Oh, now they want to get rid of me.* Roya waits for a pause in their conversation and walks into the kitchen.

"Roya jaan, where are you going?" Her father asks startled.

"The kitchen?"

"Oh. Are you hungry?"

"Yeah, a little bit."

"It's good that your appetite is back." Her mother adds.

"It's more like a sudden craving." Roya replies in a hollow voice as she turns the corner and starts back up the stairs.

She slides under the bedsheets and places her laptop on her stomach as she reaches for the peanut butter and honey sandwich she just made. She folds the bread over so that the gooey mixture falls from the edges onto the plate.

One afternoon when Roya was eleven years old, she was at the grocery store with her mother. It was one of those coveted afternoons —scarcely any homework assigned, the sunlight just warm enough without being overbearing. Maman was feeling especially cheerful. She even let Roya push the cart and ride on it down the aisle as if it were a scooter. She always said Lucky Charms were pure sugar, let alone breakfast. But that day, Maman told Roya she could take a box and Fruit Loops too. On days like this, Roya was the most excited. Her mother's presence was palpable and her laughter like a field of sunflowers.

*"Roya jaan, Roya jaan. Azize delam. My sweet girl."* She sings as she places the items in the cart and turns to her daughter. *"Roya, what shall we make tonight? I was thinking maybe albaloo polo? Or Baba can make those burgers you and Azadeh like?"*

Roya giggles and points to the Wonder Bread toast and peanut butter in the cart.

Maman walks over and looks at her daughter. *"Ah and how did these get in here, may I ask?"*

Roya laughs once more as she hides her face behind the cart's handle.

*"May I?"* Maman takes the cart and leads them to the previous isle. She scans the shelf of peanut butter but doesn't put it back. Instead, she walks over to the next row and scans the selection of honey. She picks out the one where the bottle is in the shape of a bear and places it into the cart.

*"Peanut butter and honey?"* Roya looks at her mom confused. *"No jelly?"*

*"This used to be my favorite snack. Well, minus the Wonder Bread. When we first moved to the States, I used to eat this when I lived in the university dorms. A big spoon of peanut butter, like a mountain, and just a little bit of honey drizzled on top. The honey is the best part —always reminded me of breakfasts in Tehran. Some sarshir and honey back in the day. Mmmm! My favorite."* Her mother replies sweetly.

Together, they'd push the shopping cart, stacked with Roya's boxes of candy coated grains and Maman's jars of memories. Those afternoon errands were like time warps. They'd get lost in those aisles of canned chickpeas, refrigerated dairy, and shelved sweeteners. Loading the groceries into the car became a game too. Eager to show her mom she was a big girl, Roya would always reach for the heaviest items to carry. Together, they would unload each bag at home. Azadeh wanted to help too. Roya would tell her to gather the bags as if she were passing down the torch of grocery duty glory.

The funny thing about these special occasions was that they weren't extraordinary at all. There wasn't a celebration or an event to be had. It was just that on some days Maman decided it was okay, as if she too was living her childhood. They'd sit on the countertop, even though Maman normally said they shouldn't. She'd hand them their homemade sandwiches. The peanut butter was always too thick, and the honey slid off from the edges. Roya would laugh with her mother and sister as the afternoon rays winked through the kitchen windows and casted a warm glow. Somehow, Maman always got honey in her hair.

Roya now wipes the corners of her mouth with the side of her hand. She drags the folders on her desktop from one side to the other before opening one labeled "Miscellaneous, Things, and Dreams." She closes the folder again. The mouse hovers over it for a moment. *Bing.* The volume had been left on high, and the obnoxious noise is just another confirmation for *delete.* Her desktop is relatively organized now with the icons decorated along the screen like a border. She stares at the wallpaper. The photo of her and Cyrus had been recently replaced with an image of a pigeon.

*"That's literally a pigeon just sitting on a bench, Roya."* Azadeh critiques with a disgusted look.

*"Yes, Azadeh. It is literally a pigeon."*

*"You didn't want to pick like a dove? Or an eagle? Or, I don't know, like some dragon bird?"*

*"A dragon bird? Are you referring to a phoenix?"*

*"I mean, whatever. Something cool or magical. I feel like you're into all that symbolism. A pigeon is, well, kinda just a pigeon. And gross. And just everywhere. And annoying."*

*"First of all, a dove is just a bougie pigeon. An eagle is a bit too aggressive. And a phoenix...is just too cliché. Pigeons are super*

*underrated. I mean, c'mon. They are bold as hell. Have you walked down Hollywood Boulevard lately? Do you see those pigeons move out of the way for pedestrians? Hell no! They have claimed their space, and they aren't afraid of homosapiens! Insane. Doesn't get bolder than that."*

"So, this is what it has come to? You've moved on from Cyrus to becoming a pigeon lady? Should I tell Baba to save the bread, so you can go be Mother Teresa for the birds?"

"Ha ha, Azadeh. HA HA. So funny, you are."

"And now you're talking like Yoda. You've lost it."

"I don't remember asking for your input. Maybe I'm forgetting, because as you say, I've lost it." Roya says with a hint of sarcasm laced with playfulness.

"It's really weird how you can say something pretty rude and make it sound nice." Azadeh laughs as she lightly pushes her sister. "If you and Cyrus ever get back together, in like some parallel universe, I'm going to tell him he was replaced by a pigeon."

"Azadeh, I AM the pigeon. Don't you get it? It's like being the underdog, but way cooler than all the other mainstream, fancy birds."

"Oh, I see. You are the pigeon. Right. Well, now that you've demoted yourself to a street bird, I guess I'll be leaving!"

Roya shuts her laptop and places it on the floor beside her bed. She sits in the darkness. The room comes to life as her eyes slowly adjust. Even with her window blinds tightly sealed, the room is never completely black. She can still make out the silhouettes of items in each corner. She tosses around and finds a position she is comfortable in. Sliding her hand under her chin as she rests, she feels the tips of her hair clump together in a coarse ball. *Ah, shit. How did the honey get there!*

****

"I think my parents are trying to get rid of me —send me off somewhere for the summer." Roya holds tightly onto the rope as she sways back and forth on the swing set. She had called her childhood best friend, Atefeh, the next morning for an emergency pep talk.

Atefeh is a shy girl, reserved and grounded. Delicate in her mannerisms, yet she speaks with conviction and a quiet inner strength.

As Roya had once said to her, *"If I am the ocean, then you are the boulder that withstands the tests of time."*

Their personalities cannot be more different, yet they find comfort in each other's acceptance.

*"A boulder is strong, but the ocean is a force of its own. There is more than one way to be strong."* Atefeh would reassure her friend.

The two of them move on the swings like young children do when they want to feel close to flying —with the wind against their faces. Except for, now they have grown, and the weight of their adolescence presses down against the plastic seats. The park was once filled with summer picnics, Easter egg scavenger hunts, and afternoon joggers. Now, the weeds have outgrown the cracks in-between the pavement. The playsets have been abandoned for the newer park built a few blocks away. Yet, Atefeh and Roya still prefer their childhood spot. Despite its faded paint and worn woodchips, it remains and is theirs.

"What do you mean by get rid of you?" Atefeh asks facing her friend. "Don't be dramatic. Just ask them what's going on."

"I mean, not literally get rid of me. But, clearly, they think there's something wrong with me. Like, is it not okay to be sad? Why do we have to fake being happy all the time, anyway? I can't stand all that pretending. Whatever. I don't mind getting away from home either."

"There's nothing wrong with you. You're going through some stuff. It happens. But, that doesn't mean you're alright either." Atefeh knows that she is the only one who can tell her friend the blunt truth without upsetting her.

Roya doesn't even try to fight off her remarks. "I know that. I just don't know what to do. I feel like no one understands how I feel. My parents think I'm being naïve. Azadeh is too young to get it, so she's just quiet all the time when I talk to her. The only person who tries to get me is Mamani. She really tries. But, there's only so much she can do. I'm on my own in this."

Atefeh extends her hand to Roya and holds it for a moment before letting go. "Hey, I know I don't get how your mind works, but I'm always rooting for you. I don't think what you want is wrong. But, I think you're looking for some formula to make it work when there isn't one. I hate to say it, but you're right. This is all on you. But, that doesn't mean you're alone."

"Thanks, Atefeh."

"For?"

"For not judging me."

"Why would I judge?"

"I don't know. Just seems like what most people do, but you're not like that."

Atefeh smiles.

Roya pushes her weight forward, jerks back, and jumps off the swing. "Want to grab some FroYo?"

"And then go for a drive?" Atefeh adds.

"You read my mind."

The two of them climb into Atefeh's silver, convertible Volkswagen. Roya plugs the aux cord into her phone, but all she hears is static.

"Hold on a second." Atefeh presses a few buttons and adjusts the volume. "There we go! It should work now."

The tires hit the pavement and make the noise they do when they are rolling over small rocks. San Diego is extra warm today. The drought has left the air feeling arid and unmoving. The greenery has turned to a faded yellow. Even the wind feels like a blow dryer. But today, there is something oddly comforting about the stillness, as if life is being played in slow motion. Once they are on the highway, Atefeh turns up the volume.

Muse's Exogenesis Symphony Part I moves through the air like a river gliding in-between stone mountains. In that moment, not another word is spoken.

****

"Hiya there! You can pick three toppings. Which ones would ya like?" The overzealous high schooler holds Roya's FroYo and smiles, proudly exposing his metallic silver braces. His sandy blonde curls barely fit under his work cap, yet he wears it with a sense of purpose.

*Alright buddy, easy there with the spunk. Wait until you graduate. You're going to need it later in life.* Roya ignores her thoughts and attempts a genuine half-smile. "Yeah, uh, can I just get some gummy bears, strawberries, and cookie dough?"

She looks up to see Atefeh giving her a weird look as she pays at the register. Before Roya can ask what's up, she hears his voice tickle her back and send goosebumps.

"No Hershey Kisses, today?"

Now Roya understands Atefeh's expression. Her nerves are doing somersaults. Her hands are slightly trembling like some Pavlovian reaction to being caught off guard. Then, her usual defense mechanism kicks in, and she snaps out of it.

"Oh, hiiiiiii." Roya says with an exaggerated enthusiasm trying to play it cool. "What's up! How ya doing?" *Now, I sound like this FroYo kid. Someone pass me the uniform, and let me hide under that cap.* She turns around to look at him.

Standing face-to-face for the first time since their breakup throws Cyrus off too. "Hey, uhh, not much. Just getting something to snack on." His eyes begin to scan the room the way they always do when he's nervous.

"Cool, cool." Roya nods like a bauble head doll.

"Umm...well... how have you been? How's the fam?" He says looking down and back into her eyes.

The distance between them feels so weird ––like there is a clear glass separating them from making contact. Yet, there they stand looking into each other.

"Good! Great. Everyone's great. You know, same old." Roya hates the way her voice sounds right now. "What about you? How's your family?"

"Good. Everyone's good, I guess."

"That's good."

There is a brief pause. Finally, Cyrus speaks.

"Hey Roya, I just wanted to say.. I'm...I... I feel bad. Can we maybe talk..."

"Hiya, ma'am! Will that be all? Your total is $4.07." The teenager holds Roya's FroYo in the air and tries to get her attention.

Roya turns to face him. "Yeah, that's all."

After she finishes paying, she walks back over to Cyrus. She wants to hug him tightly, the way she used to, but her pride holds her back. His presence makes her both happy and angry at the same time. "So, I just wanted to say bye before I head out."

"Oh, you're leaving?"

"Yeah, Atefeh is waiting for me outside."

"Oh."

*He is standing in front of you, Roya. This is your chance. One more chance to hold him.* She pushes the thoughts away. "Well, I... I hope you have a good summer."

Both of them feel the fragile tension ––the weight of suppressing what really wishes to be said.

"You too." He says flatly.

Roya walks outside and feels like she can breathe again.

Atefeh rushes up to her. "Can't believe he was right there! I tried giving you a heads up! Um, so how did that go?"

"I mean, it went as well as it could have."

"You really think that? You both looked like deers standing in a forest with a Hummer coming full force."

Roya smiles with an underlying melancholy mixed with amusement. "Yeah, I guess it could have gone better. But, I don't know. I just legit froze. He's the only person that makes me feel that way."

"Yeah, girl. You aren't alone. I think he scanned every corner of that store before he could look you in the eyes."

Roya now laughs. "Were you hardcore watching us or something?"

"Uhh, yeah! Of course. Gotta watch over my bestie. And plus, this shit is too juicy."

"Oh, gee thanks! How sweet. Turn me into your own sitcom, huh!"

"No. This is some HBO stuff right here —something intense. Top quality performances either way, of course."

Roya is still coming down from the high of running into Cyrus. She looks at her friend, and a feeling of gratitude washes over her. "What would I do without you, Atefeh?"

Atefeh swings her arm around her friend's shoulder and walks her to the car. "No, no Roya. What would I do without you? Be bored out of my mind!"

They jump back into the car and set off again. This time they ride with no music. After several minutes, Roya speaks with her face turned towards the passenger window.

"You know...I know this sounds so lame...but I kinda wish I gave him a hug goodbye. It's weird to feel like strangers."

The tires continue to skip over the pavement with a steady rhythm.

"I had a feeling you'd say that." Atefeh says softly with her eyes on the road.

**\*\*\*\***

Roya walks in through the front door and hears her father's voice from the living room.

"Roya jaan, is that you?"

"Hi Baba, yeah. It's me."

"Can you come here for a minute?"

"Sure." She sets her jacket down and begins to walk over.

"And please take off your shoes when you're in the house." His voice echoes once more.

*How does he always know.* Roya wonders. She takes off her shoes and neatly places them in the corner of the hall before walking into the living room.

"Hi, how are you?" She asks still standing.

"Good, my dear. Come sit for a moment."

Her father sits on the couch with one leg crossed over the other. He takes off his reading glasses and places them on the coffee table.

"Is everything okay?" Roya sits next to her father. He is acting strangely careful around her.

"Yes, yes. I just wanted to have a chat with you. Your mom and I were thinking..."

*Oh, here it goes.* Roya sits up straight and waits.

"...that it might be a good idea for you to go on a vacation. Get some fresh air. Try something different. What do you think?"

"By myself?"

"No, no. Mamani will be with you."

"Me and Mamani? Are you sending me to London to see Khaleh Farnaz again like that one summer you and mom had back-to-back conferences? I actually liked it there."

"No, no. Not London." He says calmly.

"Oh. So, where?"

"Iran."

"Iran?" Roya was not expecting that at all. "You want to send me to Iran, of all places, for a vacation? How is that a vacation? Are you and mom trying to teach me a lesson? Look, I get it. I was being a little rude the other day. I'm sorry, but I—"

Roya's father touches her arm to quiet her. "No, no. It is not like that. I think this would be a great chance for you to see where you come from and spend some time with our family there. It was actually your Mamani's idea."

*Why would Mamani do this to me?* "Dad, I don't even know those people. I barely remember them. I was a kid the last time we were there."

"Exactly, and now you're all grown up. You can have a real chance to get to know them. Aren't you curious about your roots?"

"What do you mean? I was born here. That's my roots. And I mean, I eat Persian food and all that. I like being Iranian. It's cool. I guess. But, I don't see why I have to go to Iran to do that."

"Yes, *azizam.* You are born an American, and you are an American. But, you also carry your Persian heritage in your blood. This, too, is a part of your identity. Our history is so rich in culture. I want my daughter to see that too and be proud."

"How long is this trip going to be?"

"Just a few weeks."

"A few weeks? That's half the summer, Dad!"

"Time always goes by much faster than you think. So, how does it sound?"

"Is this a trick question? I feel like there isn't really a choice being presented here."

"You're a smart cookie. Well, I thought if I got to you before your mother did, you could at least be a bit more enthusiastic. All it takes is a change in perspective."

"Well, thank you for the heads up. Can I please go to my room now? I don't feel good."

"What's wrong?"

"I'm just tired. Want to go read or something."

"Start packing, maybe?" He gives her a thumbs up. "We will need to get you a *monto* and *roosari* too."

"A what?"

"The head scarf and longer jacket you will need to wear while you are there."

"Oh, right. And when are we leaving? I mean, this is kind of happening all so fast."

"This weekend. That will give you a few days to prepare."

*A few days to prepare.*

# CHAPTER 3

Azadeh pops her head into Roya' room. "You ready?"

"Uh, almost! Are mom and dad ready to go?"

"Yeah. They're waiting for you downstairs, but I'm driving you and Mamani to the airport."

"What about mom and dad?"

"Dad has a faculty meeting with the Dean, and mom has a last-minute seminar she has to attend. She's trying to prep now."

*Of course.* "Okay, well thanks then. I'll be down in a minute."

Roya looks around the room to make sure she does not forget anything. She forces the pile of clothes in her suitcase to close the zipper and then picks up the *roosari* and *monto* Mamani had bought her from H & M. The *monto* is like any other knee length coat and the scarf like any other large scarf, except for now she is required to wear them when she is in public in Iran. She folds the *monto* gently. Holding the scarf in front of her, she examines how she's supposed to wrap this loose cloth around her head so that it won't fall off.

"Royaaa." Her mother's voice trails off as she calls her name while moving from the bottom of the staircase back into the kitchen.

*Alright, here it goes.* Mamani had said they would need to put them on as soon as their plane lands in Tehran. With this in mind, she shoves the items into her carry-on and hurries downstairs.

"There you are! What took so long?" Roya's mother stacks her folders neatly and places them in her purse.

"I was just packing a few last things. It's hard to pack when you don't know what to expect."

"Do you have your passport?"

"Yes."

"Did your father give you the Iranian money he had exchanged?"

"Yes."

"And you downloaded WhatsApp?"

"Yes, mom. I did everything you had said."

"Okay, okay. Good. I just... you know... I worry. I want you to be safe." She touches her daughter's chin and just looks at her.

"Why are you looking at me that way?"

"What do you mean?"

"The way you're staring at me."

"I'm just admiring my daughter. *Mashalla*, how fast times goes by. You've grown so much." She leans in to hug Roya, but Roya's body feels stiff. She wants to embrace her mother like she used to when she was younger. But, the way their bodies mold into one another feels forced and awkward. They hold onto each other for a few seconds before releasing.

"Roya jaan, you ready? How are you feeling? Excited?" Roya's father walks into the room adjusting his tie.

"Yeah, sure. I guess so. A bit nervous."

"Ahh, nerves. That's a good sign —-means something different is just around the corner." Roya's father now leans in for a hug. "We are going to miss you. The house is not the same without you here."

Again, even in her father's arms she feels out of place.

"I'm going to miss you too." She leans her head against his chest before pulling away.

"This is sweet and all, but you are going to be late, Roya! Where's Mamani? Can we get this Quran tradition, throwing water thing out of the way, so we can head out?" Azadeh picks up the car keys.

"She's waiting outside. Let's go get her." Roya's mother replies.

Roya whispers to Azadeh. "Why do we do this whole tradition, again? We don't even really pray."

"I don't know. Just do it. Mom says it's for safe travels, good luck, all that stuff. You know how she is." She replies. "We are really going to be late if we don't leave soon."

"I mean, I'm going to do it. I was just wondering."

"Have you ever thought of writing a book just full of all these questions you always have?" Azadeh remarks impatiently as she grabs the Quran from the drawer.

"Now, why would I write a book full of questions? People want answers."

"Omg, Roya. You're being annoying. Do you ever stop overthinking?"

"Do you ever actually care about something?" Roya responds irritated as she pushes her luggage towards the door.

"Well, that was rude."

"And what you said wasn't?"

"Eh, eh. Can you two get along? This is not the time." Their mother interrupts their bickering. "Let's go get Mamani, so you can leave soon."

They walk outside to find Mamani standing by the bed of flowers she had newly planted last season. Her back is facing them, but they can tell she is in her own thoughts.

"Are you ready?" Delband says quietly as she walks up behind her mother so that she doesn't scare her.

Mamani turns and gives her a warm hug. "After all these years, I'm finally going back." She says as she holds tightly onto her daughter. "I can finally go home."

When they pull apart, Mamani wipes her wet eyes with a tissue.

"Please watch over Roya. Don't leave her alone too much. She's so stubborn sometimes. Always wants to try this and that ––explore everything. She thinks she can handle it all, but she is still my baby. I just want her to be careful." Delband sighs.

Mamani now looks at her daughter the way Delband had been looking at Roya. "And after all these years, you are still my baby. Take it easy, *azizam*. Everything will be alright."

They walk back to meet everyone. Roya and Mamani take turns walking under the Quran three times before kissing the leather binding and pressing it to their foreheads. Roya's father holds the bucket of water they will splash after they have departed.

*This custom is for blessing the journey for safe travels.* Roya's parents had always said.

*It's not always about being religious. It's just one way of reminding ourselves that there are some things greater than us. Good to have protection for the things we cannot control.* Mamani had explained.

They say one last round of goodbyes and begin their ride to the airport. Azadeh drives and skips through songs on her playlist. Mamani, in the front seat, is busy looking up the flight information for what seems like the tenth time that morning. Roya leans her head against the window, puts her knees on the back of the seat, and plugs in her own headphones.

****

They arrive at the airport, check-in their baggage, and walk over to the security line.

"Well, here's where I leave you off now!" Azadeh looks around. Her lips are doing that thing where they twist and press into each other to shut in her emotions.

"*Merci, azizam* for bringing us."

"Of course. No problem, Mamani!" She presses her lips together harder as Mamani comes in for a hug. "Well, have a safe trip and have fun." Azadeh looks over to her sister. "Finally, no one here to annoy me for three weeks!" She says unnaturally.

"Hey, Azadeh." Roya leans in for a hug. "I'm going to miss you." She feels her younger sister's cheek wet her shirt as her face presses against her shoulder.

"Sorry, I got my mascara on your shirt."

"It's okay." Roya smiles, but her heart is also feeling tight. "I'll be back soon. Don't enjoy me being gone too much. Okay? She now presses her lips like her sister and gives her one last squeeze. "Drive home safe."

The plane roars as they gear up for takeoff. Once in the air, everything quiets down, except for the sound of the engines now gently humming. The clouds are extra white today as if an Instagram filter has been swiped across the entire sky. Roya squints her eyes to avoid looking directly at the sunlight. After a few minutes, the clouds pass over. She can open her eyes wide again. Peering down at the rolling hills and city lights, she watches them grow smaller and smaller the higher up they go.

****

"Ladies and Gentlemen, please put your trays up. Make sure that your seats are in upright position. We are now preparing for landing." The flight attendant's smooth voice sounds on the intercom in Farsi.

The Iranian airline they had transferred over to for their connecting flight from Turkey is fairly small. Almost every person on the flight is Iranian, except for a few European tourists Roya had heard speaking French and Swedish. She leans forward to look through one of the open windows, but sitting to her left is a tall, round-bellied man whose frame blocks the view. She tries leaning to her right, but Mamani has already placed her purse on her lap with her elbows in Roya's face. Feeling defeated, Roya pulls out her *roosari* and leans back into her seat. She can't help but fidget from side-to-side.

*I guess I'll just wait patiently now.*

The green unfasten seatbelt sign dings on. Suddenly, the motionless bodies all jump to grab their baggage from the overhead compartments. The women begin adjusting their headscarves. The children sitting behind Roya now laugh and sit with their knees on the seats. The elderly man one row down stretches his back. The abrupt change in pace makes Roya feel unsettled and tense. As she bends down to pick up her bag from the floor, she feels a hand pat her head.

She turns around and sees a four-year-old leaning over her seat laughing contagiously. "*Khanoom! Khanoom!*"

"Yes?" Roya pulls her headscarf over her head and tries tucking her long hair underneath, so that it does not fall from the bottom.

The kid reaches for her head again and pulls the *roosari* down. She laughs with a mischievous grin. "*Salaaam.*" The young child mumbles in-between her uncontrollable giggling.

"Roya, don't bother the young lady." The child's mother turns now. "I'm so sorry. She gets restless on long flights. She seems to have forgotten her manners." She speaks in English, but with an Iranian accent.

The little girl stares at Roya with a goofy look, completely unfazed by her mother's scolding.

Roya is confused, but can't help laughing too. "No worries. It's all fine. I understand." Turning her attention to the young girl, she crosses her eyes and makes a goofy face back. "My name is Roya too." She responds in Farsi. "Aren't Royas the best?"

Now that the attention is on her, the little girl shyly nods her head and buries the side of her face into her mother's stomach. She removes her curls out of her dark brown eyes, but remains staring at Roya.

"Oh, how nice! Your name is Roya too? Beautiful name. One of my favorites. My husband and I went back-and-forth for a while. Of course, I won. Roya, it was, for us! My little dreamer." She strokes her daughter's hair endearingly as she chats.

"I see you've made a new friend." Mamani chimes in as she stands up to leave the plane. "Come, dear. It's time to go."

Roya takes one last look at the little girl. "Nice to meet you both." She waves goodbye and exits the plane.

****

As soon as they turn the corner at the arrivals pick-up line, Roya hears the deep, raspy voice of a woman in her sixties booming from the distance. She is penguin wobbling over to them with her hands holding her cheeks like winners do in beauty pageants.

*Oh, God. Oh, God. Here it comes.*

When she gets closer, she throws her arms around Roya. "*Salaaam, ey vay!* It's been so long!" She holds onto her tightly and kisses her on both cheeks. Her lipstick leaves a faint, brown stain on Roya's face. "My! Look at the woman you've become! So beautiful. When did you lose all that weight? Where are those chubby little cheeks you had as a kid?" She pinches Roya's face with both hands. "Can't believe how much you've grown!"

"*Merci, merci.*" Roya has no idea who this woman is, but she replies politely nodding her head.

"And you, my dear cousin! How many years has it been since we last saw you? It's been too long. I have lost count." She now throws her arms around Mamani's delicate frame and lands another round of kisses on her cheeks. "Everyone came here to see you both. They were too excited to wait at home." She points to the group of flailing arms and wide smiles near the exit door.

From the distance, a woman appearing to be in her seventies waves gracefully. She is one of the most beautiful women Roya has ever seen —like pure kindness personified in human form.

Catching the direction of Roya's eyes, Mamani wraps an arm around her while waiving at the woman. "That is Afrouz back there. She was and still is one of my best friends —my soul sister. She is the wise one. Here, they call her Khanoom Jaan."

Two men start walking towards them. The first is an older man, his hair more salt than pepper but still full and thick. Walking beside him is a younger guy with the same thick hair, except for his is jet black. He's not too tall, but definitely not short —perhaps close to six feet. His jaw line is defined, and a five o'clock shadow makes his boyish face look more mature.

"Why hello there, our American friends! Welcome, welcome." The young guy says bowing down like a performer. He greets Mamani respectfully with a light air kiss on her cheeks and turns to look at Roya.

She can't tell if his eyes are green with swirls of brown or brown with swirls of green, but they look so familiar.

"Hi, you must be Roya? Yes, of course. I know you are, because my father told me. What a silly question. I'm Omid." He extends his hand to shake Roya's. "I know in the United States, you shake hands. Right?"

Roya composes herself and shakes his hand. "Hi, well yes, but I'm more of a hugger anyway."

"So, a hug then?"

"Sure." *Where do I know him from*? She wonders as she gives him a light hug. His body is warm and comforting. She pulls back to greet the older man chatting with Mamani. "*Salam*, how are you? Thank you for coming to the airport."

"*Salam*, dear Roya. Of course. Welcome to your second home. Now, come on! Let's get these suitcases to the car. Everyone is waiting to say hello!"

The man and Omid carry their suitcases off as Mamani and Roya follow.

"That is Darvish. He was good friends with your *dayees* when they were growing up in Tehran. That young man is his son, Omid. Such a lovely boy he was. Seems like a lovely man even now. His mother was also good friends with yours. We have known their family for many years."

"Oh, maybe that's what it is! He felt so familiar. I knew I must have met him before."

"Omid? Hmm, I'm not sure you've met him actually."

Before Roya can reply, Omid calls out to them. "Hey Roya! There's not a lot of room in this car. Want to ride with me?"

Roya looks at Mamani.

"Sure, go ahead if you like. I trust Omid. I will meet you back at the apartment. The whole family will most likely be there. Maybe a quick break with Omid wouldn't be such a bad idea."

"But, I don't even know him."

"You can get to know him. I have a feeling you two will become great friends. Give it a chance."

"Okay, we will see." She hugs Mamani goodbye and adjusts her *roosari* again. *This damn thing won't stay on. I need to find some bobby pins. How does everyone else make this look so effortless?*

****

"Here you go, madam." Omid opens the door of his black Peugeot sedan for Roya and closes it behind her before getting into the driver's seat.

"Thank you."

Roya is bombarded with sensory information. The air has its own distinct smell ––a mixture of gasoline, parchment that has been sitting in the sun for too long, and smoky men's cologne. Some women are dressed more traditionally with longer *montos* and hairs strictly tucked under their scarves ––not a single strand peeping out. Other women are dressed in modern skinny jeans, shorter *montos*, and *roosaris* that barely cover half their hair. If it weren't for the garment on their heads, they would look like a walking Zara ad. Even Omid is dressed in skinny jeans and a gray v-neck shirt.

"Windows down or up?" Omid interjects Roya's thoughts.

"Whichever! Either is fine with me, really."

"Oh, c'mon now. You're the guest. I just need to know do you want the dry wind blowing in your hair or would you prefer the air conditioning chilling your face?" He playfully responds while adjusting the steering wheel.

"Normally, I'd take the air conditioning, but let's try the dry wind then."

"Good choice! That will give you a real nice introduction ––sounds, smells, and all. I heard it's your first time visiting in a while?"

"Yeah, we used to visit more often when I was a kid, but then my parents got really busy. They're both professors, so their life is basically seminars, classes, conferences ––all that stuff. I don't remember much from those trips to be honest."

"Ooo, so you're from *that* kind of family. A family of academics! You must be intelligent too then. Dr. Roya, Ph.D and all. One day maybe, huh?"

Roya smiles, not really sure what he means by *that* kind of family. "My parents want me to be a doctor for sure, but not that kind. I'm supposed to begin applying to medical schools soon."

"See... I knew you must be smart." He says smiling as he faces the road. "So, tell me, is that what you want too? Become a doctor? I always thought their white coats were nice. I could see you in a white coat like that. I mean, any coat would look nice too."

"What?"

"No, no. I just mean I can see you looking all professional if you wanted to. That's all."

"Oh, right. Yeah, I mean I guess it was always part of the plan."

"What plan?"

"My life plan."

"Oh, those things still work in this day and age? I thought plans were a thing of the past. Seems like all of life is happening in-between the cracks these days, if you know what I mean."

"I'm not sure I do?"

"Well, I mean there is life, a plan, and living. Life is like the entire field." Roya watches nervously as he takes both of his hands off the steering wheel to create a circle in the air. The highways are well paved and newly painted, but the drivers ignore the lines as they swerve in and out of each other like stitched thread. "Then, there's the plan. You can plant those seeds, pour the pavement, build the roads -- whatever. But, you can't control the earth like that --the rain, the sun, the erosion. Life breaks through what it must. But ah, what is there between the crevices of things?" He now places his left hand on the steering wheel and uses his right hand, pressing his fingers together and opening them like a young bud. "That is nature --making its way-- sometimes even in the most unlikely places."

"So, you're saying we should never make plans, because they aren't perfect?" She can hear her parents in her voice.

"No, no. All I am saying is that there is your plan, and then there is life's plan. And sometimes it can surprise you in beautiful ways. That's all. Not everything that falls apart is broken. Sometimes you just need some, how do you say it, fertile ground to begin. Did I say that right? Fertile?"

"Yes, that is correct. You said it perfectly right." The word *fertile* sticks in Roya's mind. "So, what about you? Tell me about yourself."

"What would you like to know?"

"Anything. What are you studying? What do you like to do for fun?"

"Me? Go to the movies, spend time with my friends, take weekend trips to the mountains, sometimes just drive around at night with the windows down and feel the crisp night air. The usual kind of things."

"Oh, okay."

"Did you expect a different answer?"

"No. Well, I don't know, actually. It just sounds like the kind of normal stuff I do back at home."

"We may live across the ocean, but we are not so different here from your America. The things we enjoy are very much the same." Omid smiles with understanding. "I must say, here we can ride a donkey around the hill at this one place. Not too far away. Can you ride a donkey in your city?"

*Is he for real, or is he making fun of me now?* "Sorry, I didn't mean it like that. I don't know what I expected. This is all so new for me."

"No apologies needed. That is why you are here, no? To explore. To see the real Iran."

Roya feels stupid for having made that comment. She awkwardly tries to change the subject. "So, what are you studying? You never said."

"I am actually not in school right now." He is still smiling, but his voice sounds flat. "Had to take some time off. It's a bit complicated."

"Oh, okay." Afraid to make another wrong comment, she sits

quietly. This time Omid slices through the silence.

"So, do you recognize anyone? You must have seen some pictures before you came?

"Yeah, that would have been a good idea. But, no I didn't, so I really don't know who is who."

"Not even on Facebook? What kind of Millennial are you?"

Roya laughs. "Not even on Facebook!" *Should I tell him this whole trip was a last-minute surprise?*

Omid suddenly turns sharply around a corner into an alley and then turns once more. "Well, Ms. Americano, we have arrived. Are you ready to meet everyone?"

*Not really.* She hesitates for a second before she replies. "Ready as I'll ever be."

Omid drives the car through a black, metal gate into a narrow parking garage.

"Careful, it's a tight space." He runs around the corner and opens the door for Roya acting as a buffer between the door and the wall. He grabs her luggage, and they squeeze into the elevator. The apartment reminds her of older New York flats with modern interiors. The hallways smell like leather and paint --a combination Roya finds oddly nurturing.

"Thank you."

"For?"

"For carrying my luggage."

"That deserves a thank you? Of course." He ushers Roya down the hallway. "After you."

As they approach the door, Roya can hear the buzzing sound of laughter, loud chatter, and the shuffling of feet. Omid steps forward now and knocks on the door. No one answers. He rings the doorbell, and a musical chime begins playing. Moments later, the woman with the booming voice --Mamani's cousin-- answers the door with the same level of excitement as when she had first seen them at the airport.

"*Salam*, welcome! Everyone, Roya jaan is here! Her and Omid have just arrived."

Roya takes a step inside the home, but notices rows of shoes parked outside on a plastic rack. She steps back, slips her shoes off, and places them in an empty spot. A sea of smiling faces —young and old, both inviting and eager— peer from every corner of the room as she enters. She is relieved to see a familiar face when Mamani pokes her head out and walks up to greet her. Holding Roya by the hand, she takes her around the room and introduces her to each individual —some with hunched backs and skin aged with experience and others looking like the first blooms of Spring.

*Dayee Alborz.*

*Khanoom Ferideh.*

*Ali.*

*Ali.*

*Ali Reza.*

*Atossa.*

*Dayee Behrouz.*

*Khaleh Parvaneh.*

*Agha Hamid.*

*Her son, Amir.*

*Your second cousin, Shahin.*

*Your third cousin's daughter, Donna.*

The list continues. Three respectful air kisses on each cheek for every person as she makes her way around the room.

"Mamani, are there really that many *dayees* and *khalehs*?" Roya says quietly before she leans in for another round of hellos.

Mamani laughs. "It's more a term of endearment. Just go with it. I'll explain everyone to you later."

"If you say so!"

*"What are you studying? Do you have a suitor? Last time I saw you, you were this tall! My, you've grown up! Where did your cheeks go? How's*

*school? Pre-med? Bah, bah khanoom doctor! How old are you now? Are you looking to get married soon? No, no focus on school first. But, don't want to get married too late! How's mom? How's dad? How's Azadeh? Have you eaten? Are you hungry? You should eat. Let's eat!"*

There are so many discussions going on at once. Roya manages to give a few word answers before moving on to continue the hellos.

After her last greeting, she turns to find an empty seat and sees Omid standing behind her.

"Here you go. Try this." He holds a tray full of tall glasses with a red liquid in it. "I think you need this after all that."

"Cranberry juice?"

"Nope! Better. This is *sharbat*, pomegranate flavor. I think you will like it."

"Alcohol?"

"No."

"Oh, right. You can't drink in Iran."

Omid grins. "Don't be silly. Just because we can't drink doesn't mean we don't. This just isn't that kind of party."

"Oh." Roya takes a sip of the syrupy drink. "Well, thank you. It's super sweet, but definitely delicious."

"Just a little something until dinner is ready."

"Dinner this late?" Roya looks at her iPhone. "It's almost 9:30pm?"

"Late?" He gives her a funny look and rubs his stomach. "It's right on time! And I'm sure you must be hungry from all that traveling."

He sets the last cup on a coaster and heads back to the kitchen with the tray. Roya looks around the room and decides to follow him.

"Can I help?" She says to the woman emptying a large pan of rice onto a silver tray.

"No, no, Roya jaan. There's no need!" The woman replies as she holds the oversized pan by its two handles and flips it over so that the *tahdig* now sits on top of the rice.

"Are you sure? Really, I'd like to help!"

"Don't even think about it. You are our guest of honor! Go have a seat!" Shooing her away emphatically, she sprinkles some saffron on the rice and smoothes it over with a spoon.

Roya is about to insist again, but Omid pops back up. "You don't want to mess with these women. They are fierce, and they mean it when they say guests are guests!"

They walk together back to the living room just as Khanoom Jaan walks in through the door. Something is different about her presence. Roya can feel it, but she can't quite place what it is about her. Everyone around her is animated and loud. But, Khanoom Jaan's presence is a subtler joy. She almost seems like she's floating by —the way she stands tall with her shoulders back, poised with effortless elegance. She takes off her pastel orange *roosari* and places it around her neck with her *monto* still on.

"*Salam* Roya jaan, I have known your family for many, many years. It is wonderful to finally meet you." She gives Roya a tight hug as if they had known each other their whole lives.

"Thank you." Roya replies politely. "Mamani said you two were best friends growing up. You must be Khanoom Jaan."

The woman smiles. "Yes, it seems as though that has become my name. It started many years ago and somehow remained."

The food is now neatly decorated on the long, wooden table. Large, circular trays towering with bright yellow and white rice are placed in the center. Dishes filled with various stews and skewers of meat too. The elders and younger children pick up their plates first and scoop food as they walk around the table. Then, it's time for the rest of the adults to take their turns. Roya fills up her plate with a few spoonfuls of rice and some skewers of meat. She is about to complete her rotation around the table when someone grabs her arm.

"That's it? You must be starving!" The woman with the booming voice aims for her plate with a large spoon of stew, as if it were a melting meteor crashing onto her plate. She adds another skewer of meat and sprinkles some *sumac* on top. "There you go! Much better. Don't be shy to eat! A young woman needs energy!"

*Uhhh.* Roya serves an uneasy smile. *"Merci.* It all looks really great."

Roya reaches the end of the table and notices there are no more spoons. She is about to walk over to the kitchen when Omid hands her one.

"Here you go!" Omid grins.

"Oh, thanks. How did you know I needed one?"

"Well, because I took the last one and saved it for you. And then I saw you look around the room and thought to myself, *she must be looking for her spoon.* So, here you go."

"Well, that's nice of you. Are you always so thoughtful?"

"Na, not thoughtful. Just observant."

"Are you trying to be humble about being thoughtful?"

"No, I just thought I wouldn't get your expectations too high. Next spoon, you're on your own!" He laughs like a child would after they successfully execute a rehearsed joke. "Are you going to sit down?"

"Here? At the dining room table? Don't we have to sit with the kids? I don't know if there are enough chairs for everyone?"

"Do you consider yourself a kid, Roya?"

"Uhh, I mean. I guess not. But, I just thought that there wouldn't be enough space."

Omid looks her up and down with an increasing curiosity. "Well, there are enough chairs actually. And you don't look like a kid to me! And I might act like a kid sometimes, but I promise I'm not. I think we're allowed to sit here. What do you say?"

"Alright. Sure, let's sit here."

"So, tell me. What's your thing you got going on?"

"What do you mean?"

"Your trip to Iran. I have a feeling this wasn't your idea."

"Why do you say that?"

"At first, I thought maybe you came to see family, but you don't seem to know anyone. And then I thought maybe you're doing the whole *Eat, Pray, Love* find yourself thing."

"You know what that is?"

Omid gives her a look and smiles. "Roya, do you think just because our governments don't dance together that we don't hear the same music?"

"Wait...what?"

"Okay, never mind. Not the best metaphor. Anyway... I'm sensing this is all a bit of a shock for you. I mean, if you were trying to go on an adventure to find yourself, I feel like most people would go for Europe. Or, let's say, a tour in Asia. I would. I hear it's amazing. A little bit of fun, a little bit of meditation. I've read some of those zen living books."

"I think you are assuming way too many things. The Middle East is cool, and you can definitely explore yourself here too."

"Oh, Roya. The Middle East is much more than cool. It's fascinating. I just didn't think it would be your first choice or even your second."

"If you must know, which I'm guessing you do, it was my parents' idea. Well, my grandma's technically. I don't know, but they all seemed to think a trip to Iran was the way to go. So, here I am."

"And why is that? I mean, why did they suggest Iran now? You could have also come a few years ago, but you didn't then."

"I think they just thought I'd appreciate it more now that I'm older." She tries to avoid the topic and circles her fork around the plate like she always does. "Plus, I have more time now that undergrad is almost over."

"Hmm, okay then." Omid takes a big bite of the kabob and washes it down with an orange Fanta.

"What? Why do you say okay like that?"

"Like what?"

"Like the way you just did."

Omid takes another gulp of his Fanta. "Because I think you're interesting."

"What have I said that is interesting?"

"No, no. It's not what you are saying. It's what you are not saying." He smiles again. "So, I just said okay! Because I can't read your mind after all."

"I feel like you think you can."

"It doesn't matter whether I think I can. I want you to tell me when you want to tell me. I don't need to know more than you want to tell."

Roya is surprised. "Okay then." She looks around the room and takes a bite of the minty greens sitting in the corner of her plate.

# CHAPTER 4

The distant prayer songs from the speakers of the nearby mosque are muffled against the clashing noise of Tehran's morning traffic. Roya wakes up in the spare bedroom of Mamani's condo, an investment property she had saved for when she had dreamt of eventually returning.

Now, it has become a place for temporary visitors ––businessmen and their families passing through months at a time, students in need of a room to sublease. Occasionally, even a free place to stay for the various employees that manage the land. The space is small and old. Despite the bathroom renovations and fresh coat of paint, the walls reveal their age, or as Mamani had said, their history. Roya walks to the edge of the window and rests her chin upon her hand as she gazes at the street below. Busy little bodies scurry from one sidewalk to another. The apartment buildings across the street are much taller than Mamani's and the exteriors obviously newer ––more glass windows, fancy columns, less rain-stained cement.

The good part about Maman's building is its proximity to Khanoom Jaan's home. *"We thought we'd raise our families together, so our children could be close."* Mamani had told Roya the night prior. After all these years, Khanoom Jaan remained her neighbor and was witness to the various humans that sought comfort in the apartment ––a lot of land that would always belong to Roya's grandmother, but never become her own home.

The other plus side to its location is the fresh smoothie store just below the building.

*"But, aren't there smoothie shops like that on every corner? It's like Starbucks or bodegas in New York. They're everywhere!"* Roya had asked.

*"Ahh, yes. But, this smoothie shop has been passed down from one generation to another. I knew the owner's father and his father. Their youngest daughter now studies in Turkey, but the eldest son is taking over the shop. I have always believed their cantaloupe smoothies were that much sweeter. Perhaps, it is because I know the heart they put into their work."* She had looked at Roya with doe eyes, implying that she was of course biased.

Sitting on the dressing table diagonal from the window is one of those wooden Russian Matryoshka dolls. Its exaggerated eyes and rosy cheeks draw Roya in closer. She picks it up with two hands as if it were made from glass and turns the top off. Inside were replicas of the same painted face, each figure smaller than the other. She places the original top back on and sets the doll on the table where she found it.

*"What happened to Maman's childhood home? Why didn't you and Baba Bozorg keep that one?"* Roya questioned as they unpacked their bags when they arrived.

*"The government took that property from us shortly after the Revolution."* Mamani had replied as she hung her clothes one-by-one in the closet as if they'd stay there forever.

*"Just like that?"*

*"Just like that."*

The air smells like handwoven Persian rugs and rose perfume blended with lit esfand. Grabbing her toiletry bag, Roya walks to the bathroom just around the corner. Her head feels dizzy. There is a faint, throbbing sensation reaching from one temple to the other across her forehead. She turns on the faucet and catches the cool water in the cups of her hand before splashing it across her face. Tilting her head back, she presses down on her temples and rolls out her shoulders to relieve some tension.

"Roya jaan, are you ready!"

Mamani's voice calls out from the kitchen. Roya feels an unusual sense of anticipation, but her thoughts are hazy.

"Coming! Just a minute." She finishes washing up and heads to the kitchen.

"Good morning, *azizam*. How did you sleep?"

"Good morning. I slept fine." This is a lie, but she does not want to alarm her grandmother. "How long have you been awake?"

"Oh, just a couple of hours. Not too long. I couldn't sleep much for some reason."

"How come?"

"Must just be the jet lag." Mamani is lying too. Her body feels hot and clammy. "Here, have some breakfast. I had them drop off fresh *barbari* bread from down the street! The temperature is going to be a record breaking hot in Tehran today. I was thinking maybe we could go to the mall? There is a place called the Palladium. I think it will remind you a bit of Beverly Hills. How does that sound?"

*Beverly hills in Tehran? Right.* "Sure, that sounds nice. What time are you thinking?"

"Whenever you are done with breakfast. Maybe we can beat traffic." Mamani's hands slightly tremble as she pours sugar into her chai.

"Are you feeling alright?"

"Yes, dear. Why do you ask?"

"Your hands—" Roya feels the throbbing pressure in the back of her scalp now. "—they are shaking."

"Oh, that. I didn't even notice. Must be all the excitement of being back after all this time." Mamani rests the spoon on her plate and tucks her hands underneath the table. "What do you think so far?"

Roya's eyes search for her grandmother's hands before she looks back up at her. "It's nice. Everyone seems nice. Very hot though. I wish we didn't have to wear these things." She points to her *monto* and *roosari* hanging by the door. "Mamani, are you sure you feel okay? Your face looks a bit pale."

"Yes dear, I feel fine. And I know what you mean." She places her hands back on the table, but they no longer tremble. "The dress code certainly doesn't help with the heat."

They put on their layers one-by-one and enter the awaiting taxi. The driver has his windows down. The heat is sticking to everything — their faces, the ripped parchment of the interior seats, their clothes. All are absorbing the arid texture.

"Last night, my cousin invited us to attend her employee's wedding with her. Would you like to go?"

"Who?" *Oh, wait. The woman with the booming voice.* "Does her employee want us at her wedding? We can't just go, can we?"

Mamani holds Roya's hands. Roya feels the trembling again. Suddenly, Mamani pulls away.

"Yes, it's different here. They won't mind. We would be my cousin's guests."

"Whatever you want. We can go if you like."

"I think it would be a nice chance to meet some of the younger crowd. I want you to enjoy yourself while you're here. I know you feel like this is some punishment, but just be open to it. There are so many wonderful things here to experience."

"Please don't say that. I don't think it's punishment. Just different. That's all. We can go to the wedding."

"Wonderful. That makes me happy to hear. How about we look for a dress then? Right after we stop by the nuts boutique!"

****

Roya can't take her eyes off of the endless rows of pistachios, cashews, almonds, and dried fruits. *She calls this a boutique. This place is huge.* Stacked containers, bins brimming with food, and shelves of packaged goods line the store's walls. Sweet and salty delicacies in colors like roasted orange, velvet burgundy, and forest green. A skinny man with a thick mustache curled to the side passionately weighs the baggies on a scale and punches buttons on his calculator. He calls out prices to the customers, who have created a disorderly line that trails to the entrance of the store.

"Umm, there's barely room to walk in here! How are you going to shop?"

"Oh, *biya* Roya! It's part of the fun. We're going to squeeze and wiggle our way through."

Roya's headache had subsided, but now the pain is back. Her heart is beating quickly, and the same feeling of anticipation takes over her. They walk sideways through the crowd to avoid bumping into anyone.

"Shall we begin?" Mamani pulls two plastic bags from the hanging dispenser and hands one to Roya before scooping a shovel of dried apricots into a bag.

Roya searches for an empty corner and walks over to the basket hosting a mountain of pistachios. She picks one out from the top and opens the shell. Just as she is about to eat it, a man walks up to her.

"STOP! *Khanoom,* vhat are you doing? NO!" This man is also skinny with a mustache, except for his is straight and connects to a goatee just underneath his chin. "Excuuuse me. You are trying to eat dat pistachio, eh?"

Roya looks nervous. "Uhh, *salam.* I was just trying it out. I wanted to taste it first."

The man's furrowed eyebrows scowl at Roya. He is about to say something, but can't contain himself. He bursts out laughing, a high screeched noise of self-induced amusement. "Oh em gee, I am just kidding with you! You look like a tourist! I knew it. So fun joking with you foreigners. Of course, you can try it. We want you to try it! You are American, correct?"

"Yes. Wait, how did you know that? I am Iranian."

"Ah, yes. But you are Iranian and American. I can always tell when I see someone not from here."

"That obvious?"

"Maybe. Who knows! Or maybe, I just know how to read people. Anyvay, go ahead. Have that pistachio. Those are some of the best in the world. Do me a favor. Take a bag, even if it is small, for your American friends. Tell them these pistachios are from Iran! And they are the finest in the world." He grins proudly. "I was raised in this industry. My father used to export pistachios to your country back in the day before there were sanctions. Times are different now, but maybe one day our two worlds can be friends again. Not because of the money. I am serious." He picks up a pistachio, examines it, and places the interior in his mouth. "But, because food is like language. It is a shared understanding. I want them to taste our true culture once again. Delicious, no? Try a dried kiwi before you leave too. They are both perfectly sour and sweet. And welcome to Iran. We are happy to have you."

Roya smiles. Before she can respond to the man, a customer calls his attention, and he is gone. She scoops some pistachios in the bag and looks for Mamani. She spots her across the room with three boxes in her arms. They meet at the line for the cash register. The store is even busier now. The bodies weaving in and out start pushing against the crowd. The room now feels hot too. Roya feels suffocated the way she did in the taxi. Mamani, too, is disoriented and pale again. She notices her shifting the weight of the boxes from one arm to the other.

"Here Mamani, let me hold those for you." Roya reaches for the boxes.

"No, no. It's fine, *azizam*. Don't worry. I am old, but not that old."

All of a sudden, she remembers. "Oh, Mamani, I'll be right back! I forgot to try the kiwi. The man working here said they were really good."

"Okay, dear. I will be waiting here." She points to the curving line. "There is no rush."

Roya walks to the towering bin of dried kiwis and puts one in her mouth. *Mmm, damn. These are actually so good.* She grabs another small bag, scoops some in, and twists it shut with her fingers. As she begins walking back towards the line, she hears the loud thump of a body hitting the floor. Then, a high-pitched scream from someone in the crowd.

Another deeper voice yells. "*Khanoom, khanoom!*" A man is kneeling beside someone on the floor and checking for a pulse. "Someone call an ambulance!" Another woman's voice commands in Farsi. The throbbing pain now consumes Roya's entire head. She feels dizzy again. She scans the room frantically for Mamani, but can't find her. *Wait, Mamani.* She pushes against the crowd with her forearm and cuts through to the front. Mamani is lying on the floor unconscious. Her face is a dusty yellow. Roya runs over and kneels beside her.

"Mamani! Mamani! Wake up!" She grabs her grandmother's cold hands. Her hands are never cold.

The man turns to her. He is asking questions quickly in Farsi. Roya is having a hard time understanding everything that is going on.

"That's my grandma! Is she okay? Is she going to be okay? Mamani, can you say something!" She keeps repeating herself as the man tries to ask her questions again, but she can't process anything he is saying. The ambulance arrives, and emergency responders ask Roya to step aside. A woman presses on Mamani's chest, kneels beside her, breathes into her mouth, presses again, and checks for her pulse. Two men place her on a stretcher and carry her to the ambulance. The woman rises from the ground and finds Roya crying with her eyes fixated on the floor.

"Hello, young lady. Are you coming? I'll take you to the hospital." She asks in Farsi as she offers her hand.

The crowd has dispersed, except for a few kids watching her cry from a distance. Roya scans the room and reaches for the woman's hand. Mamani's boxes are now exposed on the floor. The employee has yet to clean it up. The pistachios are left scattered everywhere.

****

When they arrive at the hospital, Roya is instructed to wait in the lobby. She sits in an empty chair in the far corner of the room. Her eyes are red and her nose stuffy. She doesn't have a phone and doesn't even know who she would call if she did. Nurses rush back and forth down the hall, but none of them are there to update Roya. She gets up and walks to the front desk.

"Excuse me, ma'am. My grandmother is the woman they just rushed to one of the emergency rooms. Is there any news? Can I go see her?"

The woman is busy filing some paperwork. "I'm sorry, dear. No news yet. The nurses will come get you once they are ready."

Forty-five minutes go by before the doctor finally walks into the waiting room.

"Roya? Is there a Roya here?"

Roya wipes her eyes and walks over to the doctor. "Yes, that's me. Is my grandmother okay?"

"She will be, but we need to monitor her for a bit. She had a heart attack. She is stabilized now, but we found minor complications that we just want to take another look at it."

"But she is okay? Right?"

"Yes."

Roya feels her chest open up again. "Oh, thank God. How long does she have to stay?"

"We are thinking a week, maybe a bit less."

"A week! I thought you said she is going to be okay."

"She will be. We just want to be sure."

"Can I see her now?"

"Yes, follow me."

Roya trails behind him down the bleak hallway with the doors of nearby rooms left open. The fluorescent lighting is an irritating, sickly green. Mamani's room is at the very end of the hall. Nurses keep interrupting the doctor leading the way. He pauses discussing the patient's charts and their pending questions with each interference. *C'mon, man. Let's hurry up! I need to see my grandma!* Roya picks up the pace and stands beside him —hoping he takes this as a hint. Finally, they arrive at her room. Plastic tubes connected to her arms extend to a monitor, and a breathing mask is placed across her face. Roya can barely see her lips, but she can tell she is smiling with her eyes when Mamani turns around. She runs to her grandmother, but pauses abruptly at her bedside. She is scared to touch her.

"Mamani, can I hold you?"

Her grandmother nods her head up-and-down.

Roya leans over, careful not to touch any of the cords, and wraps her arms around her softly. "Mamani, I was so scared. Waiting in that room was terrible. I didn't know what was wrong. I, I, I'm just so happy you are okay. I don't even know..."

"Now, now Roya jaan. Look, look. Everything is alright, isn't it? Don't be scared. Everything is alright now."

She reaches for her granddaughter's hand. Her touch is warm again.

Roya is relieved. "How are you feeling?"

"Very much alive."

Roya smiles and wipes away a tear. "Of course you would say that. I don't know how you do it, honestly." Roya pulls a chair to Mamani's bedside.

"Do what?"

"You are always so calm."

"A lifetime of worry will only kill you faster, no? When you get to my age, you realize that. Hope it doesn't take you as long." She squeezes Roya's hand. "Don't you worry. I'm not going anywhere. Not yet, at least. I still need to see your wedding and maybe even your babies! And, of course, your grand symphony! And much more. Don't you remember what I told you? These joys God will give me. I am certain."

"The doctor said they want to monitor you for a week. Mentioned something about a complication. I'm not sure why." Roya looks at the floor.

"Yes, yes. Just to be cautious. But hey, look at me again." Mamani promisingly looks into her eyes. "Believe your Mamani when I tell you everything will be alright. It is not my time. Not yet."

Roya is about to say something when Khanoom Jaan taps on the door. "*Salam*, may I come in?"

"Khanoom Jaan, *salam*. Of course." Roya stands up to greet her and offers her the chair.

"No need, dear. I just wanted to say hello and make sure everything is alright. I must go chat with the doctor and take care of the paperwork." She walks over and touches Mamani's other hand. "My dear friend, you left so quietly many years ago, but arrive with a bang! Perhaps this is not the kind we expected, but I've always known that heart of yours to be a fighter." She looks to Roya now. "I'm sure you know that about your grandmother. Let me tell you. Back in the day, your Mamani was like a firework. Quiet at first and then *voooom*! Her personality lit up in colors."

Roya sits back down and holds her grandmother's hand again. "Is that true, Mamani?"

She chuckles under the breathing tube and looks at her. "I suppose all the secrets are coming out."

"Roya jaan, it might be good for your grandmother to rest. But, take your time. There is no rush. I know today has been a lot. Whenever you are ready, Omid is waiting for you outside in the hall. He will take you to grab your luggage and then to my place. You can stay with me until your Mamani is ready to come home."

"Oh, are you sure? I don't want to intrude."

"Intrude? Nonsense! I would love to host you."

Mamani says thank you to Khanoom Jaan with her eyes --the language of true friendship. "Roya jaan, she is right. I should rest. You can come back tomorrow. I don't want you to stay here too late. Today has been heavy."

"Okay, I will come back tomorrow. I love you."

"I love you too, my dear."

"And Khanoom Jaan, *merci*." Roya stands up.

"Anytime. You and Omid go ahead. I will finish up the paperwork and head over shortly."

"Alright."

She walks outside, but doesn't see him. She starts walking down the narrow hallway and hears whistling from the corner of the room. When she turns to look, Omid is standing with a box of pizza.

"Oh, there you are! Hello, hello Ms. Americano." He rattles the box side-to-side like a tambourine. "Hungry?"

"Hi, Omid. I don't have much of an appetite right now, but thank you."

"You sure? Because this isn't just any pizza. This is Iranian pizza, and it's quite the experience."

She smiles. "Tempting, but yes. I am sure."

"Okay! Maybe later then? That is if I still want to share." He holds the pizza box still. "I have been told to take you to your Mamani's and then to Khanoom Jaan's. No funny business, they said! But, that's no fun. Right? I was thinking we could stop by this coffee shop. I know, I know. You don't have an appetite. But, there's nice music, some interesting paintings, and you can witness some Iranian hipsters, eh? Man bun and everything. Just like in the States."

"I don't want to cause trouble. Khanoom Jaan might get worried."

"You know how in California you run on PST? We do too. Ours is Persian Standard Time. It's very real, you know. When Khanoom Jaan says she will be there shortly, that means we have at least a couple of hours." He takes a slice of pizza and bites into it.

"Well..." Roya looks nervously around. "A coffee shop does sound pleasant."

"I think, if I am correct, I just heard a yes from you? Great. Let's go! And I see you looking at my pizza. Don't worry. I'm bringing this baby with us! I'll share." He pats the box and points towards the exit. "After you."

****

From the outside, the coffee shop looks small. Its narrow door is inconveniently positioned between a hole-in-the-wall kabob joint to the right and another one of those fresh smoothie bodegas to the left. Omid parallel parks the car across the street and cautions her before walking across. "Watch the little dips."

"The what?"

He points to the open space between the road and the sidewalk. "Those areas. The drain pipelines. Wouldn't want you falling into some dirty water. Just leap over it!"

"Oh. Okay."

"And one more thing. Tehran's traffic doesn't stop for anyone. I swear it seems like they're all rushing home, because the kabobs are getting cold. Anyway, no waiting around. Once you start walking, you just have to go for it."

"Okay." Roya scans the oncoming traffic.

"Would it help if I held your hand?" Omid looks back.

"No, I can do it." The cars nearly skim one another's bumpers as they race ahead. *Alright Roya. Just look, go, leap. No big deal.*

Omid grins. "Of course you can."

They hurry across the street and slip in through the door. The inside really is small. Only a couple of dark wooden tables and several dainty chairs that look uninviting.

Omid points to a flight of spiral stairs around the corner near the back. "Up there. Let's go!"

Omid jumps two steps at a time. Roya holds onto the railing as one foot follows the other. As they near the top, she can hear jazzy electronic music with Farsi lyrics. The quiet stillness of the main floor dissipates and is replaced by the bubbling chatter of eager voices behind a door. Omid knocks on the thick exterior three times.

A short man wearing a bright, red beanie opens it. His earlobes hang slightly low because of the gauges on either side. A delicate tattoo written in Farsi sits across his forearm.

The man catches Roya looking at the writing. "*I am not what you see, but what you believe. If you wish to see me, look through me.* I just got this done. What do you think?"

"I like it. I really do."

The man's serious face folds into a half smile. "My mom hates it. The ink."

"Well, my friend. If you haven't pissed off your parents once in your life, you aren't doing it right. This was your once! Now, be good to your maman." Omid taps the man on the chest and gives him a hug. "This is Roya. She is visiting from America."

The man looks at Roya again. "Very nice. Where from?"

"Hi, nice to meet you. California."

"My sister's friend moved to Los Angeles a couple years ago. He said there's a whole area with Persian stores and markets. Is that true?"

Roya laughs. "Yeah, actually, in Westwood. It's pretty cool. How does he like it?"

"Oh, he loves it. The beach, the parties, the women. But you know, he has his moments, missing home and everything. I told him the other day —*Man! You can do anything you want. Just do it, digeh! It's America!* He knows, but he tells me he is lonely sometimes. It is hard to be a foreigner in a land that doesn't see you as its own, but I think he will be okay. America was always his dream. To make that dream work, you have to first wake up, no?"

"I think that tattoo has made you sound wiser, my friend." Omid looks to Roya. "Isn't he great? Now, let's continue this inside."

The interior is nothing like Roya had expected. Unlike the room below, the upstairs space is vast and open and modern. The only thing they share in common is that both areas are minimalistic, except for the top floor is intentional. Golden geometric designs add contrast against the dark, navy walls. The lighting is dim. There are sections with tables and corners with plush, velvet sofas. Some bodies lean in towards one another enthralled in conversation, while some sit across from one another at a reasonable distance. Others sit completely alone with headphones fastened in their ears and their eyes focused on laptops.

"Woah, this is like a coffee shop speakeasy." Roya whispers to Omid.

"A what?"

"Nevermind."

"Looks like there are no seats. Let's try over there."

They walk over to two vacant stools at the open coffee bar.

"Do you drink iced lattes?" Omid says without looking at the menu.

"Yeah."

"And do you like ice cream?"

"Of course."

"How about an iced latte with ice cream in it?"

"Like a milkshake?"

"No, an iced latte with a scoop of ice cream in it. A coffee glace. You don't have that in the States?"

"Oh, yeah we do. I just haven't really heard it called that."

"Want one?"

"Sure!"

"So, how are you doing?"

"What do you mean?"

"With everything that happened today."

"Oh, I'm okay. I'm just glad Mamani is alright. I don't even want to think about what it would be like if she wasn't."

"And in general? How are you doing?"

"Fine? Why do you think there is something wrong with me?"

"Woah, woah. I didn't say that. I just wanted to check in."

The waiter interrupts. "Excuse me, welcome. What can I get you?" He takes the pen off his ear.

"*Salam*, one coffee glace please." Roya responds politely, but flatly.

"And for you, sir?" He looks to Omid.

"Same for me. *Merci*." Omid hands him their menus and leans toward Roya.

"Why do you think I meant something is wrong with you?"

Roya's body subconsciously pulls back from him. "Why do you ask so many questions?" She can hear her parents in her voice again.

"I'm just trying to get to know you. That's what people do. They try to get to know each other."

"Why don't you tell more about yourself then?"

"You didn't ask?"

"I'm asking now."

The waiter returns with their sweetened coffee beverages topped with whipping cream and cinnamon.

"Okay, let's try this again." He extends his hand to Roya as if he wants to shake it. "My name is Omid. I am twenty-three years old. I like classic rock, electronic music, and even some opera. Yeah, yeah. Opera. I said it, alright! I like the mountains early in the morning and the beach at night. And my left side is my best side for photos. Makes my nose look smaller." He turns his face to the side showing his profile headshot.

Roya pokes around the whipping cream before taking a sip of the drink.

"No. I mean what's your story? You're so eager to know mine. What's your real story?"

Omid leans back and smiles. "Not uh, Roya. You give and you get. I just admitted I like opera. What about you?"

Roya takes a few more sips. "That didn't count."

"Okay, here's another one then. I know I talk a lot. But, I'm curious why you don't have something to say. Because I think there's more to you."

Roya is quiet.

"Not good enough? Alright, alright. This is my last one. I didn't like seeing you sad today. So be annoyed with me if you want to. Be sad if you need to. Just don't be sad all the time." He checks his phone. "We should get going though."

They finish their drinks and head down the spiraling steps. The vacant main floor now seats a couple of older men drinking chai. The car ride to Mamani's is silent. When they arrive, Roya runs upstairs, quickly gathers her belongings into her suitcase, and gets back into the car. Again, they drive to Khanoom Jaan's in silence.

Omid helps carry Roya's suitcase up the steps to the apartment. The complex is similar to Mamani's, yet looks newer and has more windows. Using the spare key he was given, Omid opens the door, takes off his shoes, and carries her luggage in. "Well, I should get going. Told you we had plenty of time."

The room is full of plants of all sizes, smaller ones lining the window sills and larger ones resting in the living room. There are photographs everywhere and barely any paintings, except for one. The 24 X 36 piece hangs just above the large sofa in the living room. It isn't really an image at all, rather a conglomeration of various colors. Brush strokes moving past one another --unclear where one shade begins and the other ends.

"Omid, would you like to stay for a bit. Maybe talk?" Roya finally speaks.

"I was hoping you'd ask. I have an idea."

Roya grabs a floor cushion and sits cross-legged opposite Omid. "What's that?"

"They say a picture is worth a thousand words. I always thought that was not only strange, but also completely wrong. A picture is more like the trailer for an independent drama. You think you know what the movie is going to be about and then *pow!* It turns out to be something completely different."

"I never thought of it that way."

"I was thinking you show me a picture, and I'll tell you what I think the story is about. And I will show you one of mine, and you can share your thoughts. A photo that means something to you. Can be of anything. Then, we will tell each other the real story."

"Alright, why not. Let's try it then. You go first."

"Hmm, let's see." He pulls out his phone and starts swiping through his album. "Hold on, hold on. I need to find a good one." He pulls up an image and turns the screen to Roya. "Okay, here you go. What do you think?"

The image is an old photograph. A boy that looks like he is around eleven years old sits on a bench with his arms crossed against his chest and cries. His hands and light blue shirt have dirt on them.

Roya holds the phone and looks closely. "I'm going to say that your mom told you not to play outside, but you did anyway. And you were playing soccer in the street, because there's a soccer ball in the corner of that photo. And you got into it with some of the kids, maybe started fighting and rolled around in the dirt. So, your mom punished you by saying you couldn't play with the kids that weekend. You were all upset."

Omid takes the phone back and laughs. "I didn't even notice there was a *fútbol* in there! Didn't belong to me!"

"Oh."

"On that day, my father came home from work upset. Not angry. I had seen him angry a couple of times before, but more disappointed this time. I don't even know why anymore. But, I remember my mom saying flowers are messengers for the words we cannot say. My allowance wasn't enough to buy him some, so I went to the best garden I knew. Khanoom Jaan's. I picked out a few. Just a few! Did not even think she would notice. When I went home, my mother asked me where I got them from. I told her the truth. *Ey vay*, she took me by the ear all the way back to Khanoom Jaan's and made me tell her what I had done. *'You don't go taking what other people have worked hard to grow, Omid!'* she had said. When I told Khanoom Jaan, she told me to sit on the bench. She sat next to me and said, *'Omid jaan, I am not upset that you took the flowers because of the time I put in. I understand why you did. But, I want you to know something important. The beauty of a flower is to appreciate it and to let it grow in its roots. You don't want to pluck them until they are in full bloom.'* She took that photo and handed it to my mother and told her, *'How lucky you are to have a son who thinks with his heart.'* Man, my friends laughed at me so much that day. That photo still makes me laugh. It is one of my favorites." He clicks his screen off. "Your turn."

Roya hesitates and picks up her phone to start scrolling. She finally chooses one and turns the screen over. In the photo, she is standing next to a tall woman with short, blonde hair in her late forties. The woman is holding onto one end of a certificate. Her arm rests around Roya's shoulder. Roya holds onto the other side of the certificate, and her smile is the kind that erupts from an innocent surprise.

"Can I hold the phone? I can't read the paper."

"Sure."

He zooms into the photo. *Award for best composition and innovative lyrical development.* He reads it out loud. "Oh shit! Look at you. I knew you were a big deal, Ms. Americano. Let's see now. You worked your ass off all day to come up with a piece. Your parents told you, *'Roya jaan, take a break from your hard work. Pre-med must be challenging enough. Come have some fun.'* And you tell them very seriously, *'This is serious! Art is no joke!'* And you go back to creating your masterpiece like some of the greatest of all time. Then, on the final day of your performance, you start getting nervous. You realize there's a lot of talent in the room. When you get on the stage, you see your parents waiving to you from the audience below. You get up on that stage, do your best, and feel relieved until... they call your name for best performance. You are shocked. Shocked! And that's your music teacher, proudly standing next to you with your award."

"Hah, right! That was good. I mean you were close, but not really."

"How do you mean?"

"I did work my ass off. Day and night. Art isn't a joke, not to me at least. Music is one of the realest things I know. I'll give you that part. But, my parents never even noticed, let alone showed up. That is not one of their priorities. Me going to med school? That definitely is. That day, I performed my first solo composition ever for a music talent show. Not some prestigious program or anything. I can't even write notes, so I just hum them and make symbols. I had a couple of people I knew in orchestra perform it from memory. That woman there is actually my biology professor. She knew how much this meant to me and had encouraged me to join the show as some kind of stress relief. I was surprised I won, but I was also so happy she came. My parents, that's whatever, right? It didn't faze me."

Omid looks away from the screen and at Roya again. "They probably just don't understand. That's like the role of parents. We're a different generation. Give them a break, maybe? Maybe they do care more than you think, but aren't sure what to make of it."

"Are you seriously defending my parents right now, and you don't even know them?"

"I just think you shouldn't jump to conclusions about your parents. Seems like they just want what's best for you. To them, what they believe is safe."

"Well, thank you for the pep talk. I think parents should at least ask their kids what happiness means to them before they force their own ideas."

"I agree with that. Just try not to act so ungrateful."

"Wow, okay. Thanks. For someone who says we shouldn't jump to conclusions, you just did." Roya reaches for her phone back, but her hand accidentally swipes through the album. A photo of her and Cyrus pops up on the screen.

"I'm sorry, Roya. I didn't mean it that way." He watches her quickly click the screen off and put her phone away. "What's that all about? The photo of you and that guy. Why are you trying to hide it?"

"Because it isn't relevant anymore."

"If something isn't relevant, people don't usually act that way about it. C'mon, I thought we were starting to get along."

Roya sighs. "That is my ex, Cyrus."

"Ohh, ex-boyfriend. It all makes sense now. Bad breakup?"

"Are any breakups good?"

"All breakups are hard. Not all end bad."

"Well, I guess you could say it wasn't an easy or good breakup."

"Ah, okay. Okay." He walks over to the sofa, throws himself into the plush abyss, and flings his legs over the armchair. Resting his head on his hands, he looks up at the ceiling like a young philosopher would

—high on his own brilliance. "Have you ever read Plato's *Allegory of a Cave?*"

"I've skimmed it years ago? Something about prisoners, a cave, some shadows? That's so random."

"Not really. There is more than one way for humans to act like prisoners. Take another look at it. I think you might see it differently now. That is if you can find a copy. I've been looking everywhere here."

"Umm, okay. Noted." Roya folds her legs up and wraps her arms around them.

"As for your heartbreak situation, I'm no Rumi, but—"

*Here it goes.* Roya waits for it.

"—I imagine that love should only ever touch, not scar. Right? Just think about it. Love hurts when it is lost. But to love itself, I often found it to be something powerful, yet subtle —like when I watch smoke bending in the air. Or watching the sunset and knowing it will rise with you again in the morning, yet finding yourself amazed by its beauty every time."

"It's not that simple. These words sound pretty, but it's semantics. Love lost, love felt. Does it matter? When it's gone, it's gone. And it hurts."

"It does. You're right. But no, real love is never gone. Even when it's lost, it simply changes form."

"Alright, love guru. Why are you single then?"

"Maybe because I've never felt true love, or maybe I'm smart enough to avoid it all. You really want to stay upset about some guy while you're on vacation?"

"I don't understand. You say you want to be my friend. You come in with all these questions. And when I tell you, you start judging and in-sulting what I have to say. You think this is who I always was? You think I'm a dumb girl crying over some boy who gave her some attention? Or has some mommy and daddy issues, because I'm a spoiled brat? You don't even know anything about where I come from, what kind of dynamics I've had, or how I really feel. I don't sit here victimizing myself. I barely want to talk about it. I know there are real problems in the world, okay? I get that me and my feelings are not big enough issues. But, don't you sit here and ask me to tell you something honest when I already feel like an idiot and then make me feel like I don't deserve to be upset. I appreciate you bringing me here and all, but I think you should go now. I want to be alone." Her voice is stern.

Omid puts his hands in his face and stands up. "Do you feel better now getting that off your chest?"

"Not even close. I feel exhausted." Roya's voice now shakes.

Omid breathes in heavily and starts walking towards the door. "Before I go, I just want you to know I would never judge you. I'm really sorry if it came off that way. Goodnight." He puts on his shoes and leaves.

Roya closes the door behind him, but feels trapped. She tries laying down and stretching her legs, but everything feels uncomfortable. Her heart feels heavy, but she can't cry. She puts on her *monto* and *roosari* and heads to the small garden hidden behind the complex's gate. The tall trees hovering over the fence create shadows on the paved cement. Roya looks around before sliding her *roosari* off and lays down with her back on the ground. Closing her eyes, she digs her fingernails into the soil. Anything to feel connected to something. For the first time in a while, the tears stubbornly refuse to come out. The numbness sinks in. She feels like her heart is a wild animal rattling in her ribcage. She digs her nails deeper into the earth. The sun has left. The trees' shadows begin to grow smaller as the night fully takes over the sky. Suddenly, she feels someone watching over her and opens her eyes.

"I must say, Roya jaan, I did not expect to find you exactly in this condition. I see you have found the garden." Khanoom Jaan is now home. She kneels down and touches Roya's shoulder. "I know today has been long. How about you go wash up and rest. I'll prepare some dinner. Tomorrow, we will start again."

# SHADE

# CHAPTER 5

The next morning Roya wakes up once more to the sound of Tehran's honking drivers, but this time the voice of Googoosh's "Gol Bi Goldoon" playing downstairs drowns out the ruckus.

Roya can feel her heart do that thing where it tightens for a moment as if two strings were tying it up in a double knot. The nervous feeling then moves to her stomach where it feels as if hundreds of fluttering butterflies all lost their wings and fell at once.     She closes her eyes and listens carefully to the lyrics. She cannot understand every word perfectly, but she can feel the way the notes rise and fall in Googoosh's voice.

She thinks of Cyrus, and her heart longs for him. Pathetic. Does he even think about me? Doubt it. She slowly opens her eyelids, turns over on her side, and stares out the window for a few moments. *Who knows.* She tries to shrug her thoughts away and sits on the bed.

Today, she and Khanoom Jaan are going to Tajrish Bazaar, one of Tehran's most famous markets. She hopes this will help take her mind off of her uneasiness.

She quickly puts on some jeans and a white button up, picks up her navy *monto* off the foot of the bed, and grabs her cream-colored *roos-ari*. She walks into the kitchen where she sees a basket of *noon-barbari* and feta cheese awaiting her on the table. Roya flashes an embarrassed smile. *I really should be waking up earlier to help prepare breakfast.*

"*Sobh bekheir*, Khanoom Jaan. *Merci* for the breakfast."

"Good morning. *Nooshe-jaan*. You will need the energy. We have a long day ahead of us. Do you have an outfit for the wedding tonight?"

"I have some options, but I'm not sure yet. We're still going to the wedding?"

"Yes, of course. Perhaps you will find something while we're out shopping today. I was thinking we could see your Mamani and then go explore the Bazaar." Khanoom Jaan's presence is always so warm and calming. Roya admires her grounded energy. Her own mind always seems to be racing from one thought to another. In Khanoom Jaan's presence, she finds herself slowing down. She feels safe.

Roya finishes her breakfast and washes it down with the cup of chai she substituted for her usual coffee.

"Shall we?" Khanoom Jaan calls for a taxi, and they make their way downstairs.

As the taxi pulls up to the front of the complex, Roya remembers she forgot something.

"Just a minute please!" She rushes back to her bedside and runs downstairs with her headphones in her hand. "You never know when the inspiration hits. I like to listen to music during the drives."

"Very good."

Khanoom Jaan sits alongside the driver in the front. Roya sits in the back and manually rolls the window down.

The taxi driver peers through the center rearview mirror to look at Roya. "*Khanoom*, the pollution is heavy the closer we get to the center of the city. Just warning you in case you mind," he says in Farsi.

Roya smiles back with her eyes. "I know, but I want to remember these moments. I want to remember these smells. Years from now, I may forget many things, but smells will always take me back in time." She responds in her elementary level Farsi.

"First time visiting Iran?" The driver rolls down his window too.

"Kind of. I have visited as a kid but never as a young adult."

"*Be salamati.* Ve are khappy to have you, our American friend."

With Roya's broken Farsi and the man's broken English, their conversation is whole. A language spoken with smiles.

"*Merci.*"

****

Khanoom Jaan begins to ask the driver about his wife and kids. Roya isn't sure if she just happens to be acquainted with everyone or if it is simply her nature to befriend every stranger. While Khanoom Jaan continues chatting, Roya plugs her headphones comfortably into her ears.

Drake's "Fall For Your Type" comes on. Roya quickly changes the song. *Not that kind of mood,* she tells herself. *This day was supposed to be a break from thinking about Cyrus.*

Next, "Lotus Flower" comes on. Radiohead —this she can handle. She raises the volume and looks out the window. She has accepted the chaotic driving and disregard for traffic lanes, but is still amazed by how the drivers intuitively maneuver the cars without hitting one another. Aside from the excessive honking and occasional yelling, the ability to handle Tehran's traffic feels like a pleasant adventure itself.

Roya people watches as the car races past the crowds, but her mind is already drifting. Radiohead always reminds her of high school. Those days already feel so distant —the innocence and security of imagining all that she couldn't wait to achieve as an adult. Her mind takes her to a memory during her senior year of high school.

She had just finished breakfast when Azadeh walked into the kitchen with a pile of mail in one hand and a packet hiding in her other hand.

"*Guess what, Roya?*"

"*What?*" Roya looks up quickly and then goes back to scrolling on her phone.

"*You're gonna want to pay attention to me right now.*" Azadeh waves the pile in front of Roya while still hiding the single packet.

"*Azadeh, what do you—*" Roya begins slightly annoyed and then stops."*Why are you hiding something? You're being weird right now, ya know."*

"*This is for dramatic effect. If this were a movie, I would say druuuum roll pleaaaase.*" Azadeh jumps onto the kitchen table and hands Roya the packet.

Roya's heart sinks. Not in the way a nervous singer does before her first solo in the school choir. Not in the way lovers feel when they long for one another. Not in the way one feels when she has something to confess, but can't get the words right. No. This is that feeling when the one thing she has ever wanted dangles in front of her eyes, circles around her, and lands perfectly in her hands the way leather shoes take form to the soles.

"*Azadeh, oh my God. That's a packet. A packet from USC. They don't send packets just to say no, ya know!*"

Azadeh smiles at her older sister like a proud mom. "*Yeah, I know. I'm not an idiot! Now, are you going to open it or what! I have things to do, and I want to watch you bawl like a freak before I go.*"

Roya slowly opens the letter and tries to prolong the moment, so she can savor it.

*Dear Roya,*

*Congratulations! We are pleased to inform you of your acceptance to the USC Thornton School of Music, Class of 2017.*

"*I got in.*" She stares at the words for a few more seconds. "*Azadeh, I got in!*" This time she jumps up on the kitchen table and squeezes her sister rocking back and forth.

"*Duh, Roya. Are you gonna cry or what! I was waiting to record this moment.*"

As Roya pulls back, Azadeh notices her sister's eyes are

glazed over with tears. Her cheeks are red. *"There we go. But in all seriousness, I'm so happy for you."*

Roya's eyes are now full and her tears heavier.

*"YES. Can I record this? I want to remind you of how happy you are right now."*

*"No Azadeh, please don't."*

*"Why?"*

*"Because I'm not going."*

*"Wait, what? Why?"* Azadeh knows what Roya is about to say.

*"You know mom and dad won't let me do this."*

*"Maybe we can convince them? Don't say that so fast."*

*"No. It just won't work."*

*"Let's just call them and share the news."* Azadeh insists.

They both huddle over the speakerphone and wait for the ring.

*"Hi, Mom! Guess what?"* Roya says excited as her tears slow down.

*"Hi, azizam. What?"*

*"Mom, Roya got into USC's School of Music. Isn't that amazing."* Azadeh blurts out.

*"Wow, Roya! That's great honey."* Her voice trails off a bit.

*"You don't sound that excited. Mom, it's actually a really big deal. One of the top schools for music. Aren't you proud?"*

*"Yes, of course I am."*

Roya can sense her mother's worry in her voice before she speaks again.

*"Roya, dokhtaram..."*

*"Yeah?"*

*"You know that you can't go. It just doesn't make sense."*

Roya knew she would say this, but hearing it still hurts.

*"But, mom…can we talk about it lat--"*

*"I have to go. I'll call you back. I love you."*

*"Okay, I love you too."* Roya ends the call and stares down.

Azadeh watches as two teardrops fall from Roya's eyes and land on the acceptance letter still in her sister's lap.

*"Roya, I'm sorry you're sad. Do you want to call Dad now at least?"*

Roya looks up and wipes the mascara stains from her cheeks with the sleeve of her baby blue sweater and jumps off the counter. *"No, I don't want to hear it twice right now. I'll tell him later."* She walks towards the door.

*"Where are you going?"* Azadeh picks up the letter Roya left on the table.

*"For a drive."*

*"Where?"*

*"Just a drive. I just need to be alone. I'll be fine, honestly."*

Roya turns on the car. "Lotus Flower" plays on the Bluetooth. Once she'd pulled out of the driveway, she begins to cry. And she cries and cries. It is that feeling when one realizes that even dead things eventually float to the surface, but the heart just sinks to the ground. It was the feeling of a dream being buried.

****

As the taxi nears the entrance of the bazaar, Roya finally notices the thick combination of gasoline and pollution in the air. She and Khanoom Jaan step out of the right side to avoid the oncoming traffic.

"Watch your step." Khanoom Jaan points to the exposed sewer drains just before the sidewalk like Omid had.

Roya carefully hops over holding tight onto her *roosari* so that it does not fall off.

As they walk into the busy market, the crowds are much like the traffic on the roads. A teenage boy carrying a large sack on his shoulder rushes from the left causing Roya to bump into a woman wearing an all-black *chador* just beside her.

"Khanoom Jaan, why is she wearing that big blanket around her? I've noticed some of the women do. Tehran is much more relaxed about its dress code, isn't it?"

Khanoom Jaan grabs Roya's arm and pulls her close so that she doesn't bump into another woman rushing by with a toddler in her arms. "It's called a *chador*. Women who are more religious or conservative sometimes choose to wear them. Sometimes, their families may force them to. It all depends."

"Oh." Roya replies embarrassed. She cannot understand why someone would choose to wear one if they are not obligated to, but also feels like she is being ignorant. *Can't someone be religious and still not have to wear that?* She silently wonders to herself. *Best not to discuss that with Khanoom Jaan right now. I've already called it a blanket. Nice, Roya. Real nice.*

The bazaar consists of arching cement walls tattooed with the passage of time. Some portions have ceilings with small openings in which sunlight comes through. The summer heat can be seen glistening on the faces of store tenders as they sit in front of their small, doorless booths.

Roya runs her hand against a wall covered with various "evil eye" key chains. She picks one intricate keychain that has a string of four red beads and a single evil eye symbol with metallic gold writing on the back. She knows the writing is a prayer written in Farsi even though she cannot read it.

Khanoom Jaan notices Roya's interest. "You like it?"

"Yeah, it's nice. I don't understand what it says, but it makes me feel good having one. I feel like I'm being protected."

Khanoom Jaan calls over the young man working the desk. His white shirt is tucked into his black dress pants. A silver chain with similar Farsi writing hangs from his neck on top of his black chest hair that's poking out. As Khanoom Jaan pulls out her wallet to pay, Roya gently touches her arm.

"Khanoom Jaan, please. You've already done so much. This is something small. I would like to get it myself."

"Don't be silly, Roya. You are my guest!"

"No, honestly. Please. I will feel guilty. This is something personal I'd like to buy for myself. No *tarof*."

Khanoom Jaan looks into Roya's eyes and senses her sincerity. "Alright, just this one I will allow. Only because it is personal for you."

"*Merci*."

"But!" Khanoom Jaan's lips stretch into a playful smile. "We might as well let you have the full experience. Today, you will learn the art of *chooneh*."

Roya's body tenses. Her ears move back and forth like they always do when she gets nervous. She knows *chooneh* means *bargaining*. And bargaining over prices is something she does not have the courage to do.

"I mean, it's just a small keychain. Really can't be all that much. Plus, this is how they make a living. Right? I say we save the lesson for another day." Roya lets out a nervous laugh hoping Khanoom Jaan is convinced.

"No, no. Today seems like the perfect day. After all, it's only a small keychain. Should be simple knocking off a few dollars." She can tell Roya is uncomfortable, but she wants her to learn to assert herself. The amusement of watching is a bonus.

"Right. Well, okay. I, I–– okay how do I start this?"

"First you need to call him back over."

"But how do I *chooneh*? What price is too low? How high is too high?"

"Think about it this way. Ask yourself how much do you think this keychain is worth. Then, decide what is the highest you'd be willing to pay for it and the lowest ideal price, even if it sounds crazy at first. Then, you approach the employee with those considerations in mind and ask for the selling price."

"When should I compromise?"

"When it feels right."

Roya's eyebrows bend forward again as she gives Khanoom Jaan a confused look. That answer doesn't help her at all.

*When it feels right? What does that even mean? It's just a keychain.* "Okay, I'm going for it."

"Be confident."

Roya flashes her a closed lip smile. "I will try." She tugs on her *roosari* once more and tries to stick her hair back under the cloth. She takes a deep breath and approaches Mr. Chest Hair. "Um, *salam.* Excuse me!"

He does not hear her.

Roya taps him on the shoulder. "Hi, um, could you tell me the price for this keychain please?" She says again in elementary Farsi.

The man steps around the counter and walks over to the dangling blue wall of charms. "*Salam khanoom,* this one?" He takes the keychain from Roya and holds it up under the light as if it would make a difference. "15,000 toman."

*15,000 what? Oh shit. Wait. I don't know how this monetary system work.* "Could you please tell me how much that is in U.S. dollars?" Roya gives her best doe-eyed impression.

The man hands the keychain back to her. "Hah! I knew you were not from here."

*How can everyone tell?*

"Your accent for starters."

*Wait. Is he reading my mind now?*

"And I have had the same price for these keychains since I can remember. That's how I know."

*This is weird. Focus Roya.* "Oh right, yes I'm visiting! But 15,000 toman is way too much. How about 8,000 toman?"

"No way! Too low." He scoffs as if Roya is offering him lint in exchange for the item. "13,000 toman."

"10,000 toman." Roya replies back like a game of verbal ping pong.

"12,000 toman."

"Okay, deal. I'll take it."

The man places the keychain in a clear plastic bag and hands it to Roya. She walks proudly waiving the little baggy in the air as if it were a victory flag.

"So, how did it go? What was the final price?"

"12,000 toman." Roya brushes her shoulders like a Jay Z music video.

"Hmm. And how much did he offer it to you for?"

"15,000 toman."

"Hmm." Khanoom Jaan makes that noise again. "Not bad for your first time."

"What do you mean? I don't even know how much that exactly is in dollars, but from what I can tell, that's pretty cheap for this keychain!"

"Well, for starters, everyone in this bazaar knows he sells those keychains at a standard price of 12,000 toman. If you bargain, you can get it for 10,000 toman. My God, one time I saw a woman get two of those from him for a deal of 8,000. I think she drove him insane that day!"

"He told me his standard price for locals was 15,000 toman?"

"Because he knew you are not a local. You see why this is amusing now?" Her gray hair is peeking out from the top of her *roosari* and sweetly falling in her face as she smiles. "It's alright, dear. Now you know for next time. Let's see if we can find you a dress for the wedding!"

"I think I'm good for today with the bargaining lesson. Can you tackle the next round for me?"

"I make no promises!"

# CHAPTER 6

Roya's dress keeps getting stuck under her heels as it drags slightly on the floor. *Ah, shit. I knew I should have got this hemmed!* Growing impatient, she finally grabs the edges and holds it to her side as her and Khanoom Jaan enter the venue. The wedding ceremony is hosted in someone's backyard gazebo. Positioned at the far end of the room is the bride and groom's *sofreh aghd*––decked out with metallic silver and rose gold centerpieces, each symbolizing an aspect of marriage. A medium sized mirror sits in the middle of the setup. Its thick metal frame has little crystals that seem to sparkle as if they were flirting with the lighting of the room.

Khanoom Jaan and Roya take their seat in the fourth row. To Roya's surprise, the men and women sit intermingled in the room. Only a few of the elderly women keep on their headscarves. The rest have stowed them away. Their hair, in shades of blonde, black, and everything in-between, is free in the open air for all to admire. The man officiating the wedding is short and what little remains of his hair is gray. His voice is deep with fervor as he recites a poem of wisdom for the couple. He then turns to the groom to ask if he accepts the bride. The groom, a man in his late thirties, dutifully responds yes. Next, it is the bride's turn to accept the marriage.

"The bride has gone to pick flowers!" shouts a bridesmaid rubbing the traditional cubes of sugar over the couple's head.

The officiator asks the bride once more.

"The bride has gone to bring rose water!" shouts another brides-maid holding a corner of the *toor*.

The officiator asks once more.

True to tradition, the bride answers on the third try. "With the permission of my parents, I say yes."

Flower petals are thrown in the air as the couple lick honey off one another's pinkies in well wishes for a sweet marriage.

Khanoom Jaan leans sideways next to Roya. "Only in the Iranian tradition does the woman still play hard-to-get even at the wedding!" She laughs quietly like a young girl instructed to remain silent in class.

"I can see why they say us Persian women are high-maintenance." Roya mumbles.

"You think the men are any less? And besides, it's all in good fun. I think it makes it that much more engaging." She smiles the way Mamani does, and Roya wishes she was there too. "Shall we head to the reception?"

"Sure." Roya stares at the bride and groom now greeting their guests. They stand only a foot apart, but their bodies are turned away from each other like two strangers standing in line. Neither of their eyes show emotion despite the half-baked smiles they have managed the entire time.

****

The salon is a short drive from the ceremony. Khanoom Jaan leads Roya past the buffet of appetizers to their assigned table.

"I will be right back!" She hangs her purse on the back of the chair. "When I return, we can go get something to snack on together? Dinner will be late tonight." She waves to a woman across the room and rushes over.

Roya pulls out her phone and begins scrolling through Instagram. The reception is spotty, and the photos refuse to load. She clicks her phone off and sets it back on the table. Music is playing, but the dance-floor is empty. Resting her chin on her hand, she scans the room. Her chest feels tight again. Sometimes, it just does that. Suddenly, she watches a couple walk past her to the dance floor. The woman holds the man's hand and cajoles him forward. He looks as though he is in his early forties, and she is in her mid-thirties. The man now wraps one of his hands around her waist and gently grabs her hand as he dips her slowly to the music. He pulls her in close to him, looks into her eyes, and spins her around. He smiles this time as she turns to face him again. He has that look in his eyes ––that look when men know they have given their heart to a woman. That look of awe when one knows what he feels is much greater than he can control ––something almost divine.

Roya notices his vulnerability as he holds her in his arms. The woman knows this too. Roya stares at her radiating sensuality and confidence. She stares at the way their bodies move together ––forward, backward, around, and back. The woman moves her shoulders and hips, pulling away and then leaning forward into his arms again. In this moment, time feels as though it has slowed so that this couple could move in complete unity.

*This. This is what I want.* Roya thinks to herself. All her life, people's words made her feel as though she misunderstood what love should look like.

*Love should be fast some would say. So fast you don't even know what happened. Love should be slow others would say. So slow that you don't make mistakes. You must learn to fall in love. Love is for fools.*

All these words seem so distant to what Roya feels love should be like.

As she watches the couple, she feels a certainty in the core of her stomach. She may never understand the many shades of love, but she knows what love should look like for her.

*Love should be movement. Love should be forward, backward, and back around. I don't want your promises. I don't want your words. I don't want to need you. But, I want you. I want to feel you. I want to feel a part of you and you a part of me. Love should be timeless. Love should be music. Love should be strength and vulnerability intertwined, like limbs that curl into one another. Love should be simultaneously fast and slow —felt so much that time bows to its presence. Love is two people holding one another and saying —my love, we don't belong to one another, but I will hold you with all that I have. Will you hold me too? That's what I want.*

The song finishes, and the couple walk to Roya's table with their arms wrapped around each other's waist. They point to the center-piece labeled "Table 24" and smile at Roya.

"*Salam*, looks like we are sitting together! You must be Roya, Del-band's daughter? *Vay*, you look so much like her." The woman says as she places an elbow on top of the chair and her other hand on the man's lap. The man wipes sweat from his forehead and tries to catch his breath. "Shayan, let me introduce you to Roya. She's Delband's daughter!"

The man looks up to greet Roya. "*Salam*, it's so nice to meet you. Wow. You do look like your mother. Copy! Both of you are beauties."

Roya has no idea who these two people are or how they know who she is. Yet, she finds herself mesmerized by their presence together. The way their body language is in sync even as they sit still.

"Hi, thank you. It's really nice to meet you too. I am sorry. I don't mean to be rude, but how do you know who I am? Are we related? Be-cause I seem to find out I have new cousins every day!"

The man and woman laugh. "Seems that way, doesn't it? But, no. We are not related by blood. Maybe by souls!" says the woman.

Roya smiles at her use of the word "souls." Seems like everywhere she goes in this country, there is a discussion about souls and the heart.

"That's a funny way to put it." Roya replies.

"Sorry, didn't even introduce myself. My name is Azar. I'm Arman's daughter, and this is the love of my life, Shayan. Our parents were very close growing up. My father speaks very highly of your mother. The best stories!"

Roya has never heard her mother mention anything about Arman. She doesn't want to be rude, so she pretends to know who Azar is refer-ring to.

"Right, right. Arman! Of course." Roya nods her head politely. "So, what kind of stories?"

"Oh, so many!" Azar looks to Shayan. "*Azizam,* doesn't my dad tell the greatest stories about Delband? They were really something." She flips her long hair to the side as she flirtatiously smiles.

Roya is so curious about this Arman guy. *Who is he and how was he so close with my mom?*

"Roya, if you are anything like your mother, I'm sure you find yourself in some trouble from time-to-time." He laughs as he wraps his arms around Azar. "Arman and Delband sure did. Skipping school for secret dates. My favorite is that time Khanoom Jaan caught them at the café. Azar and I laughed quite a bit at that one."

"*Eyyy vay!* Even my mother enjoyed the stories about her. I think she understood that he and Delband shared a deep past, one that would always be woven into his identity. God, my mom loved him so much. She lived for his stories."

Roya's thoughts are running in circles. *Who is Arman. What past? What happened to Azar's mom? My own mom, a trouble maker? Do they even know her?* She simply nods and smiles.

"They sure were something! Wouldn't really consider myself a troublemaker, but I have my moments." She says with a cheeky shrug.

Shayan excuses himself from the table and goes to greet an elderly man that had just walked into the salon. Roya and Azar lean back into their chairs and watch the bride and groom sitting at their table in the center of the room. After a few seconds, Roya leans towards Azar.

"Do you think they are in love?" she asks Azar.

"Who? Them?" Azar says gesturing to the bride and groom.

"Yeah, them."

Azar giggles. "Eh, not sure. Doesn't seem like it, does it?"

"I mean, I'm not sure. I guess it doesn't. But, hey, what does love look like anyway?"

"Great question. I suppose it's different for everyone. When it's not there, you can tell though."

"So, why would someone get married if they aren't in love now-adays? It's not like it was before."

"Like what before? Power? Money? Security? Convenience? Duty? People still want the idea, the safety, or the control. These things still exist. They just look different now." Azar looks at Roya with a kindness in her eyes.

"Why did you get married?"

"Me? Hah, I didn't!"

Roya raises her eyebrows. "Oh, sorry. I just thought you and Shayan would be married. You said he is the love of your life. I just assumed."

"He is the love of my life." She places her hand on Roya's. "And that's enough."

"Yeah, that makes sense. I feel similar. But, do you ever want to get married?"

"Sure, maybe! If it feels right, then why not? I just don't want to do it, because we feel like we have to. I want it to be, you know, the cherry on top of what we already have together. Just something extra to what is already real between us. When I met Shayan years ago, he was the first man I could see myself marrying. Even then, I knew it was the love that felt right. Not that he was this perfect person. But, his presence intrigued me at first. Then, it just pulled me in and wrapped itself around me. It's difficult for me to explain, but I've never been good with words! I just let it be."

Roya listens closely as Azar speaks. She, too, had always felt that the way people treated marriage seemed odd. Like some transaction or check list of criteria. But, she had not expected a woman Azar's age to be so carefree about it, especially in Iran. Her perspective goes against everything Roya had ever heard about marriage.

"I think what you are saying makes perfect sense. I am just sur-prised you feel that way too."

"I told you we could be soul sisters. I just felt it. So, what about you? Do you have a boyfriend?"

"Not right now. I recently just had a breakup actually." Roya's tone shifts. She shuffles in her seat uncomfortably.

"Oh, what happened?"

"Long story. Probably not the best time to talk about it now."

"I understand. Well—" Azar pauses for a moment. "Wear your heartache as a badge of honor!"

"Honor?"

"Yes, of course. It's a privilege to feel a love so deep that your heart aches in its aftermath. Better than never having experienced love at all." She gestures to the bored bride and groom once more as she gets up and pushes her chair in. "For now, try to enjoy yourself tonight. Be here if you can, not in your mind. Magic happens when you stay in the now."

She turns to walk off but spins back around. "Oh, one more thing. Open hearts ache sometimes, but only closed hearts break. Hope that makes sense. Now, let me go find Shayan. He promised me one more dance!" Azar winks at Roya and adjusts her dress. "I'm so happy I could finally meet you."

"Yeah, me too. I'm really happy. I like your vibe." *Open hearts ache sometimes, but only closed hearts break.*

"My vibe?" Azar smiles. In fact, she hasn't stopped since the moment she sat down.

"Your energy."

"Energy, interesting you mention that. Seems like you're an old soul, Roya. It's lovely. I'll be back!"

Azar sneaks up behind Shayan, and he subtly kisses her cheek.

Roya watches them for a few seconds before getting up to pour herself some chai. She reaches for the petite glass cup, slowly turns the knob of the kettle to pour tea, and adds a few drops of rose water. She peers across the room. A young couple flirt. The men chat under the gazebo. The elderly women stare down the kids, who are throwing themselves onto the dancefloor. The pop singer Arash blasts from the speakers.

She checks her phone and sees Atefeh has sent her a message on

WhatsApp. The reception is back. Roya puts her phone away and tries her best to take Azar's advice. *Be in the moment.* But, all she can think about is —*who the hell is Arman?*

# CHAPTER 7

The next afternoon they walk past the burgundy albaloo trees and enter the covered patio. Roya grabs the pitcher of pomegranate *sharbat*, pours some in a cup, and adds water. The dense syrup is still too sweet for her taste buds.

"Would you like to help me in the garden for a bit before we eat?" Khanoom Jaan reaches for her watering pot.

"Sure. I'd love to." They walk around the patio back under the open air as Khanoom Jaan hands Roya a spare pot.

"So Roya, what are you studying?"

"Well, I'm in my last year of undergraduate school."

"University, right?"

"Yes, university. Right now I'm studying pre-medicine."

"And then?"

"And then I become a doctor."

"And then?"

"Then, I spend the rest of my life as Dr. Roya."

"And then?"

"Then, I get married, have kids, and wait until they're teenagers, so they can tell me I'm being annoying." Roya lets out a playful laugh.

The old woman smiles with her eyes intrigued by the young girl sitting before her. "Sounds like a wonderful plan then!"

"Yeah, wonderful." This time Roya mumbles with a look of uncertainty on her face.

"Is that not what you dreamed of? What's wrong?"

"I have thought about it. A lot. It's not exactly what I have dreamed of."

"And what is your dream? What makes your heart feel alive?"

"Isn't that a little cliché?" Roya replies innocently.

"Would you rather me ask what makes your heart feel dead?"

"Well, no." Roya smiles. "I love to create music. Every time I feel lost or my chest feels heavy or I'm just moved by emotions I don't understand, I begin to hum to myself. Slowly, the hum turns into a melody. And then I begin to sing random words that just flow from me. It's weird."

"That's because they flow from your heart, not your mind. They are your soul's art."

"I guess so. It just feels good, you know? I can go into my own world and create something for myself. It's when I feel the most understood. It's always been kinda my secret thing."

"So, why not pursue music in university or take classes?"

"Music in school? There's no way to make a living like that. I thought about some classes. I just don't have time."

"And why pre-medicine?"

"I want to help people. Medicine heals. It makes people better."

Khanoom Jaan continues to pluck the overgrowing mint leaves and collect them for dinner later. She is thoughtful, examining each leaf and gently placing them in her bowl.

"Roya––" she finally says softly as she tilts her head and looks at the young girl from the corner of her eye.

"Can you hand me those scissors please?"

"Sure."

The elderly woman cuts the stem of a white rose and hands it to Roya.

"Omid mentioned you had said we should appreciate flowers as they are and to let them grow in their roots?"

"Yes. But, I want you to appreciate its beauty and take care of this one."

"Flowers all eventually dry out Khanoom Jaan. I will water it, but it's not going to last very long now."

"Exactly."

"I don't understand." Roya's eyebrows bend downward.

"The branches and petals of a flower can grow as long and as far as they may. When the seasons change and their time arrives, all will wither to make room for the new blooms in Spring. But, a flower cut from its source will dry out much faster than that connected to its roots."

"Right…"

"In some ways, this is how us humans are too. Our source is our soul, and our heart is our root. What a shame all those dry petals that long ago forgot the soil from which their dreams were born. They become so quick to fall apart."

Roya sits quietly and runs her fingers through the dirt, exfoliating her fingertips as she slowly brushes the residue off. She is trying to understand the weight of the woman's wisdom.

"Oh Roya, one more thing."

"Yes?"

"Music, too, can heal. You, too, can heal. Helping someone is not just keeping them alive. Sometimes, it is helping them to feel alive."

****

Khanoom Jaan stands up and mixes the mint leaves with the rest of the *sabzi* sitting on the table. Just then, the patio door abruptly opens. A gust of wind blows through the room startling Roya.

"Omid joon, *salam*. You are just in time. I am setting the table for dinner. Please join us."

"*Salam. Merci.* My mother asked me to come by and see if the pistachio cream puffs are ready for tomorrow's *mehmooni.* You know her. She gets nervous."

"Ahh, yes yes. Your mother, such a wonderful host, but she overthinks every detail. I'll give you the desserts after dinner. For now, join us."

Omid smiles and pulls a chair next to Roya.

"Mmm, *kabob koobideh* and *barg.* My favorite!" He rubs his belly and grins leaning closer to Roya. "Hi, by the way."

"*Salam.*" Roya is still annoyed with how their last conversation ended.

"Oh, there we go. Thought for a second you forgot how to speak. And in Farsi, too? Look at you. So cultured!"

Roya rolls her eyes but finds herself softening up to his presence. "So, your mom is having a *mehmooni*?"

"Sure thing. Would you like to come?"

"Khanoom Jaan is already invited. She invited me to come along too."

"Oh, did she now? Well, doesn't a personal invitation feel even better?"

"Basically, you want me to come?"

"Basically." He reaches for one of the mint leaves and pops it in his mouth. "Mmm, so fresh. Nature's gift to mankind."

Khanoom Jaan walks back into the room and places down the skewers of steaming red meat, sandwiched in-between pieces of tomatoes and onions.

"Bah, Bah." Omid eyes the juicy piece of *barg* dangling from the top.

"Tell me, Omid *joon.* How's everything? How's life?" She asks while breaking up the pieces of *tahdig* into imperfect slices.

"You know, the same. Helping mom and working at the store." He changes the subject before Khanoom Jaan can ask about school. "But, I am veeeery excited." He stretches out the syllables as he does a silly shimmy nudging Roya.

"And why is that?"

Khanoom Jaan always enjoyed Omid's quirky enthusiasm. Since he was a young boy, she had always felt that he was special. Tough, always finding himself in some sort of mishap, but also tenderhearted.

*"He will be quite the ladies' man."* She would say to his mother.

*"Oh, will he now. How so?"* His mother would stare at her young son and know the answer.

*"Because he has the strength to see beyond his own ego."* Khanoom Jaan would reply.

"Well, I was going to wait and tell Roya tomorrow. But, I might as well say it now! I have officially organized our annual trip to Shomal. And I figured since Roya hasn't been, she should come along. See Iran's oceans. Maybe let us know if they are more beautiful than her California coasts."

Khanoom Jaan looks over to make eye contact with Roya and see how she feels about it.

Roya looks hesitant but intrigued. She, too, looks up to meet Khanoom Jaan's eyes and receives a nod of approval.

"I have actually heard a lot of good things about Shomal. Not sure if it can beat those Malibu waves, but I'd be open to exploring what Iran has to offer." She playfully nudges Omid back.

"Great, it's a date then."

The word "date" jolts Roya, and she shoots Omid a blank look.

"As in, the date is set. Not a date, date. Don't flatter yourself, Roya. You American girls." He says knowingly trying to get a reaction from her.

Khanoom Jaan places a piece of *tahdig* on Omid and Roya's plates and pushes the last of the *koobideh* onto the *noon lavash*, so they can easily scoop them from the platter.

"Here, take some mint too. It helps you to digest the meat." She then leaves the room to finish preparing the cream puffs.

"Hey, Omid." Roya speaks softly.

"Yeah?"

"I'm actually really excited about going to the beach."

"I figured you would be. Happy to hear that. You know, this won't be like that American show with the girls running on the beach in a one piece though, right?"

"Baywatch?" Roya knows he is teasing. "Yeah, but still. I've always loved the water."

"Oh, the water, the trees, the flowers, the views overlooking the hills —so green. The absolute greenest of hills. You will love it. Very different than Tehran. Here, the people see a different kind of green. But in Shomal, it's the kind that makes the long drive worthwhile."

# CHAPTER 8

"Thank you for dinner tonight. It was all lovely. Marzi, your *fes-enjoon* will always be my favorite!" Khanoom Jaan says as she begins cleaning up the plates that had been left on the table while they chatted.

"Anytime. Please take some leftovers with you." Omid's mother playfully pushes Khanoom Jaan's hands away and takes the dirty plates from her. "And absolutely no cleaning while you are here! Don't even think about it. Please."

"Alright, alright. I know how you are. Thank you." Khanoom Jaan checks her watch and starts putting on her *monto*.

"Leaving so soon? At least stay for another round of chai! Or fruit! I just sent Omid to buy some more. It's only 10pm."

"*Merci*, but it has been a long day. I better get some rest."

"Roya jaan, you are more than welcome to stay longer if you like. Omid can drop you off home later." Marzi looks to Khanoom Jaan.

"If that's alright with Khanoom Jaan, I'd love to stay for a bit longer." Roya replies.

"Very well then! Enjoy your time. I will see you back at the apartment. Not too late, eh?" She air kisses the women goodbye and waives to the men. "*Merci* again for the evening, Marzi joon."

Omid's mother heads back to the kitchen to finish clearing the table while the other women join the men in the living room. Marzi has successfully fought off all helpers. Roya lingers around, but feels out of place without Omid there. She notices some dirty plates still left on the table and walks over to retrieve them. As she carries them to the kitchen, she hears the men discussing politics. She stops before entering and tries to listen.

Darvish, Omid's father, dips his sugar cube into his tea and places it in his mouth. That's how her father drinks his chai as well. Growing up, she would watch her father place one sugar cube in the tea and stir. Then, he'd dip a second one only to directly place it in his mouth.

*"Baba, why don't you put both of them into the cup at once?"* Roya asks.

Her father hugs her tightly and looks at his daughter. *"Roya jaan, you ask so many questions. You always have."*

Roya rests her head on his chest and wraps her small arms around his stomach.

*"I know."* She says knowing very well her curiosity. She was always wondering why and how. Knowing the answers wasn't enough. She wanted to understand the things that puzzled her. *"So, why do you do that with the sugar cubes? You never answered!"*

*"Because this way I can enjoy the taste of sugar without it becoming lost in the cup of tea. And then, I can enjoy the tea without it becoming overly sweet."* She raises his two hands and moves them up and down like a scale. *"Balance, Roya jaan. Everything in moderation."*

Roya then picks up a sugar cube and dips it into the tea just like her father. She mimics his behavior sometimes just so she can feel closer to him. Her father is a sensitive man with difficulty showing too much emotion. Whether it was his heritage, his childhood upbringing, or the weight of both over the passing years, he wore his big heart within his armor.

*Maybe if I act just like him, he will at least understand me better.* Roya thinks.

With this thought, she squeezes him tighter until he has to finally get up and move. She is never the first to let go. She would have held on forever with her head on his chest just to hear his heart beating. Just to know he, too, can feel emotions just as deeply as her. That the blood that runs through his veins and gives him life runs through hers as well.

Her father holds her close and simply says, *"When you were a baby, your whole body used to fit across my chest. Look at you now growing up so fast. Slow down, dokhtaram. Slow down. Life is moving too fast."*

And Roya knows that means ––*I love you.*

Just then Marzi pops up. "Roya, please no need to clean! Come along now."

"Marzi joon, I'm not cleaning! I'm just… bringing these to you. Can I keep you company please? I can just put some of these away for you. No real cleaning. See?"

"Alright. Only because Omid is not here to keep you company!" She wipes her hand on a cloth and returns to washing the dishes.

As Roya empties the leftovers into small containers, her attention returns to the men's chatter.

"Darvish, I'm telling you. The people are getting restless. The youth will not tolerate the restrictions. They have had enough. They feel suffocated." Mahmad shifts in his seat as he leans forward to set his tea cup on the wooden table. He brushes his thin mustache with his fingers to clear the crumbs from the tea cookie he just ate.

Mahmad had once jumped into the wrong taxi on a busy, arid day in Tehran. In his frantic hurry, he sat on an item that cracked underneath him. Seconds later, Darvish, who had also been sitting in the backseat, let out a howling laugh. *"I have been looking for a reason to buy new glasses."* And so, they became friends much to the cab driver's surprise.

"What do you mean suffocating? Things are getting better. Can't you see? Change takes time, Mahmad. It will come." Darvish now replies calmly.

"*Areh digeh*, you see what happened with the Revolution after the Shah. Same thing with all these governments. Sure, they might offer different perks here and there. But underneath, they are all the same." Dariush chimes in.

Roya has barely heard Dariush speak all night. Instead, she had watched him politely nod from one encounter to another. For the first time, she hears the texture of his voice. His tongue seems to hug his lips when he speaks, but his voice does not quiver.

Darvish turns now directly to Dariush. "You are being very negative. Can't you see as a society we have made progress? The times are complicated. I am not saying that what we have now is perfect. Certainly not. All I am saying is one cannot rush social change or else the pursuit will become contorted and consume you. Change must happen over time."

"But, what is enough time?" Dariush sits up in his seat and leans closer to Darvish. "When has it been enough time? We are old now. Our time has passed. But, the youth are living in a different world. A globalized world. Don't we want our beautiful country to be a part of the global markets? Don't they deserve to be integrated into the international fabric of our times?"

Mahmad picks up his tea again and takes a small sip. "Mathematics, poetry, the arts, philosophy! Our culture has given birth to so many ideas."

Roya finishes placing all the food containers in the fridge one-by-one while Omid's mother separates the pomegranate kernels into a bowl. She leans closer to the doorway, so she can hear the men more clearly. Until now, she has not heard anyone discussing politics in Iran.

"Dariush jaan, of course they do. Our people are brilliant. They are resilient. They are creative. They are sophisticated. They are good people, kind people. But, change must be rational. We don't want to repeat the mistakes of the past. Do we? If you want to fight for a cause ––for true progress–– you cannot become lost in the cause."

"*Ey baba*, you and your turtle pace philosophy." Dariush takes a big bite into the piece of fresh baklava and places the remaining portion on the ceramic plate in front of him.

Darvish laughs and shakes his head. "You two are not hearing what I am trying to say. You are misunderstanding me. I want what is best for everyone, but I know that aggression is never the answer."

Mahmad finishes his tea and slowly wipes his mouth with a napkin. "What do any of us know! This is all chatter. Dariush, why don't you play the *tonbak* for us? You really have a gift."

Dariush blushes like a shy child. "Darvish, do you have your *tar*? We can play together, like the old days, remember?"

"Ah, yes. It must be somewhere around here. Let me go find it. The old days, such good times we had. But, today can be just as good. Friendship, food, warm chai, and good music. This is a moment to cherish."

Darvish walks to his room to look for his *tar* as Marzi finishes preparing the pomegranate bowls.

"Come, Roya jaan. Shall we join the guests now? I see Darvish went to get his *tar*. I think you will enjoy this."

"Yes, of course. I love the sound of *tar*. But, Marzi joon, I just have a question."

"Sure."

"What do you think of the *times*? You know...how things are going here?"

Marzi smiles warmly. "Oh, I see you heard the men talking. They are always chattering away. They love to hear themselves talk as if they're lecturing a room full of Ph.D candidates." She laughs.

Roya smiles back. "But, really. What do you think?"

"That is a discussion for another day. You sure are curious, aren't you."

Roya blushes. "Yeah, sorry. My father always says that to me too."

"Sorry? *Azizam*, why sorry? You ask, because you are searching for truth. Your mind wants to fill the gaps in the spaces it has yet to imagine. Don't apologize for wanting to learn and understand things.

But, do not burden your mind with worry right now. This is a discussion for another day. Just simply seek wisdom, and it will seek you in return."

"What you seek is seeking you. Rumi. I read all his poetry."

Marzi giggles. "I am impressed. He is one of the greatest. Speaks right to my heart. May all our lives be poetry, so we can share it with the world. Wouldn't that be lovely? Now, come. I see Darvish has found his *tar*, and he sure loves an audience."

Just then Omid walks in carrying the two bags of fruit his mother had requested. "Maman, here you go. Bought extra just in case."

He sets the fruit on the kitchen counter. He then walks over to his mother, gives her a warm hug, and whispers something quickly in her ear. As he walks over to Roya, his eyes are sparkling.

"You can thank me later."

"For?"

"Saving you from this boring *mehmooni*."

"What? Saving? Um, I'm not that bored."

"Okay, sure. So, you want to stay or... would you rather go to a real party?"

"A real party? Where?"

"Underground."

"Are you kidding me? Khanoom Jaan told your mom to watch out for me. Your mom will never let us go. It's like you don't even know your own mother! *Divooneh hasti*."

Omid grins. "Um, Roya. I know you think you know everything. But, I think just this once, you're wrong. I do know my mom. That's why I told her we are going to my friend Sepideh's house." He raises his hand in the air and mimics a light bulb going off.

"So, you lied? Great. Honestly did not expect that from you of all people."

"No, we are actually going to Sepideh's apartment. We happen to also be going out after."

"That is still technically a lie." Roya crosses her arms half-intrigued by the idea and half-bothered by Omid's approach. "I do not like lying."

"You are so noble. Now that we have confirmed that, you down for it? I'm not going to force you. Seriously. It was just an idea. But if you don't want to just because you feel bad, then blame it on me."

Roya is nervous and excited. Her mind is telling her this is not the safest idea, but her instinct is pushing her to take the chance. She knows despite his white lie, she can trust Omid.

"Okay, just for a little bit. I'm curious."

"You might want to change your shoes and wear some sneakers or something."

"What's wrong with heels? Sneakers don't go with my outfit."

"Just in case we have to run."

"Run?" Roya's heart starts beating faster. *Maybe this isn't actually the best idea. I don't think this is what Marzi joon exactly meant when she said it's okay to be curious. Then again, it could be interesting.*

"I mean, it's only happened to me a couple of times. People here are used to it. You, not so much. But, don't worry. You're still lean enough where I could just throw you on my back and run carrying you."

Roya's face falls flat. She stares at Omid for a few, long seconds.

"Relax. I'm kidding."

"About having to run?"

"Oh no, about you being lean enough. You're actually really lean. We might need to fatten you up with some *kabob* and *polo* while you're here." He teases. "Okay, okay. Seriously. We will be fine."

Omid and Roya start making their rounds of polite air kisses goodbye.

When Darvish notices them preparing to leave, his smile droops. "Eh, where are you two going! I was just about to play a song."

Roya and Omid look at each other with guilt and then back at Darvish.

"Will you listen to just one song?"

Roya can sense how much his performance means to him. Her and Omid share another glance with an understood agreement.

"We would love to hear one of your songs before we leave." Roya sets her *monto* and *roosari* temporarily aside and sits on the vacant Victorian couch closest to the door.

Omid leans against the doorway.

Dariush begins the beat on his *tonbak*. First, he slowly taps on the instrument with his thumbs and then increases the speed with the impact of his palm. After a few moments, Darvish joins with his *tar*. The combination cradles Roya. The sound of hands hitting against the aged leather creates a consistent rhythm, but the *tar*'s high pitch breaks through.

Roya focuses on Darvish's face as he plays. His eyes are closed. With each pluck of the strings, he moves his head gently side-to-side. In that moment, there is no past or future concerns for Darvish. It is just him and his *tar*.

When they complete the song, Roya jumps and claps with sincerity. "Beautiful! Really. That was so beautiful."

"*Merci*, Roya jaan." Darvish and Dariush look at one another with contentment. "It is your ears that choose to hear the beauty in our simple performance."

Roya walks over to Omid. Before leaving, they both give Marzi a big hug.

"Sorry that we are leaving early. Thank you for having me as a guest. *Merci* for everything."

"Thank you for being here. There are no such things as guests in my home. We are all friends." She then looks at her son with a certain look in her eyes ––eyes that reveal *I know what you are up to, but I will keep it to myself.* "Omid, *pesareh sheytoon-e-man,* be careful when you go to Sepideh's. And whatever you do, watch for Roya. Remember, she is still a foreigner in this land. She does not know the ways."

Omid blushes knowing that his mother is aware of his little lie and that she is being gracious. "I promise, maman."

"Good. Enjoy yourselves, and don't be home too late. Nothing good happens too far into the night." She gives her son and Roya one more hug and watches them leave into the taxi before closing the door.

When she walks back into the living room, Darvish calls her over and whispers in her ear. "My love, you know they're not just going to Sepideh's. Why did you give them permission to go?"

Marzi rests her head next to his. "This physical world already has its limitations, no matter where we are or what country we live in. But, we cannot chain their souls. They are young. Let them be. I trust Omid will be careful."

"And Roya? She is our guest. This is unlike you to be so lenient. I am surprised. Her grandmother has entrusted her to Khanoom Jaan. Will she be okay with this?"

"It was Khanoom Jaan that first spoke those words to me many years ago. I have a feeling she will understand. I am surprised with myself as well." She kisses him on the cheek. "After all these years, watching you play the *tar* is still my favorite part of our *mehmoonies*."

"You're not just saying that to make me feel good?"

"No, my love. That is not what I am here for. I am just here to love you."

****

"So, where is Sepideh's apartment?"

"It's in Elahieh. It's actually her parent's apartment. Since they are never home, we just treat it like its Sepideh's."

"Elahieh. That sounds so familiar. Isn't that fancy mall there? The one with all the European brands?"

"Yeah, that's the one. Only the upper-middle class and elite of Iran can really afford to regularly shop there. But, everyone loves to go walk around. Its architecture and design is magnificent, isn't it?"

"Yeah, I was surprised."

Omid laughs. "Oh c'mon. You weren't expecting camels and a desert here, did you?"

"No, of course not. I just didn't think Tehran's architecture was so modernized either. It reminds me of New York —the Middle Eastern version."

"Does NY have fresh cantaloupe smoothies too? Or kabobs on skewers fresh off the fire on corners of the street?"

Now Roya laughs. "They have their own spin on those things. But, I'll tell you one thing. They definitely don't have grilled corn on the cob soaking in buckets of salt water in the open streets."

"Did you try one?"

"At first, I was worried about getting sick. But, then I figured why not!"

"And what did you think?"

"It was delicious. One of my favorite things I've eaten here so far."

"You wanna know the secret ingredient?"

"Sure."

"Dirt."

"Dirt?"

"Yeah, a light seasoning just before serving."

"Ha ha, very funny."

Omid smiles as he looks out the window. "Well, it's not too far-fetched to think about. But, who cares? You said it tasted good. And you didn't get sick. All is good!" He leans forward and taps the cab driver on the shoulder. "My friend, it's the apartment complex here to the left. You can just drop us off at the corner right there." He points to a side entrance. "*Merci.*"

"Why are we going through the side door?"

"So the doorman doesn't make it a big deal. We don't want him to know there's that many people in the apartment."

"Oh, right. That makes sense."

They walk past the mail room and towards the elevators. Roya tries to walk on her toes so that her heels don't make a loud clinking noise on the pearly marble floors. While they wait for the elevator to arrive, she gazes around the room. The walls are bordered with a thin line of metallic gold lining. Every corner is decorated with intricate ceramic pots brimming with vibrant flowers —magenta, deep greens, and white ones with yellow centers.

The subtle *ding* of the elevator sounds, and the two of them step in. Roya pulls out her phone, turns it on selfie mode, and checks her makeup. As they exit the elevator, she takes a deep breath and exhales. *Here we go. Be cool, Roya. Everything will be fine.*

Omid opens the door. Before they step inside the room, Sepideh pops up. Her eyelids are covered with smoky eye-shadow, a thick coat of eyeliner, and mascara. Her eyelashes are so long and curvy, they look as if they are going to touch the top of her eyelids. She is wearing a low cut white blouse tucked into a pair of dark denim jeans. A light brown Hermes belt hugs her hips, and her feet are fitted into a pair of Valentino studded heels. A glimpse of her cleavage is visible, but not too much. She looks like she has stepped out of a Vogue magazine.

"Omid, *azizam*! Hii! So happy you two can make it." She wraps her arms around his neck and pulls him in for a tight hug.

"Hi, Sepideh. Thanks for having us. This is Roya by the way! She's visiting from America."

Sepideh pulls away from Omid, turns to Roya, and grabs her hands. "Roya, welcome! It's sooo nice to meet you!" She pulls her in too and squeezes her tight.

Roya is shocked by Sepideh's enthusiasm. "Hii, so great to meet you. Thanks for the invite. Your place is really beautiful. I love the interior design."

"My parents will be happy to hear that. They're barely ever here, but this is their home." She looks around the room and sighs before perking up again. "Let me introduce you to everyone!"

Omid walks next to Roya. "Sepideh is a lot, but she's sweet. Her friends… they're okay too I guess. Some better than others. You're probably wondering how I even got involved with these people." He pauses. "I'd like to think I'm an entertaining guy, and I guess our family does okay for themselves. But, these super rich people take themselves so seriously at times. Every group of friends needs a clown, right? That's what I'm here for!" He crosses his eyes and sticks his tongue out.

Roya is distracted but turns halfway towards Omid. "Not to build your head up anymore, but I just want to say you're not a clown. I think your sense of humor makes you wise. Now, don't hold that compliment against me!"

Omid is about to respond when Sepideh pulls Roya towards a group of people.

"Hiii everyone, this is Roya, Omid's friend from America. She's never had the *real* Tehran experience." Sepideh winks and begins pointing towards each person. "This is Leila, Niki, Reza, Saman, and Roozbeh."

Roya smiles and nods at the group but pauses when she makes eye contact with Saman. He grins, and his dimples make their appearance. He walks up to her and kisses her on the cheeks --the Persian way. "Welcome to Tehran," he simply says as he swirls his whiskey on the rocks. "We are happy to have you."

His Tom Ford cologne tingles Roya's nostrils. His scruff is perfectly groomed. He's wearing a black v-neck with a blazer, fitted jeans, and velvet loafers. He too looks like a GQ ad, but Roya has seen that before. It is his presence that gets her attention. Unlike the other men dressed handsomely in the room, Saman truly does not care what people think. He is the kind of guy that does what he wants --a sense of freedom Roya seeks.

She smiles at him, returns his wink, and walks away.

As she approaches the dessert table, Omid comes up and offers her a glass of champagne. "Here you go. Oh, and I saw that thing going on with Saman."

"What thing?" Roya blushes.

Omid pretends to flip his hair like a diva and exaggerates a wink. "That thing." He laughs. "I get it, Saman is a handsome guy. I mean look at his hair. It just perfectly stays like that. I think he spends more time fixing it up than Sepideh does with hers."

"Yeah, he's cute. And he knows he's cute. Anyway, where does all this alcohol come from? *Aragh* is one thing, but champagne? Whiskey? They have everything."

"There's ways to get it in. Most people know someone who has a connection. If you're from here, you know where to get it. How do people in the States get weed? Similar idea."

"Oh, right. I see. Well, thank you for the champagne."

Omid discretely points to the tall guy with a clean-shaven face and gelled hair. "You see that guy?"

"Yeah. I just met him."

"That's Roozbeh. He's one of my good friends. We used to play soccer together before him and his family moved to Toronto. He still visits every summer. Most of these kids have homes in Toronto."

"I've never heard you mention him before."

"There's a lot you haven't heard me mention! I'm sure it's the same with you." He then continues pointing to a woman. "The girl standing next to him is Leila, as you know. She lives in Paris, and she makes sure you know it within five minutes of talking to her. I swear, go start a conversation. It's the first thing she brings up." He laughs as he bites into a macaroon.

"So, which one of them don't you like?"

"It's not about who I don't like. I don't mind any of them. I just don't particularly care for them either, except for Sepideh and Roozbeh. They have their flaws, believe me, but their heart is good. I think you can always tell when someone's heart is in the right place, even when they act up. Right?"

"Yeah, I know what you mean."

Sepideh's voice can be heard yelling over the music. She turns down the volume and waves her hands in the air to get everyone's attention. "Hey, alooooo, everyone! In about five minutes, we're going to head out. Be ready!"

Roya looks to Omid. "Should I be worried about tonight?"

"Do you ever stop worrying?"

"Well, I..."

"Never mind that question. We will be fine. I got you."

They all head down the elevator together, out through the side door, and into the two private cabs Sepideh had called for them.

Piled on top of each other in the back of the cab, they squeeze as the car winds down the busy Tehran streets. The night is late, but the city is alive. The lights of nearby, hole-in-the wall restaurants twinkle as they speed by.

Roozbeh turns in the passenger seat and looks over his shoulder. "Roya, did Omid tell you where we are going?"

Roya looks to Omid. "Yeah, he said we are going to an underground party. I don't know what that exactly means."

Roozbeh now looks to Omid. "Omid, you didn't want to explain to her? Give her a heads up?"

"That'd be no fun, now would it? I thought it'd be better to put away the expectations and just experience it all." He flashes a quick glance at Roya. "Plus, I didn't want to freak her out. She worries all the time."

Roozbeh turns so far in his seat as if he were a human pretzel. "Well, it's not actually underground. But, Omid is right. Better to just have the experience. Anyway, are you liking Iran so far?"

"Yeah, I am. It's, uh, really different than I thought it would be. In a good way."

"What do you mean?"

Roya blushes. "Well, I don't know. All I really knew about Iran was from my parents' stories and stuff on the news. I didn't think it'd be so fun. So modern. So lively. Maybe I didn't expect to feel like I belonged here."

"And do you now? Feel like you belong?"

"I'm not sure really. I mean, not completely. It's still different. But, there is something about being here and walking these streets. It just feels familiar to me. Like I found the missing piece to something that I didn't know I was looking for. Does that make sense?"

"As long as it makes sense to you. That's all that matters." Roozbeh laughs.

"Oh, don't get her started. Roya's mind has a mind of her own." Omid teases.

"Isn't that so for all of us? We're all caught up in our own heads at times. But, enough of that tonight! We're here." Roozbeh unfastens his seatbelt.

Roya peers out the window to what looks like a rundown warehouse. "Here? This is where we came all dressed up for?"

"Just wait." Omid and Roozbeh say in unison.

They unravel out of the cab and meet Sepideh outside the door with the rest of her party. There are no signs, no windows. Nothing but a tall, gray door and a building made of cement. The night is quiet, except for the gentle booming of a bass sounding from behind the walls.

A man wearing ripped denim jeans, a charcoal leather jacket, and a well-groomed beard opens the door.

Omid ushers Roya in front of him. "After you."

The energy in the air is heavy, dangerous, and exhilarating. The *montos* are peeled gently off revealing tight dresses and bare skin. Pedicured toes and arched feet are tucked in heels like weapons of seduction.

Roya's eyes widen as she struggles to see among the clouds of thick smoke.

"I'll be right back. I'm going to get us some drinks. Stay with the group please. Okay?"

"I'm not a kid, Omid."

"I didn't say you were, but you're not from here. Just please don't wander off."

"Got it. No wandering."

Roya turns and sees Saman pull out a bag of white pills. He signals his entourage to come close.

"What is this?" Roya squints with curiosity for a better look.

"C'mon Roya, it's M. You don't have this in your America?"

"What! Of course we do, but I don't do those kinds of things."

"So, you've never tried it?"

"No."

Saman grins with his signature, elusive charm as he downs his *aragh*. He leans over and kisses Roya softly on her cheek —so softly it almost feels like he kissed the air and not her skin. His scent is intoxicating. He whispers in her ear. "Would you like to try?"

"Ehhh, pass me one of those!" Leila calls over to Saman. Without hesitation, she pops one into her mouth and chases it with champagne.

"See, Roya. It's fine. Actually, it's more than fine. It feels great. *Akheeeey*." Leila moves her shoulders and hips with the music.

The beat of the Iranian rap breaks out of the speakers like a rebellious child.

Everything is happening so fast. Roya doesn't know what to do. Fear isn't holding her back, but she knows better. Her whole life she has known better. This night feels different. This night feels surreal. Suddenly, she feels within her years of knowing better raging into a desire to be reckless.

*Roya, think about this. You're in a foreign country. You barely know these people.*

She can hear her thoughts begging for her attention. But, she doesn't care anymore. She takes one of the pills and pops it in her mouth. "How long does it take for this thing to work?"

Saman smiles. "Roya, relax. Just take it easy."

Roya grabs Saman's *aragh* and takes a sip. The bitterness of the pure alcohol burns her throat and makes her squint her eyes in disgust. Saman reaches for her hand and pulls her slowly into a haze of strobe lights winking at them from every corner of the dance floor. Pairs of curling bodies press against one another the way stacks of wet paper become one. Roya can sense her body slowing down, but her heart is beating fast. It feels like her limbs have turned into a cup of jello and someone is stirring it all up. The music feels like its running through her veins. She can feel the thump of the bass in her chest. In between the strokes of flashing light, Roya can see Saman's smile. He is dancing solo now as if he is the only one in the room. As if there aren't eyes peeking at him from all over the dance floor.

He leans in close to Roya's ear. "You feel it yet?"

"I think so! I don't know what it's supposed to feel like. But, I feel like all my cells are dancing inside of me."

Saman pulls back and laughs moving his head side-to-side with the music. "Well, that's good then! Let's enjoy it. Let's be free."

The way he raises his eyebrows and smiles reminds Roya of Cyrus.

*"Roya, if you could try a drug, any drug, what would it be?"*

*"What? I would never try that stuff. Why?"*

*"I don't know. I was just wondering. Sometimes I wonder how much we will change. What kind of adults do you think we will be?"*

*"Hopefully, the kind that are actually still happy. All I know is I'm so happy right now. I'm so happy that I can already miss this moment. Cyrus, what if I don't want things to change? What if we change too much? What if we don't even recognize each other anymore?"*

*"I don't know."*

*"What do you mean you don't know?"*

*"I get what you're saying. It's just strange to think about ––a life in which we don't recognize each other. But, I don't think that will happen."*

*"How can you be sure?"*

*"Because I know that even if it's years down the road and we haven't spoken, even if we're old with gray hairs or fat or whatever, I will know one thing."*

*"Mhm, what's that?"*

*"That you can't even lie if you tried, because your smile gives it away. And your laugh. I will always know you by your laugh.*

*That sound could fill any gap in time. What will you remember me by?"*

*"Hmm, I guess I'd say your eyebrows."*

*"My eyebrows? Really?"*

*"Yeah, the way you raise them when you're trying to charm someone. You do this thing where you will make a point and then raise them as you grin. It's just the way your whole face moves when you do it. I can't explain it. But, that's something I'll always remember. The way your face moves."*

*"See, we wouldn't be able to forget each other even if we tried. No worries."*

*"So, what about you?"*

*"What?"*

*"What drug would you try?"*

*"I don't know. I guess Molly."*

*"Why Molly?"*

*"Not sure. I heard it was supposed to make you feel good."*

Just then she feels a hand on her shoulder.

"Roya, what the hell. I asked you to please not wander."

"Um, I didn't wander. I've been here dancing. I feel gooooood. Like real goooood. Don't be all grumpy."

Omid gives Roya a suspicious look. "Shit, Roya are you high?"

"Define high..."

"Dammit, Roya. What did you take?"

"M. I got it from Saman. Can you chill. You're the one who said I should stop worrying and now you're getting all worked up."

Omid presses on his temples and wears a distressed look on his face.

"Yeah, Roya. I said have fun. Relax. Do your thing. Whatever. But, I can't take you home high out of your mind. Khanoom Jaan is going to kill me if she finds out."

"Oh, now you're worried about them finding out? It will be fiiiiine.

Come on! Let's dance. This music is so good. Who knew Iranians could rap? This is edgy." Roya closes her eyes and waves her arms in the air.

Omid tries to fight back a smile. "Roya, this is serious. Have you ever tried M before?"

"No waaay." Roya makes an *s* shape with her hips, moving along to the rhythm of the music.

"Oh, that's good. Really nice." Omid mutters under his breath.

Just then Saman walks up to Omid. "Hey man, so you and Roya. What's the deal?"

"There's no deal. Saman, what the hell. You gave her M?"

"Yeah? What's the big deal? Anyway, look, is she yours or what?" Saman rests his hand on Omid's shoulder. The smell of his vodka infused breath makes Omid want to gag.

"She's not something to be owned, Saman. She's not mine. She doesn't belong to anyone."

"Dude. You know what I meant. Don't act like you're the only good guy around here. You don't have to be an asshole."

"If I'm an asshole Saman, then you're a jackass."

"It's all the same, isn't it then? At the end of the day, we're both asses." Saman laughs as he spills some of his vodka on the floor. "Look, I'm not trying to be rude. I think she's cool. Just didn't want to get in the middle of anything."

"Yeah and you thought giving her M was a good idea, right?"

"Omid, you can be a real hypocrite sometimes. You know that, right? She doesn't belong to anyone, remember? I didn't force her to take one. She wanted to. Get over it. You don't have to babysit her." He points to Roya. "Plus, look at her. She's enjoying herself."

"Whatever, Saman. That's not what I'm trying to say. She's not from here. Things can get out of hand if we aren't careful." Omid feels the need to justify himself but realizes Saman has a point.

Suddenly, they hear the loud bang of a door being kicked open. A team of *basige* rush through the doors with their flashlights invading all corners of the room.

"You have got to be shitting me right now." Saman throws his bag of M in the nearest corner and places his glass of *aragh* on the floor."

"Look, I'm going to find Sepideh, so we can call our father. He will handle this. You and Roya should leave. Hurry!" Saman's speech is slurring.

"Are you going to be okay? What about everyone else?"

"Yeah, man. We will just have to sort it out —come to some under-standing." He winks at Omid and hurries away.

Only seconds have passed, but it feels like hours. Omid runs over to Roya, grabs her hand, and starts ushering her towards the back of the warehouse, so they can slip out the side door. The energy of the room has completely shifted. The underlying danger that felt exhilarating now feels palpable and threatening.

Roya can sense something has gone wrong, but is still lost in her own headspace and slow to react. "Why are we running? And why is it so bright in here? It's really killing the mood."

"Roya, I need you to please just run and not ask me any questions. Just this once. And, uh, you might want to take off your heels."

"My heels? You want me to walk on Tehran's streets without shoes on? Or any street for that matter? That is gross. I would never."

Omid is growing impatient. "Oh, man. Fine. Can you run in your heels?"

"I can try."

"Great, so let's go. NOW."

Holding her hand and pushing through the frantic maze of bodies, he leads her to the gray door on the opposite end of the warehouse. He pulls on the handle, but the door doesn't budge. He takes a step back, leans in, and pulls the door knob back again with all his strength. Sweat marches down his neck.

"Omid!" Roya taps on his shoulder.

"Not now!" Omid scans the room as he runs his hands against the door and tries to find a way to open it. His heart is beating wild. His fingers are beginning to cramp as he looks over his shoulder to see if the *basige* have seen them yet.

"Omid!" Roya now taps harder on his shoulder.

"Roya, just wait a min–– OW!" He turns around to look at her. "Why the hell did you pinch my shoulder!"

Roya, with her pupils still sparkling under the bright lights, points to the bottom of the door. "Look!"

Omid looks down and sees a lock on the bottom of the door. Half-annoyed and half-relieved, he reaches down to release the lock and leads Roya out through the door before closing it shut behind them. He can hear the bickering voices and thumping of footsteps in the background, but the roads ahead are empty. Not the kind of empty where there is simply no one around, but the kind of empty where the air is dead still.

Reaching for Roya's hand again, Omid makes sure no one can see them. "Are you ready to run?"

Roya looks at him and smiles. "Omid, I've NEVER seen you this serious before. It's kind of...interesting." She squeezes his hand.

Omid notices the softness of her hands. Roya's eyes are warm and sincere ––both familiar to him and completely unique. "Alright, so that's a yes? Let's go!"

****

They cross the uneven road careful not to trip over the broken pieces of pavement. The moon is whole and full and seems to follow them with its light. Omid can see the neon signs of the stores closed shut. The tired bodies of its owners must now be sinking into their mattresses for a deep sleep. The beating in Omid's chest begins to slow to a gentle, consistent pulse. He knows once he can see the lights, they are close to home.

As his mind begins to ease, he notices Roya's hands have turned damp and cold. She hasn't spoken a word since they first ran from the warehouse. He turns to look at her as she gazes off into the distance with her head facing away from him.

"Roya?" Omid lightly squeezes her hand, but she doesn't turn around. He touches her shoulder. "Are you feeling alright?" He stops walking and waits for her to respond.

"While we were running, just before, my heart felt like it was going to scatter into a thousand directions at once. The sound of the *basige* and their boots felt like they were stomping in my ears." She still does not turn to face Omid. "I had no idea what was going on. Everyone was moving so fast, blurring back and forth in front of my eyes. I know I should have been scared, but I wasn't. I was confused. I'm still a bit confused. But––"

She turns to look at Omid as she holds his hand. He notices her eyes are filled with water, but there is not a single tear drop that has fallen. Omid can't help but gaze at her with curiosity. Something about her sadness is so beautifully unfiltered.

"But–– " Roya continues. "It was the first time I've felt something...anything...in a long time. I've cried, sure. But, lately, I just feel numb. Neutral. Not in pain or joyful. Amused, but detached. I think I've tried to hold myself together for so long. Now what? Look at me. There's something wrong with me. I took a pill from a guy I just met. Our lives could have been at risk when the *basige* got there, and I couldn't process anything. To be honest, I don't even know if I cared all that much. Why? Because look at the world we live in. What is the point of all this anyway? People are so selfish sometimes. So greedy. So cruel to each other. There are people suffering. There are people just trying to stay alive. There's people trying to live. And here I was thinking I was going to be a somebody. I was going to be the one to make a difference. I was going to be different. I wasn't going to give up on my dreams. I wasn't going to be that adult."

A few tears finally fall on her cheek.

"Omid, I wish you met me a couple years ago. That girl was going to be somebody. That girl believed she could walk on water, move through mountains, and carry the weight of the world on her pinky. That version of me was going to show everyone it was possible to create things in this world from your very own mind ––things that reach from heart-to-heart and touch people's souls."

She now looks up and straight through Omid's eyes. "Sometimes, I feel so damn dead on the inside. And I hate myself for saying that. I fucking hate it. And I know hate is a strong word. But, I mean, how ungrateful can I be? Maybe you were right the other day. That's why I'm messed up. I feel this way. I feel so trapped sometimes, like I can't move forward or backward. I'm just suspended into this nothingness waiting to be moved along. I don't want to hurt my parents and tell them all this. That I am not okay. Not after everything they have sacrificed for me. It isn't their fault honestly. They just don't understand. My problems aren't real problems ––not like what they've experienced at least. And my sister? I'm supposed to be the strong, older sister. You know? I'm not supposed to be the one falling apart. Do you ever feel like everything in your life plays like a movie trailer before your eyes? It's so close. I can imagine it all ––what it could be, what I could be–– ever since I was a kid. But, it seems like another life now."

More tears begin to fall. Roya lets go of Omid's hand to wipe them away.

"I worry that what I feel is wrong. Am I being selfish? But, then I worry that giving up on what I really believe and want is wrong too. In a world where every fairytale has a villain, I feel like I'm not even my own savior. Maybe I've been the villain to myself. Betrayed myself for what I thought I had to be to please others. All these life choices. Then, there's him. Cyrus. I can't get his damn face out of my head. I try. Believe me. The more I run from it, the more it lingers closer to me –– this truth that maybe what we had wasn't even the love we thought it was. What love should be like. The right kind of love. The truth that it wasn't even his fault or mine. No one to blame. Maybe we were just two broken people trying not to cut each other with the shattered pieces of ourselves. It's like I'm grieving the loss of someone I never really had to begin with. I've been running from myself for all these years, and here I am ––so far from the person I once was and so lost. And I just keep pushing everyone away, because I feel like they're looking at me with disappointment. You know what the truth is, Omid? I try to smile my way through the day and listen to others so they feel heard. I tell them *everything will be okay!* They believe me, and everything is okay.

But deep down, I am sad. I'm not okay. It all hurts. It feels good to say that out loud."

Omid wants to wrap his arms around her and comfort her, but stops himself. He opens his mouth to speak, but he is speechless. He wants to say the right words, but can't find any. All he can think to do is reach for her hand again. He is about to say something when, suddenly, a flashlight blinds them.

"Alo! Alo! What are you kids doing there!"

Omid's body shuts down as a frenzy of nerves start colliding inside of him. He wants to run and take Roya with him, but he's frozen in fear. The light comes closer.

Roya's body continues to turn cold in the summer heat. Her head feels heavy. Still blinded by the lights, she squeezes Omid's hand tightly and manages to muster a faint, "Omid…Omid…we need to go…we have to go."

"You're right. Roya, I need you to run as far as you can. Okay? We're going to get out of this." A surge of adrenaline jolts through him again.

The footsteps rush closer. The light flashes on them in zigzag lines. Omid holds onto Roya, and the two of them run with every bit of power they have left.

"Ehhh!" The voice of the *basige* can be heard hollering at them with disdain. "Wait till we get you. You troublemakers!"

They hear his voice chasing them, but they don't look back.

Omid guides them out of the street spotlights and into the nearby park. They crouch in the bushes hidden by trees ornately trimmed into geometrical shapes. He hears the footsteps of the irritated officer hit against the park's paved steps. Pressing his hands over his lips, Omid signals Roya to remain quiet. The only sound is the crunching of a few dried leaves under the officer's boots.

"Aaaaagh." The officer peers past the bushes and grunts before leaving the park.

Roya's heart is burning.

"Omid, I don't feel well…I think I'm going to faint…"

Roya's weight collapses into Omid's arms.

"Roya! Roya! I need you to wake up. Come back to me!"

He carries her to one of the small stone benches under a gazebo. Dangling yellow flowers shield them from the open landscape.

"Roya! Wake up. C'mon!" Omid cradles Roya in his arms and tries shaking her back into consciousness. "This is not how tonight was supposed to go. C'mon! I need you to come back to me right now." Omid feels crippled with guilt. He looks around to see if anyone is near. He doesn't know if he should pick her up and run for help or if that would worsen her state. A heavy weight presses on his heart. His hands are moist now too. He places two fingers gently on Roya's wrists and is relieved to find a steady pulse.

There is a fountain several feet away. Too scared to carry Roya into plain sight, he rolls her *roosari* into a ball and rests her softly on the ground with the thin scarf underneath her head. Omid's thoughts race as he runs over to the fountain, takes off one of his shoes, and fills it with water. He runs back to her and desperately uses his hands to throw some water onto her face ––hoping it will wake her up.

After a few moments, Roya gasps for breath and opens her eyes. "Omid? What's going on? Where are we? Why is there water on my face?" He places his hand on her back and helps her to slowly sit up straight. Roya takes a minute to reorient herself and notices Omid's shoe filled with water. "Why is there water in your shoe? Did you put that on my face? I feel so dizzy."

Omid quietly stares at Roya with relief and embarrassment. He simply puts his arms around her and holds on. "Roya, are you okay? I'm so happy you're awake. Thank God. I'm so sorry for everything. This whole night was a bad idea. This is my fault." His hug feels like embraces given to loved ones at the airport.

"Yeah, I'm okay. Just feel a bit weird. Everything is kind of hazy." She takes her *roosari* off the ground and wipes her face. "I remember being in the warehouse with everyone. Then, I took molly from Saman. I mixed it with vodka or something. And then there were people chasing us? And we ran. Now, we're here under this gazebo. I just don't get what all happened."

"I think you might have had a bad reaction with the M. How are you feeling now?"

"Not too great. But, a bit better. What happened with everyone else?"

"Do you know who the *basige* are?"

"Yeah. Mamani had mentioned them. They're like religious police officers who enforce the rules."

"Yes."

"They crashed the party? I thought that doesn't happen too often?"

"It doesn't. But, that doesn't mean it can't. I honestly didn't think it would --not at the warehouse."

"What happened with Saman and Sepideh and everyone else?" Roya says as she presses her temples with her fingers.

"I'm not sure. But, I know Saman and Sepideh will be alright."

"How do you know?"

He rubs his fingers, indicating money. "Their father is a well-known and powerful businessman."

"And that's enough?"

"It can be. Money talks. And can shield too."

Roya's arms look like the legs of a skinned chicken.

Omid's phone lights up with three missed calls. "I think we should get you home. Khanoom Jaan must be worried by now. Maybe we can figure out an explanation by the time we get back." He raises his head to make sure the road is safe. "Are you okay to walk?"

"Yeah." Roya starts to slowly get up, but her legs still feel like jello. "I'm just really cold."

"You're still cold? It's summer in Tehran. I think your blood pressure has dropped. We can stop by my place. Get you something sweet."

****

Omid helps Roya sit on the steps and tiptoes into his home. He slowly inches the cabinet drawers open so that he does not make any noise.

"Omid jaan?" She says his name like it is a question, but he knows it is not.

"Maman, you are still awake this late?"

"I couldn't sleep. I had a bad feeling." Her eyes redirect to the chocolate in Omid's hands. "Is everything alright? Where is Roya?"

Omid tries to answer, but can't think fast enough.

"She's here, isn't she?" Again, she already knows. "Khanoom Jaan had called looking for her."

She walks outside to find Roya leaning her head against the door. Bending down, she touches her forehead and turns her chin to look at her. "Roya jaan." She says her name as if she were cleaning up glass with bare hands. Her voice is delicate and unassuming. "You will be alright. Would you mind if you slept here tonight?"

Roya forces her neck to hold her head up, so she can face Marzi. She opens her mouth to speak, but her voice drowns out in humiliation. "I'm so sorry." She finally whispers a few words.

"Shhh. No need for apologies." Marzi helps Roya stand up and supports her weight. She turns to her son. "Omid, take Roya to your room. Get her some water. You can sleep on the couch tonight. I will call Khanoom Jaan and then come check on Roya."

Omid helps Roya to the room.

As he walks into the kitchen, his mother is walking out. He keeps his head down in shame. She raises his chin up the way she held Roya's and looks into his eyes. "My son, I am so relieved you are both safe."

Omid's eyes have tears in them now. He wraps his arms around his mother and sobs. His tall frame collapses onto her shoulders. "I'm so sorry, maman. This was all my fault. I was so scared."

She touches his head the way she would when he was a child. "I love you."

"How are you not angry? I don't understand."

"Because I know the man I raised. And I know, in this moment, you are more disappointed in yourself than anyone else." She pushes his shoulders back so that he stands up tall again. "My son, I am not angry at you for wanting to live. I want you to experience the full palette of life. But, I just want you to be safe. To make the right choices. As you know, things are a bit different these days."

"Are you going to tell baba?"

"You know I cannot hide things from him."

"He will be upset."

"Perhaps, but this will pass. And you are here. Come, let's go check on Roya."

They walk into the room to find her sleeping. Her breathing is slow and steady. Marzi touches her hand and checks her pulse. "She will be okay. In the morning, you can take her to Khanoom Jaan's. You should rest if you are driving to Shomal tomorrow."

"Shomal? We can still go?"

"If Mamani and Khanoom Jaan are still alright with Roya going, I do not mind."

"And baba? He will."

"How about we tell him once you have returned?"

"But why? Why are you alright with me going after all this?"

"Because I trust my son. It is in youth that we make our mistakes and as adults that we worry. You will stand one day in my shoes and know how it feels to make your maman stay up late, eh?" She lays a blanket on the couch and hands him a pillow. "Goodnight."

Omid takes the pillow from his mother and lays on his back staring at the ceiling. Usually, at this hour, his mind is running through all his thoughts. Tonight, all he can focus on is the sound of his own heartbeat finally slowing down, so he can sleep.

****

Roya rises before the sun has come up. The sky is still dark, but the black is transitioning into a lavender gray. She gently turns the knob of the door and sees Omid laying down. He is awake too.

"Omid." She sits on the floor near the couch and whispers. "Can we walk together to your mom's favorite bakery? I feel terrible. I'd like to get her something and leave a note."

"The sun isn't even orange yet, and you're already asking for favors." He smiles.

She touches his hand and looks at him, resting his head on the sofa. His face looks different today. There is a closeness between them. "Thank you for last night. Really."

"For what? Does taking care of a friend deserve a thank you?" Omid sits up now and places his other hand on top of hers. "Sorry by the way."

"For?"

"For the dirty water in the shoe thing. I panicked."

"Ahh, I almost forgot about that. I'll just have to wash my face ten times today. No big deal!" She stands up still holding his hand and pulls him up too. "Was your mom mad last night? My mom would have lost it if I came home like that."

"Actually, she wasn't."

"Really?"

"Yes, it was strange. She seemed to understand."

"Well, let's hope Khanoom Jaan feels that way! We're supposed to see Mamani today. You think she will tell her?"

"Looks like we will soon find out."

****

Omid drops Roya off in front of Khanoom Jaan's home. "Let me know if Shomal is still happening. I can pick you up later today."

"Okay, I will." She takes a deep breath before walking up the steps and ringing the doorbell.

Khanoom Jaan answers immediately. Roya opens her mouth to speak, but Khanoom Jaan simply puts her arms around her the way Marzi had. "Roya jaan, thank God you are alright."

"I'm really sorry. I know this looks bad. I promise, I—"

"Roya, you are not a kid anymore. And I am not your mother. Please do not keeping apologizing. Just come inside. Hurry up and change. I told your Mamani we will be there in the next half hour."

Roya's headache has subsided, and Tehran's heat has caught up to her again. *Well, looks like things are somewhat back to normal.* She quickly washes up and changes into fresh clothes before meeting Khanoom Jaan again.

They arrive to the hospital just as Mamani begins her physical therapy exercises for the day.

"I told you they can't keep this woman down for long!" Khanoom Jaan calls out to her friend.

"You look great, Mamani!" Roya runs over to her grandmother, but slows down when her head starts to feel dizzy again. "I've missed you."

"*Salam*, my love. So good to see you." Mamani asks the therapist if they can stop and begin again in a few minutes. "Tell me, tell me! How has everything been? What all have you done since the last time I saw you."

"I, uhh, well... actually...so..." Her eyes look for Khanoom Jaan.

"Oh yes. Go ahead, Roya! Tell her about what a master gardener you've become lately."

*Huh? I've helped you water your plants. I wouldn't call that a master.* She smiles quietly.

"Is that right, Roya? Has she been teaching you her secrets? She is the best of the best. We used to call her the plant whisperer. The way she can bring even a dainty shrub to life again, it's an art. Lucky you!"

"Oh right, yes! I have been learning a lot. Spending a long time under the sun."

"Explains that tan you've got going on now! Looks good on you." Mamani moves around on the edge of her hospital bed.

The nurse taps on the door before walking in. "Ma'am, we need to complete your therapy session. You may have visitors again later." She closes the door behind her and waits.

"Oh, oh. Looks like I must go now. As should you. I hear you have a trip to Shomal?"

Roya's almond shaped eyes widen into a hazelnut. "I can go?"

Mamani takes a deep breath and slowly lifts herself using her walker. "Took a bit of convincing from Khanoom Jaan, but yes. I think it will be nice to see more than just Tehran. Now, come give a big hug and be safe."

Roya waits until they're in the taxi before she turns to Khanoom Jaan sitting beside her. "Thank you for not telling her. But, why would you still persuade her to let me go?"

"The same reason Omid's mother is allowing him." She rolls down the window. "You should ask him what she told him. That's how I feel about you."

The all too familiar smell of car exhaust fills up the air, but Roya doesn't mind. "I thought you said you weren't my mom?"

"Well, thankfully, I don't have to discipline you like one. But, I can care for you as one."

"*Merci*, Khanoom Jaan."

"Oh, don't thank me! When you come back, I'm taking you to the bazaar again for round two of practicing your *chooneh* skills."

"Hey! I thought you said no discipline?"

"No young lady. This is entertainment for me."

As the taxi drives past the city streets and nears Khanoom Jaan's home once more, the textured smell remains. Yet, the air feels cleaner.

# CHAPTER 9

Asal and Bijan, two of Omid's friends, both fall asleep on the floor shortly after they arrive at the condo.

"Should we wake them up, so they can sleep in their rooms?" Roya suggests to Omid.

"Them? Na, let them sleep. Tomorrow will be a long day. They look comfortable to me."

"Where's Roozbeh?"

"He's probably going for a walk. He likes to do that sometimes. Says it helps him feel sane --walking along the shore under the dark night sky. He's a romantic."

"Oh, I see. Maybe that's why I like Roozbeh."

Omid laughs. "Why? Because he reminds you of yourself?" He teases.

"Maybe! But no, I feel like he gets it. I guess that makes me a romantic too. I just love the night. It's so quiet, so mysterious yet comforting. There are certain types of people meant for the night. You know?"

"Mhm, yes. I can see that. I think that's nice."

"What is?"

"That you notice the beauty in things others take for granted."

"Wow, look at you. Giving me some credit! I thought you said I was ungrateful."

"No, I said you were acting ungrateful. Plus, that's before I knew you. You're different than I thought."

Roya grins. "I have heard that one before."

"Would you like to go for a walk? Indulge your love for the night?"

"Is it safe to do that?" Roya asks nervous. "You know, a young guy and a girl walking together at this time?"

"Here, you are fine. But, if you want, we can stay in." Omid doesn't want Roya to feel uncomfortable.

"Yeah. Maybe after the night we had, that's a better idea. Let's go on the balcony. I like the view and my night." Roya slips on her hoodie and grabs her glass of *aragh* mixed with pomegranate juice.

Omid heads to the kitchen while picking up the dirty plates on the way to place them in the trash. He returns to the balcony with a bag of *pofak namaki* and his glass of *aragh*.

"Want some?" He extends the bag of snacks to Roya while using the side of his hand to gently wipe the cheesy residue from his lips.

"Thanks." Roya pops one in her mouth. She lets the single *pofak* dissolve on her tongue.

The snack reminds her of her mother's childhood stories growing up in Iran. How she would use her allowance money, rush to the nearest store, and finish the entire bag before she got home.

Mamani would catch her walking through the door and scold in Farsi. *"Delband, why did you eat all those snacks before dinner?*

*"How do you know!"* Delband would ask shocked.

*"Because a mother always knows what her child is up to. And because your mouth is covered with cheese flakes.* She would admit and soften her voice.

Omid now sits on the chair opposite from Roya. They stare at the blanket of trees surrounding their condo on the hill. He connects his phone to the portable speakers and plays Faramarz Aslani's "Age Ye Rooz."

"I love this song!" Roya says with a youthful excitement. "It is one of my dad's favorites."

"Me too. I'm pretty sure all of Iran loves this song." Omid sips his drink. "That's the power of good music. Each person takes away what they want from it. They feel what they feel. Who can say what they feel is right or wrong? It just is."

"What do you feel when you hear this song?" Roya looks at Omid curiously. He always has an answer for everything. Always talking about his philosophical ideas but never personal details about himself.

"Regret."

Roya is surprised by his response. Omid looks away again with his head facing the trees. Roya can sense a shift in his energy and body language. She can only see the corner of his eye, but can feel his sadness. He turns and looks at Roya.

"Yeah, regret." He says once more. "They say alcohol makes you speak the truth. No wonder all those Sufis engaged in so much *darde-del*. All that wine!" He smiles in the way people do when they are hiding pain.

"Why regret?" Roya is still waiting for an explanation.

"Remember when you were talking about Cyrus?"

"Yeah."

"Well, I had a similar heartbreak. I messed up."

"Why didn't you tell me this that day?"

"Because that day you were sharing your pain. And sometimes it is better to simply listen and let that pain be heard."

Roya never thought about it like that, but she understands what he is saying.

"So, tell me about it. I want your pain to be heard too."

"Her name was Elaheh. I called her Ela. We knew each other since we were teenagers. She attended the all-girls private school, and I attended the all-boys academy nearby. The kids from our schools hung out together often. When I first met her, I thought she was a pretty girl. All the guys seemed to think so too."

"Was it one of those moments in the movies where you were like —–*woah, she's beautiful!*" Roya interjects.

Omid grins. "No, not that feeling exactly. But, she was definitely beautiful. She—–"

"So, when did it change? When did you feel something?" Roya interjects again. She catches herself. "Sorry, it's a habit when I get excited. I will let you tell your story."

"Our group of friends would spend time together. Normal teenage stuff. Elaheh and I would talk, but always with other people around. She was one of those girls, I don't know how, but you just felt good by her being there. One day, we all decided to go to Goftegoo Park after our exams. I was running late for some reason. When I get there, the first person I see is her. She was laying on a blanket with her head resting on a textbook. She was holding a novel in one hand and eating *pofak* with her other hand as the wind kept blowing in her face. She kept trying to move her hair out of her eyes with both her hands full. I don't know why I remember that moment so well. But, I do."

"And then what?"

"I walked up to her and said hi. She just looked up at me, raised her hand to block the sun, and smiled. *'Hi Omid, pofak mikhay? The weather feels warmer than usual today,'* she said. I didn't even like *pofak* all that much, but I took a couple."

"No, I mean. What happened next!"

"Oh, right. Well, we spent more time together. We laughed a lot with each other. We eventually dated for three years. But then, I became scared and just messed it all up. We would argue over the smallest of things, and I stopped being able to see her worries. I could only see my own. It's a strange thing, isn't it?"

"What?"

"Fear. What it does to people in love."

"Do you still love her? I thought you said you hadn't been in love before."

"That's an interesting question. I was always in love with her. That rush of feelings that you can't explain. Just wanting to be with her and know more and more about her. Know her thoughts and her hopes. Going to the nearby market and helping her decide which cantaloupe seems most fresh. Holding her close and feeling so happy that it freaks you out. But, I don't think I knew what it meant to love her until I lost her. Typical, I know. But, you know what I realized?"

"What?"

"That you can't choose who you fall in love with. It's one of those things that just hits you and you fall into it. But, you can choose how to love someone. And you can't really love someone if you're scared all the time."

"Why were you so scared?" Roya already knows the answer. She understands Omid's words. She resonates with his pain.

"Because when you have everything to gain, you have everything to lose."

The words land on Roya's chest as if someone had placed his hand and pushed down firmly. *Because when you have everything to gain, you have everything to lose.* The words loop in Roya's mind. "Well, what does it mean to love someone now?"

"I don't think I have an exact answer to that. But when it's all gone, the fear is gone too. So, in the place of those old fears, I guess you fill them with memories. Maybe things were worse than I remember. Maybe not. But, I guess to love her now means holding on and setting her free at the same time. To want her to be happy whether it's with me or not. It's like closing the door to the past but leaving it unlocked."

The two of them sit in silence before Roya finally speaks.

"I'm sorry if I was harsh with you when we met. It just sounded like you thought life was always so simple."

Omid snaps out of his thoughts and returns back to the moment. "The truth is often simple. Accepting it is complicated."

"Do you miss her?"

Faramarz Aslani's voice gently streams in the background.

"Honest answer?" Omid takes another sip of his drink.

"Obviously."

"Only when I can't help but think about her."

"And how often is that?"

He slightly turns up the volume on the speakers. "Sometimes, every day." He says as he reaches for another *pofak*.

****

The late-night rain now leaves the roads of Shomal wet, but it has brought with it a wave of cool, crisp weather —the kind of weather that begs to be felt. The winds are whistling. The air smells like fresh dew and salt. The five of them walk over to the open garage to a large, charcoal tarp covering a few large items.

"What's under there?" Roya nudges Omid with her elbow.

Omid leans into Roya with a playful smile on his face without turning to face her. His eyes are set on the tarp. "It's a surprise."

He walks over with the eagerness of a child on Eid. He peeks underneath the tarp without lifting it entirely and looks over to Roya.

"You ready?"

"Mhmm!"

"Alright!" He whips the tarp off. Basking in the morning sunlight, stand three, newly shined motorcycles. One green, one red, and one white. Omid does a little dance, which makes Roya laugh. "Yeah, yeah… I know. It's the colors of the Iranian flag. You can make your jokes. But hey, we are *bachehaye Irooni* after all."

"How did you know I was going to say something!" Roya pretends to be offended with her hands on her hips.

"Only because you always have something to say." Omid responds with a wink.

Roozbeh looks over to Asal and Bijan with mischievous eyes. "Good God, you two flirt like kids on a playground. I swear. Just look at Omid's goofy face. Haven't seen him this goo-goo eyed since his last birthday when he was gifted the poster of Googoosh."

"Me? Flirting? This is just my personality! I can't help it!" Roya insists.

"Well, I am flirting!" Omid says without looking up as he examines the red motorcycle carefully.

"Omid jaan, you flirt with everyone." Roozbeh teases.

"This is true." Omid laughs

"Roya jaan, Omid thinks he's a real Casanova. Except for, the only thing he's playing with these days is himself."

Now Roya bursts into a loud belly laugh, half in amusement and half in surprise.

Omid shoots Roozbeh a semi-serious scowl, and then relaxes his lips into a smile. "Oh, oh, oh. Somebody is making jokes today...you just wait."

"For what!" Roozbeh eggs him on.

"Right now you may be the jokester, later just the fool." Omid looks over to Roya with a look of satisfaction on his face.

"Ehhh, look! All your solo time has even made you wittier. *Mashallah!*" Roozbeh pats his friend on the shoulder.

Bijan and Asal have been standing there the whole time giggling to one another as lovers do.

Asal finally rolls her eyes for dramatic effect. "Okay, okay boys! Shall we get going?"

Omid hands the red motorcycle's spare helmet to Roya. "So, what do you think?"

"All jokes aside, this is awesome! I have been wanting to ride a motorcycle for a while!"

"I had a feeling you would like it. That's why I polished these up."

"For me?"

"Well, for all of us. But...because of you." He smiles warmly.

"What about my *roosari*? Should I wear it under the helmet?"

"Ehh. We're not going that far, and no one is really around here at this time. You'll be fine, but bring it with you. Come, let's give it a try?" He gestures for her to come sit behind him.

Roya ties the *roosari* around her waist. "I want to drive it! Why do I have to sit behind you?"

"Do you know how to drive one?'

"No."

"Do you feel comfortable navigating the roads here?"

"Well...I mean... no."

"That's why! Believe me, I rather you drive. I get quite lazy sometimes. Better to let you do all the work!"

Roya rolls her eyes.

"Kidding, kidding. How about I show you how to drive one later? Deal?"

"Fiiiiine. Deal!" Roya swings her legs over and adjusts to the cushion on the bike. She wraps her arms around Omid's waist. This is the first time she's really held onto him. "So, Googoosh, huh? That's your celebrity crush?"

Omid laughs. "Oh yeah, young Googoosh was a babe. All of Iran knows it too." He pushes back the brake pedal with his foot and revs the engine ––signaling to the others that he's ready to go if they are.

Bijan and Asal ride on the blue motorcycle together, except for Asal is the one driving. The wind makes her hair dance around her face. She looks over at Roya with a contagious excitement. "Bijan taught me last summer! It's a thrill."

Roozbeh takes the white motorcycle. He adjusts the helmet softly to avoid pressing on his gelled hair.

The engines are revved one-by-one and then all together. Their noise sounds like how violins in a quartet begin separately and end in a unified crescendo. The wind has now gone from whistling to howling. There is a current of adventure in the air.

They begin down the winding path, spiraled around the tropical hills of Shomal. They zigzag in front of one another turning the roads into a playground. Roya is scared and excited at the same time. She turns around to look at the humps of lush, green forest behind them. The wind draws her backwards, and she tightens her grip around Omid's waist.

"You okay?" He asks with his hands firmly on the wheels.

"Yeah, just lost my balance for a second."

"Hold on!"

Omid presses on the gas pedal, and the motorcycle flies forward. Roya feels her heart drop. Her hairband has fallen out, exposing her loose braids. Her thick, black hair is now dancing in the wind under the helmet just like Asal's. The sunlight chases them as they ride without a care in the world. In this moment, none of them are concerned with anything but the fresh air now mixed with the pungent scent of exhaust. They feel the smooth texture of the road as their bikes glide on the pavement —interrupted only by minor bumps and the cushion of leather, pressing into their skin beneath them.

There is no Cyrus in this moment. There are no pending medical school applications. There is no anxiety about suspended dreams. There is no insecurity about not being enough. There is this moment —just five individual bodies in motion, moving along.

****

The houses tucked in-between the hilltops now look like those used in doll houses. Omid releases his foot from the gas pedal and lightly presses the breaks, bringing the bike to a natural stop. Roya catches her breath, and for the first time takes in everything around her fully. She turns her head gazing in awe. Swinging one leg after the other, she jumps off the bike. They have reached a valley. A large body of turquoise water moves before them in-between the vastness of the towering hills. Everything looks bigger to Roya from down here.

She takes her helmet off. The wind cools the thin layer of sweat on her forehead.

"Isn't it something?" Asal says in a calm, yet emotional tone.

"Wow." Roya sits on the ground. She folds her legs into a pretzel like a kid. "This is everything."

Asal joins Roya on the floor. She has wrapped her *roosari* now like a bandana around her forehead and unbuttoned her *monto*. "It's even more beautiful at night. I bet you have never seen so many stars in one sky."

"I don't know, Asal! The California sky can hold many stars. Might be a close call!"

"No way." Asal tilts her head like a schoolgirl. "Here, it's like the stars are kissing you goodnight."

The boys take out the blankets from the carrier boxes they had attached to the back of their motorcycles and place them on the sand. Roya and Asal help bring the last of the items. They had spent the morning packing chicken kabob sandwiches so that they could enjoy them for lunch. Once everything has been unloaded, Omid lets out a disgruntled sigh.

"Ah, dammit! I forgot the speakers." He says to himself. He joins the rest of them on the blanket with a frown on his face. "Guys, I forgot the speakers."

"We know. We heard you." Roozbeh says handing him a sandwich and a fizzy yogurt drink. "Don't worry, man. It's not the end of the world."

"I know it's not the end of the world, but it would have made it perfect."

"Hmm, what was it you had said about *living happens in the cracks?*" Roya says patting his shoulder.

They all laugh.

"You know, Roya...I'm starting to realize all those times I thought you were drifting off in la la land, you were actually paying attention."

"Well, it's hard to forget when the first time you meet someone they start comparing your life to uprooted sidewalks."

"Aha! I made an impression." Omid takes a bite of the sandwich and washes it down with a gulp of his drink.

"Roya, do you drink *doogh*?" Bijan offers one to Roya.

"No, thank you. I don't know if carbonated yogurt is really my thing."

"It's not the true Iran experience until you've at least tried it! It's like going to Australia and not trying veggiemite!" Asal emphasizes.

"When did you go to Australia, Asal?" Bijan mocks and kisses her.

"All I'm saying is if I did, I would try it!"

"No. You're right, you're right. I'll take a sip. Just one sip."

Omid offers her his. Roya pours some in her mouth. The milky fizz and sour aftertaste throws her off and makes her distort the expression on her face.

"No good?" Omid hands her a coca cola.

"It's... different. Is this officially the real Iran experience now?" Roya takes a sip of the soda to chase it down.

Asal looks to her friends and back at Roya. "I'd say close enough!"

They finish their meals and lay down on their backs. The air in Shomal is more humid than in Tehran. Usually, Roya would feel uncomfortable. But today, the humidity feels like someone is softly pressing the warm sunlight onto her face. She closes her eyes and reaches out her hand to use the sand as a natural exfoliant. Bijan rests his head on Asal's lap as she runs her fingers through his light brown hair. Roozbeh swipes through his phone for several minutes before he puts it down. He, too, closes his eyes and tilts his head like a sunflower towards the sun.

They share several moments of comfortable silence. The five of them, stretched on their backs, surrounded by the vastness of the mountains and the sea. Roya knows she will miss this moment before it is even over.

Omid begins whistling to himself quietly. Gradually, his whistling becomes louder. He begins to sing a song in Farsi.

"What are you doing?" Roya asks without opening her eyes.

"I am singing! Doesn't today just make you want to sing? Something must be in the air. My heart feels full."

"The good kind or the bad kind?" Roya opens her eyes.

"Neither." He sits up straight and extends his hands to Roya. "Here, can you get up for a moment!"

"Why?"

"Just do it, please. C'mon." He smiles boyishly.

Roya reaches for Omid with one hand and uses the other to push herself off the ground. "So, what now?"

"Let's dance."

"Dance? There's no music?"

"I'll sing!"

"You want to sing and dance at the same time? Did you smoke something before we left the condo?"

"Na! I'm just feeling a certain way. Will you give me your hand?"

Bijan and Asal smile at each other.

"Hey Omid, you start singing. We will join you! What do you have in mind?" Roozbeh sits up.

"A message to the sea. 'Darya' by Roozbeh Nematollahi. I think you will know the words of the song once I begin." He calls back to Roozbeh and extends his hand once more to Roya. "We leave this paradise tomorrow. Have to make it count."

Roya puts her hand in Omid's. He twirls her in, twists her out, pulls her in once more, and dips her down. They fumble in the sand like kids at a school dance ––laughing at nothing and everything as they awkwardly move their bodies.

"I have an idea for what we should do tonight. Since it's our last night here after all." Roya pauses to catch her breath.

"And what is that?"

"We should stay up all night and wait for the sunrise. I always love when I can catch the moon and the sun up in the sky at the same time. Even if it's just for a moment."

"Hmm, I don't know Roya... we might be too drained for that after today's adventures."

"Oh, c'mon!"

"Okay, okay." Omid's laughter is palpable. "Sing with me, and we will watch the dark blend into the morning light. Deal?"

"But, I don't know the words."

"Just go with it."

# CHAPTER 10

Omid and Roya pull up to Mamani's apartment and find her standing on the steps with Azar.

"Mamani! You're home already? Khanoom Jaan said we'd pick you up together later today." Roya covers her yawn with her hands. *Oops.* "Hi Azar, it's nice to see you!"

"That was the plan, but it looks like I could leave earlier. And what perfect timing. Azar jaan had just come by looking for you."

Omid parks the car and joins them on the steps. "*Salam*, Mamani jaan. *Salam,* Azar jaan." He greets them.

They return his hello.

Azar turns to Roya. "Roya jaan, I'm hosting a poetry reading today at my place. I was wondering if you'd like to join us."

Roya looks to Mamani and then back to Azar. "Thank you, Azar. That's really kind of you. But, Mamani just got back today. I haven't seen her for a few days. I think I should stay home."

"No, no. You should go." Mamani insists. "I mean it. We can have dinner together afterwards."

"Are you sure?"

"Yes, I am very sure. I think it will be nice."

"Wonderful. Why don't you rest, and I will be back in a bit to pick you up. Sound good?" Azar reaches for her car keys.

"Yes, that would be great. *Merci*."

Omid and Azar leave. Mamani walks over to her granddaughter and kisses her on the forehead.

Roya holds her close. "Mamani, I'm so happy you're back."

"Me too." They stand there together for a few moments before Mamani whispers in her ear. "Just one thing…"

"Yes?"

"How about we don't tell your parents about your Shomal trip."

"Why?"

"Because it won't be the heart attack that will get me. It will be your mother! For letting you venture there alone."

"Oh, right. Oh my God. Can you imagine if she knew."

"Ooo believe me, I can just hear her from here."

"Honestly, when Khanoom Jaan said you were okay with me going, I was surprised."

Mamani laughs. "I'm not sure what happened. I suppose being in a hospital makes you look at the world a bit differently."

Roya grabs her travel bag and looks over her shoulder to Mamani again. "Speaking of secrets, who is Arman? I have been meaning to ask you."

Mamani closes the door gently behind them. "When Azar showed up, I had a feeling you would ask. How about we talk about that later? Come rest."

****

Azar's apartment is small, but elegant and vibrant. A plum shaggy rug lays across the floor. The couches are the kind that beg to be sat in for hours. Shortly after Roya arrives, they hear knocks on the door. Two women arrive with pastries in their hands. Roya, too, has a pastry with her ––a cardamom cake topped with crumbled pistachios, Mamani's pick.

"Hi everyone, this is my new friend Roya. She is visiting from the U.S." Azar says as she walks the pastries to the living room.

Roya greets the women, and they walk over to find Azar sitting with her legs crossed on the fuzzy rug.

"Shall we begin?" She places pieces of each pastry onto four separate plates and passes them around. "Roya, would you like to begin?" Azar hands her a thick, bounded book of poetry.

"What do I do?" She runs her hand against the jagged edges of imperfectly sized papers.

"Usually, we just get together, read some poetry, and spend time talking. But, you could have some fun with it. Try thinking of a question you may have or a general area of your life you wonder about. See if the poem speaks to you. Just open to a random page."

"Is this like one of those fortune telling games I saw them doing at the bazaar the other day?" Roya laughs.

"I don't know if I'd say this is a fortune. Just a fun way to see what kind of words pop up. You can judge if it means anything to you."

"Alright, here it goes." Roya closes her eyes and flips to a page.

"Pick a side." Azar guides.

Roya puts her hand on the left page.

"Now, open and read it out loud."

### A Timeless Youth

*In the depths of the unknown, the seekers shall find truth.*
*Others may jest that the wanderers have lost their minds.*
*Day to Day, Night to Night*
*The ordinary play among shadows and call it light.*
*To lift the veil in search for truth, requires a courage*
*The sage called youth.*
*To the seeker newly plucked and the seeker grayed,*
*Youth is not a time*
*But an essence, a way.*
*Dear wanderer, open your eyes.*
*Buried in your pain, there is a window beyond the lies.*

*You are the healer within. A co-creator with the universe.*
*Those who wander will find everything a wonder.*
*Do not look beyond you for what lies within.*
*There is a fire in your heart.*
*It is time to tune in.*

"Oh, I love that one." One of the women says with her mouth full of cake.

"Me too. To hell with ordinary! Give me that fire." The other woman rubs her hands together as if she is holding them over an invisible fire pit. "Azar, what is it your mother used to always say when you were a kid? Something about flames and blaze?"

Suddenly, Azar's eyes do this thing as if a flash of sadness had played behind her eyelids ––like a memory turned into a shooting star. Her eyes become tender like a young girl. "She'd tell me, *'Dokhtaram, hold your hands like this.'*" Azar cups her hands together in front of her with her palms facing the ceiling. "And then she'd say, *'My sweet little girl, I named you Azar because you are my little flame. Use your fire as a torch to guide your way when you are lost. Turn to a flicker of a candle to bring others closer to love. One day, you will become a woman. Never close your fist. As long as you cup your hands like this, life can never burn you. And if the winds ever try to force their way, you will have the power to set them ablaze.'*" Azar's eyes look like they are traveling from a distant place back to the present moment. She looks to Roya. "So, what do you think of your poem?"

Roya stares at the words and finally speaks. "I feel like she is saying something I've never known how to say out loud."

"That's why she is one of the best." Azar smiles.

****

As the afternoon sky slips into dusk, the slices of cake now dwindle into crumbs. The two women leave. Roya now sits on the fuzzy blanket with Azar. Albums with loose photos sticking out from the corners cover the space between them.

"Look at this one!" Azar points to a photograph of a young man and woman.

"Is that...my mom?" Roya stares in disbelief.

"I believe so!"

"And is that your dad?"

"Yes."

"Wow."

"What?"

"It's just so weird to see her like that. With someone else."

"Oh yes, these are from quite some time ago. Look how yellow and aged the pictures are!"

"Azar. That day at the wedding when you were talking about your dad and my mom, I have to be honest. My mom had never mentioned Arman. That was my first time hearing about it all."

"Oh, I see." Azar's eyes fasten on Roya's expression. "That is strange. My father always spoke about her."

"Yeah, and I was wondering why. Why after so long would he still bring her up?"

"Well, my father is an interesting man. He doesn't believe in burying memories. He says that's one way life can trap you. *'Put your past in a casket, and its ghost will show up at your door. Burn it on a pyre, and its ashes will get in your eyes. But, if you entertain them from time-to-time, you realize they are no longer anything but the residual imaginings of the human mind.'* That's what he says at least. I suppose it makes sense now. We don't have to demonize the experiences of the past in order to move on."

Roya looks at the floor. "I suppose you're right."

"Here, I have something to show you. A little while ago, I found this in my father's belongings. When I saw you at the wedding, I thought how funny timing that I came across this letter. There you were sitting before me. I've been meaning to return it to him, but maybe you'd like to see it?"

She walks over to a shelf nearest the kitchen. She returns with a stained, cream-colored envelope and hands it to Roya. There is only one thing written on the outside of the envelope: *Arman.*

Roya's chest tightens before she pulls the letter out. She gets up and stands before Azar. Their bodies face towards one another like a mirror.

> *Arman,*
>
> *My love. I have thought of a hundred ways to begin this letter, yet couldn't seem to get the words on paper. I did not want to think, let alone write, these words to you. My hands are shaking. My tears have stained every piece of paper I have tried to write on. I hope this one will make it through without too much water damage. I wish you were here to hold me in your arms and tell me everything will be okay —that we will figure it out together.*
>
> *I knew if I asked you to meet me, you would. If only I had your lion-hearted strength. I could not bear the idea of facing you and looking into your deep brown eyes. I lose myself in those eyes. I was afraid that if I saw you, I would not be able to turn around and leave. Everything I could have ever wanted would be standing before me. How could I walk away? I know this is selfish, but I know myself. I know how strongly I feel for you.*
>
> *Please forgive me. As you know, there has been word that the Revolution is changing tides. Agha Firouz had come by Baba's office at the embassy and told him he must be alert. There is news that they may be coming for the diplomats who serve the Shah. Rumors say some may even be detained in jail as we speak. Baba does not scare easily. He, too, is lion-hearted. But, you should have seen his eyes when he came home. I have never seen his eyes like that. They looked as though they were fixed upon something from a distance —something that kept moving away from him as he desperately strained to catch one last glimpse. His shoulders looked defeated. He has not been feeling well, and I fear for his health. I had wanted to tell him about you today, but not with those eyes.*
>
> *He walked over, gently placed his hand on my shoulder, and said to me: "Delband, dokhtareh golam. Dokhtareh bahousham.*

*My world. You are so young, but you are my eldest child. From today, your mother and I will need you. We will need each other — all of us." He looked so far into my eyes with tears in his. "We need to leave Tehran late tomorrow night. We won't be returning for a while. Take all that you can and need in your suitcase. Please help your brothers do the same. I will explain more to you, but for now, I must go be alone and have a chai. My heart feels heavy."*

*If someone painted a canvas with the image of my heart, it would have been a burnt orange, a blood red, a wounded indigo, and then black all over. I was speechless, but I understood what Baba was trying to say.*

*I carried my weight to my room and ran my fingers against the lightly faded walls. I examined every single corner —the photos of our family tucked into golden frames, the chipped wood of the door where Arya had kicked his fútbol, the edge near my bed where I had carved a small heart without telling maman. I opened the drawers, closed them, and opened them again. I sat on my bed, and I smelled the clean sheets. I walked to the dining room and sat at the table where we gather every night for mom's khoresht polo. Where baba would ask us about our day and tell us to eat slowly and chew well. I finally walked over to our garden and sat on the swinging chair.*

*I wish you could have seen it. It is my favorite place to sit and read Hafez and Rumi. I would sit there for hours late in those summer nights when the mind is busy, but the city is at ease. I would look into the sky and pray for answers to the millions of questions I had about my life. Seems all very silly now. I could not have even imagined this —you and all the happiness you gave me. And now this —leaving and all the sorrow I will carry.*

*Arman, truthfully, I am scared. Baba says maybe we can stay in Turkey or go to Europe until we can finalize our visas to America. America! Can you believe it? I had always wanted to go and see how life is like, but not like this. I don't understand all the politics. All I know is I am sad to leave my home. This land birthed me. I am scared of what is to come and who I will become. I know everything is about to change in my life, but I am not sure what to expect. I suppose I have never been sure of much in my life, except for you and my love for you.*

*I have never been one to wear my heart on my sleeves. I always thought what a foolish thing to place something so fragile somewhere it could easily fall. But, here I am. I have taken my heart off my sleeves, placed in my hands, and given it to you. Whoever said lovers wear their heart was lying. Lovers give it away and pray to God that the hands that carry it for them do so with care. You have shown me a love that I thought only existed in poems.*

*That day when we first passed each other and you turned around to call for me, I thought you were crazy. Singing and dancing with ease in the middle of all this chaos and unknown. Now, I see that it is your courage. Your ability to bring laughter and joy even when you feel wounded and lost. You have been my light. You have shown me that a walk in the garden and a sky to look up to are enough reasons to smile.*

*If I was with you right now, I would look into your eyes and tell you, I love you. I love you very much. I would ask you to hold me. When I tried to leave, I would secretly pray that you'd just whisk me away. But, I did not want to place that burden on you. I did not want to see the pain in your eyes when I stand before you with my broken heart now cutting into yours too.*

*I wish all joys are yours and that all the stars align for you. I wish that you always have reasons to sing and dance and that when you must weep, you do so without shame. I wish that all the weight is lifted from your shoulders and placed upon your head like a crown so that you wear your challenges with grace. I wish your heart feels light so that you may love again with the same force as the winds. All these things, I wish for you Arman.*

*But, I ask you for only one thing. Please do not forget about me. Years from now, just remember there is a woman named Delband with her heart tied by strings in a bow for you. There is a girl that lives inside of her that held your hand, gazed into your eyes, and found refuge in your arms. This part of me will always belong to you and our memories.*

*I have managed to write this letter without my tears completely ruining the ink, but I was not able to prevent the stains. I don't want to end this letter. I can't sleep. I can't eat. I feel so lost. Just this morning, I was going to tell baba about you. I have a feeling maman already knows. It is strange how this all happened. We leave tomorrow night. I have asked Bahareh to give you this letter.*

*Your love has changed the core of who I am and brought me to life. I hope I have done the same for you. I hope that one day I can return to Iran, and we will see each other again. When I do, I will feel once more what it's like for the heart to be unbounded and free.*

*—Delband*

"Isn't it beautiful?" Azar has a novel twinkle in her eyes —like she is watching a play, delicately and perfectly timed.

Roya's eyes have welled up with tears. Her head is still facing down at the letter in her hands. Several seconds pass, and she looks at Azar.

"Why would you show me this?"

Azar's eyes widen. The twinkle in them disappears as if someone abruptly turned off the lights. "What do you mean?"

"Is this a joke? Is this just some soap opera to you? How do you think this makes me feel?"

"Roya. I, I don't understand. I didn't mean to—"

"I know you didn't mean to do anything. I know. But this? How could this be beautiful? You're trying to tell me my mom is married to my dad, but it's beautiful that in her letter she only has love for yours? Or, that your mom really didn't mind that there are doors closed in your father's heart that she would never hold the key to? How is this so beautiful to you?" Finally, a few tears fall down Roya's face. "I just don't understand. You know, some things are what they are. Sometimes, things are just sad. That's it. You can try to take that sadness and cut it into all these different shapes to make it something it's not. But, at the end of the day, you're just left with a mess." Roya reaches for her *monto* and throws her *roosari* on. Her hands shake as she tries to resist the tears.

"Roya, please don't go like this. I'm sorry. I thought this would be meaningful for you... maybe help you connect to her... I just..."

"Connect to her? She lost so much in her life. Her home, her childhood friends, her great love, her dreams. I don't want to feel connected to my mom through loss. That scares the shit out of me. I don't want this. Any of it." Roya wipes her tears with her sleeve. She does not want to go home to Mamani like this. "I have to go. Please, Azar, I just need to be alone. This was a lot for me."

"I can walk you out. Just a moment...let me call you a taxi." Azar looks around the room not knowing where to place her hands or what to say. She is searching for the right words, but is unable to fill the dense silence.

"No, really, it's alright. I'll just go. I have the address on a piece of paper. I'll get a taxi. *Merci* for having me over. Goodbye." Roya rushes down the stairs, grabs her shoes from the rack, and quickly pushes her feet into her sneakers. The shoe laces are tangled, but still loose.

****

Roya arrives at Mamani's home and almost trips on the mat in front of the door.

"Mamani! Mamani!" She had tried to hold in her tears in the taxi, but now they are streaming down her face. "Are you here?"

She runs to the living room, but it is empty. The kitchen is also empty and so is Mamani's room. She falls to the ground and buries her head in her hands. Just then, Mamani walks in through the front door and hears Roya's sobbing.

"Roya, what happened? Are you alright? Let's go rest on the couch. I am feeling tired."

Roya follows Mamani to the living room and helps her lay down on the couch. She grabs the worn, plush pillows from across the room and places them underneath Mamani's head.

"Come, my dear. Sit down. I thought you were spending time with Azar today? You are home early. I had just gone to see the doctor."

"Is everything okay?"

"Yes, my love. It was just a follow-up. I am feeling much better." Mamani softly holds Roya's chin with her hand. "Tell me. What is going on?"

"I was with Azar, as you know. We were having a great time. I feel very close to her, as if she were my older sister. But then, she showed me a letter that Maman had written to Arman before she left Iran. Do you know about this letter too?"

"I know of it. Your mother mentioned it to me many years later."

"It made me so angry, Mamani. I just wanted to tear it up right there."

"Angry? Anger is not an emotion on its own. It masks a deeper wound. What's wrong?"

"Isn't it obvious? My mom hasn't told me anything about her life. I feel like she's just been living this lie. Azar knows more about her than I do. I know it sounds wrong to say, but I hate that. How could Arman have told her so much, but my mom kept it from me?"

"Roya—"

"You know what else hurts? That she felt so strongly for this person. Then what? How could she just run away and give up? Who gives up like that on someone they really love? Did she even love him? Does she love my dad the same way? Is he just option number two, because option one didn't work out?" Roya's tears drip onto her lips. "You know what I've realized? No one makes sense. No one has life figured out. Not me. Not adults. No one. Life gives you a taste of something good and just takes it away from you. We're just stuck in the in-betweens trying to understand what went wrong. Azar looked so proud of that letter like it belonged in some romantic novel."

"Now, now. Calm down. There's more you don't know."

Roya looks into Mamani's eyes with a piercing expression. "Mamani, I don't want to turn out like these people. I am so scared. A life so practical that it suffocates true meaning. I see so much of my mom in me. And I love her, I really do. She's this resilient and beautiful woman. But, I don't want to make her mistakes. What if I make her mistakes? What if we are so alike that her sorrow becomes my sorrow too?"

Mamani hands Roya a tissue and gently moves her hair out of her face. She patiently stares at her granddaughter. "My, my. You sure do have your mother's eyes. And the shape of your face, just like your father. Copy! They used to bet with each other who you would look like more when you were first born. Did you know that? You should have seen their faces as they huddled over your crib. You would cry and cry."

"Guess that hasn't changed, huh." Roya says calming down.

Mamani smiles. "I had never seen either of your parents more patient than when they were trying to pacify you. You taught them how to really love —a love so selfless and pure in those moments where they held this new life in their hands. You sure have your mother's perseverance and your father's bravery within you. But, my love, you have something not I nor they had."

"What is that?"

"You have this awareness beyond your years. You think of things so deeply in a way unlike I have seen in others when they were your age. What others must live through, you imagine and feel through. This is why you feel so conflicted. I can say you have the gift of being born at a time in which you have the freedom to choose what you want as a woman. I can say you are privileged to have options. But, let me tell you, that is not what makes you different. Your heart craves more. Remember what I told you that day by the lake? You have a poetic soul, and a poetic soul is restless unless it finds its truth. Others think so much, they can't hear their heart. But, you! You live from your heart. Making a mistake is not wrong, but it's when people stop listening to their heart that they become lost. Now, what is all this concern about Arman?"

"I just thought it was disrespectful to my dad for her to show me that. I could have handled it better though. I know. I'm still learning how to deal with my feelings." Roya folds her tissue and places it on her lap. "Do you think my mom made the wrong choice marrying my dad?"

"Why do you think she made the wrong choice?"

"I don't know. The way she wrote about Arman seems like he meant everything to her back then. Do you think she still wishes she could see him again?"

"She did."

"She did?"

"Yes. When your mother was getting her engineering Ph.D, she attended a conference in London where she ran into Arman. He had been in town for a friend's wedding. His hotel was the same building where the conference was hosted."

"What happened?"

"They saw each other as she was leaving the lobby. He was arriving through the doors. I still remember the phone call from her. She didn't have much money for the international calling cards back then, but we spoke on the phone for a while. Arman had asked her to meet over chai. She asked me what to do. This was the first time I learned about Arman. I had known my daughter for so many years, yet failed to notice the hidden burden she had carried." She places her hand on Roya's hand. "That is a guilt I lived with for many years. There was something I did not recognize in your mother's voice that day. She was elated, yet frantic. Her nerves were all over the place. She kept telling me why she thought she shouldn't meet him, as if she were trying to convince herself out loud."

"What did you say to her?"

"I must admit I was overwhelmed by all that she had shared. But, I told her she should meet with him. I let her finish talking herself in circles and told her she must be brave enough to face her greatest weakness in the eyes. Roya jaan, you cannot live inside your fears or lie to yourself. I told your mother the same. That she must step into the situation or else she will always have questioned what could have been. It is those question marks that make us resentful."

"They saw each other and then what? I can't even imagine after all those years them sitting before one another. Did they just leave each other then?"

"Yes. They were both in town for a few days and spent time together. When she returned home, she sat down next to me like you and shared the story. Now, I know your mother is logical, so I said, '*Delband jaan, what is your heart telling you? What is it that you want? I don't want you to end up like me —married without a choice. I want my daughter to feel freedom.*' She spoke in a tone full of enchantment and sorrow and confessed to me. '*Maman, it just didn't feel the same. We are different people now. We both felt it. Those few days together meant everything to me. We laughed over the past. We cried over the passage of time. Our last embrace was like holding onto another life. But maman, that life is over. We have changed. It's like two characters meeting again. Only the shells of us remain the same.*'"

"Wow. I didn't expect that at all. That was her chance to be with him."

"It's quite interesting. The ending always holds a lot of truth. It's raw and vulnerable. It's why loss molds us so deeply. It creates a space within and turns us into these human vessels that we must fulfill. Sometimes, people grow apart and eventually grow back to each other. Other times, their lives are kept in parallels."

"How do you know which one it will be?"

"We don't. We can't predict it. Only in the moment can we decide. For your mother and Arman, the love was not lost. It had just changed into another form of love —the kind that intertwines a shared history but frees the present for new beginnings."

"Do you think she loves my dad the same?"

"Why do you ask that?"

"I don't know. I can't explain it, but I feel like there's something missing. I don't see happiness in their eyes anymore. Not like the old days at least."

Mamani looks at Roya with eyes that want to cradle her. She admires her granddaughter's curiosity. "One relationship can go through many cycles. I cannot tell you whether your mother made the wrong or right choice. What I can tell you is that the day she met your father, I saw a light in my daughter's eyes that I had not seen since we lived in Tehran. She never shared many details, but that look said it all. But, love is a thing to be nurtured and an action to be lived every day. Time takes a toll on anything we do not tend to —much like our health, our homes, our dreams. Your mother and father have much to learn from one another. This is a part of their love story. After all, they are only human. Right? They do not have all the answers and nor will you. Life is about learning to ask the right questions."

"What's the point of asking all these questions if there is never a right answer?"

"One day you will understand. Now, enough of this crying! You care so much for others' wounds. I need you to focus on yourself. There is a time to release and a time to pursue. Look where you are —in our beautiful homeland. Allow yourself to outgrow the past. These hurts are not the end of your story."

"And you, Mamani? Are you happy?" Roya tries to scan her grandmother's expression and understand what her life must have been like.

In the past, it was typical for young women in Iran to have arranged marriages coordinated by their families. Mamani was one of the few women who had the privilege to receive higher education. She was finishing her last year of high school when her parents married her to Roya's grandfather. He was a good man. An intelligent and hardworking man. A gentle man. She was lucky in this sense. But, they were never in love.

*"It could be worse! You could be married off to an aggressive man or an ugly man. He is tall and broad shouldered. So handsome!"* Her friends had said when she locked herself in the bathroom on the eve of her wedding night with her hands clasped in prayer for more time.

*"Oh, you know shy brides! It's normal to be nervous. Her life will never be the same. Of course, she is nervous! When you get*

*married and start a family, your life is no longer about you. She will adjust, like we all did, of course."* The elders had said as they nudged her to smile at the *sofreh* ceremony.

Like many other women, Mamani was expected to stay home and take care of the children. True to her father's promise that she could complete school, she graduated. On the day of her ceremony, she held her head high and wore her favorite pastel blue dress from Paris. Mamani loved all the European dresses she could wear before the Revolution, and her father never returned from his travels without a souvenir. When she accepted the framed certificate, her headmaster had whispered in her ear. *"Mobarak, young lady. You were one of my favorite students. You will go far in this life. I know it. Anything you want will be yours if you dare to seek it."* Mamani left the stage with tears in her eyes, but she kept her head high. She knew her future was no longer hers.

"Mamani?" Roya softly touches her grandmother's shoulder.

"I am grateful. God has blessed me with my health, my family, and their safety. I have done the best I can with the circumstances I was given. This is why I want you to dream big, Roya." She stretches her hands wide apart and creates a vast circle in the air. "You can achieve it all. For you and for me. Promise me."

Roya embraces her grandmother and kisses her forehead. "I promise you, Mamani. For you and for me."

****

Later that night, Mamani brings out a box from underneath a pile sitting in the corner of her bedroom. The cardboard is torn at the edges, but its base is still intact. Farsi writing is scribbled across the various sides of the box in bold, black swirls. One-by-one, she takes out each of the albums, brushes the dust off with her hand, and places it on the ground. She stares quietly at each album before picking up a faded pink one with glossy plastic covering. The black-and-white photos have aged to a faded brown. As Mamani flips through the pages, the newer photos are printed in faint shades. Colors like a salmon pink, a morning sky blue, a leafy green, and sunset yellow. Kourosh Yaghmaei's "Gole Yakh" sings in the background. Lit candles decorate the bookshelf. Small crowds passing by can be heard from the streets below. They are chanting some phrases in unison. She turns the volume up to drown out their noise and leans her back against the foot of the couch.

Roya walks into the room in her pajamas and her hair rolled into a towel. Her cheeks are still a rosy red from her hot shower. "Mamani, do you know what is going on outside? I heard people yelling, but I couldn't understand clearly." She unravels the towel and dries the tips of her hair before tying it in a loose braid.

"Don't mind the noise for now. Look what I have found for you." Mamani hopes Roya will dismiss conversation about what is going on in the streets. She flashes her signature smile, inviting her granddaughter to come sit beside her.

Roya leans her back against the couch like her grandmother and picks up a photo from the floor. "Is that…?"

"Your Baba? Yes."

"No way! That's Baba? He looks so…"

"Young?"

"…lively." Roya pulls the photo and examines it closely as if any moment it would vanish. Her father's face is clean shaven. His black, shaggy hair is full. He is wearing a pastel green turtle neck, a leather jacket, and denim jeans. The bottom of his face is covered with icing as if someone had pressed his face into the cake he is holding. A few unknown faces stand around him laughing, but Roya can't take her eyes off of her father's expression. There is a light in his eyes that she has not seen before.

"What do you mean?" Maman puts her glasses on to examine the photo.

"His eyes. He is smiling with his eyes. His laughter looks so contagious. I can't remember the last time he looked this happy. So, I don't know, energized."

"Ah, yes. This was his 30th birthday. Your Maman threw him a surprise birthday party. He had been working on his dissertation all day at the library. She had told him they would meet at the house and go out to dinner. When he arrived, she had gathered his closest friends. I wish you could have seen the look on his face! He was grinning ear-to-ear. Just before they cut the cake, your mother had one more surprise for him. She closed his eyes with her hands. The next thing your Baba felt was his father's hand on his shoulder."

"Wait, what! Agha joon came to the U.S.? How?"

"One of our friends was able to get him a temporary visiting visa. Your Baba wept tears of happiness the moment he realized his father was sitting in front of him. This photo was taken shortly after they sang him happy birthday, and your maman pressed his face into the cake."

"Maman?" Roya let's out a short, amused laugh. "My mom pressed his face into the cake? The cake everyone was going to eat? At her *mehmooni*? That doesn't sound like her."

"Oh, yes! We used to say your Maman was like one of those Kinder chocolate eggs we used to buy in Europe."

"Chocolate on the outside, confusing little toy on the inside?"

"Well, I was going to say sweet on the outside with a playful surprise. You never knew what to expect. She would be calm and collected. You know how she likes to carry herself. Then, she'd do something silly and surprise everyone." Mamani picks up another photo from the scattered collection. "Here, look at this one!" She holds the photo away from her face and gazes before handing it to Roya.

In the photo, there is a woman with caramel brown hair tied in a high ponytail. She is leaning against a tree. Her summer dress is covered in colorful powder. Her head is tilted back like she is laughing to the sky saying, *you may be vast, but I am also limitless.*

"That's Maman. I can't believe it. That doesn't look anything like her."

"This was at university when your mother was getting her masters. She was celebrating Holi with her classmate. Everyday she'd come home with a new story. A new experience."

Roya picks up another photo. This one is newer. She can tell by its texture. Her mother is holding a baby in her arms. She is kissing the baby's forehead as Baba kisses her forehead. They are both leaning into each other with the infant nestled in-between them. The California palm trees tower in the background, but a ray of sunlight manages to pierce through and create a golden glow.

"That's you, Roya. You were only a few weeks old here. Your parents were so nervous. They did not want to do anything wrong, but were so excited to hold you. Their baby. Their little world."

"What happened to them? I feel like when I see these photos, I am looking at two characters I don't even know. My father's eyes. My mother's laugh. They seemed so full, like their hearts were brimming with all the joy in the world."

"And now?"

"I catch myself staring at them sometimes. Wondering what they think about. Wondering whether they became who they always wanted to be or everything they feared. They laugh and smile. They hold each other close. But, I don't know. I guess they still seem empty to me. All their words sound flat these days."

"There are those who suffer loss, and they retreat from themselves to avoid their pain. There are also those who suffer loss and turn into the pioneers of their own souls. They become like cave divers, digging for meaning. Somewhere along the way, your parents felt loss, as we all do. But, they never looked to find new meaning. They were occupied with other worries. They never stopped to think where they were going like you do."

"That makes me sad. Sometimes when I hug them, I feel like I absorb their emotions. It's why I don't like it anymore. It just feels strange. Somehow, I feel their pain. Does that sound weird?"

"Not at all. You are, after all, a part of them and they a part of you. We tend to carry the wounds of those we love in our hearts. Sometimes, that is easier than facing our own."

"I miss how we were before real life happened. I miss them."

Mamani smiles. "Life has just now begun! Carrying your parent's emotions will not help you or them. Remember what I told you earlier? You deal with yourself first. Release your burdens and fill your own vessel. Be the best you. You will then become the best daughter, the best student, the best anything you wish. First, you must learn to take care of yourself. All else will fall into place."

Roya picks up the photo of her parents holding her again. "Can I keep this one, Mamani?"

"Of course. We had brought these albums over for the family when your parents visited. You were a couple years old then. There are more copies at home."

"I had never seen these ones before. So surreal." She squeezes Mamani lightly. "Mom was pretty cool though. Wish she wasn't so uptight now."

"Maybe we should throw some colorful powder on her when we get back. Hmm, or paint." Mamani squeezes Roya back.

"Very funny. We aren't exactly on the best of terms. She'd yell so loud. Can you imagine?"

"I think your Maman and Baba miss you even more than you miss them. Maybe if you start living your life, you can show them how to do it again too. They could use a little push. You are my young warrior."

"I'll try. By the way, Mamani?"

"Yes?"

"What was going on outside earlier? You never said."

Mamani's heart sinks. She knew it would be a matter of time before Roya would ask again. "They were protesting."

"Protesting what?"

"Protesting for their rights. To be heard."

"Isn't that dangerous? I thought you can't do that here."

"Yes, it is."

"So, what will happen? Is everything going to be alright?"

"I pray to God that it will be."

# CHAPTER 11

Roya leads the way up the spiral stairs she had climbed the first day Omid had taken her to the coffee shop.

"Slow down a second!" Omid pants as he follows her up the stairs.

Three knocks later, they are inside the hidden sanctuary. The smell of roasted coffee beans is heavy. Roya knows it won't be long before it settles onto her skin.

"How about there?" She points to a table near a window that has been slightly cracked open.

"Looks good to me. We can get some fresh sunlight."

They sit down and order their drinks, two coffee glaces like before.

"Roya, hear me out. I really think you should start composing some music." Omid leans forward in his chair.

"Woah, random. Where did that come from?"

"I've just been thinking. Imagine this. You know how in movies, the lead hero—"

"Mhm." Roya coughs. "Heroine..."

"Hero, heroine. Whichever. You know how there's that beating of the chest, running through the fields, I'm on top of the world moment?"

"You think me writing music will be that grand finale?"

"Hah, no! Not even close. Those scenes are never the ending in real life. I get why they want to leave the audience there. People want to know how things end, but that's just cheap."

The coffee glaces arrive with their mountains of whipping cream and scoop of floating vanilla.

"Where do you think it should leave off then?" Roya lets the ice cream melt on her tongue.

Omid continues. "Right at the beginning."

"And why is that?"

"Because that's the whole point. Life is a loop." He draws a circle on a napkin with his finger. "When flowers finally bloom, they're now ripe for bees to begin making honey."

"How is this related to me making music again? You lost me."

"The point is there is always more. An ending is not the end. But, you can't let things in if you don't let some things out first. When people create, they're taking all that stuff in them and unleashing it in some other form. Remember when we first met, I said I feel like you have something to say?"

"Yes. It annoyed me so much." Roya teases.

"I didn't know this then, but I think that means more. Maybe you have more to say. Things people need to hear."

"Omid, I really appreciate you thinking so highly of me and all. Seriously. But, there is nothing I have to say that hasn't been said before."

"That doesn't matter. It's not what you say. It's how you do it. To make people feel something means you can't hold back. You have to be raw and present and vulnerable and brave."

"Even if I wanted to, like I said, I can't write notes. I don't know how." Roya slouches in her seat discouraged.

"What do you mean? How do you compose music then?"

"I told you. I just hum the beat to myself and imagine how all the different instruments would sound together. Their pitch, their crescendo, the sound of the bows stroking the wood. The sound of a piano moving in-between the cries of the violins, the stability of the cello and bass, the excitement of the trumpets, the soothing touch of the flute. I imagine it all in my mind as I hum."

"Right. Why don't you have someone write these down? This could be something."

"Omid, I gave up on all that a while ago. There's no space for that in my life anymore."

"You said you were pre-med, but why completely give up on music? I don't get it."

"My parents didn't think it was practical. It wouldn't be enough. It wouldn't give me a living. Like you guessed, they want me to be secure. Maybe music really is just a hobby, you know? It's a joy. It's a companion. It's a release. But, it's a one in a million chance they said. We don't have the luxury of taking that chance."

"So what! Pursuing a dream is a reason to live and sometimes even a living." Omid looks at her in disbelief. "You don't sound like the Roya I know right now. How could you give up so easily on something you believe in? Just because it isn't going to be easy? Why can't you do both?"

"Both? How is that even possible? I can barely handle my med school applications right now. You want me to pursue medicine while chasing some illusion?"

"I'm saying do whatever you have to do, but don't give up. Make a living and also live. How you do that is part of this all. Don't you see? We make up our mind, and then make a road when there is nothing but gravel. Sometimes, we have to create ships with bare hands to travel the seas and climb mountains on bare feet. When we've done all that we can, we bow our heads, touch the ground, kiss the Earth, and raise our hands to the sky."

"And then what?"

"Then, we trust. We trust with our entire heart. We make hope our wings and give ourselves at least the chance to soar ––a chance, however small, to be what we want to be."

"You know humans can't actually fly, right?"

"No one said jump off a building and freestyle. All I'm saying is give yourself the freedom to try."

"Okay, I will try! Enough about me now. What about you? What are your grand dreams?"

"My dreams? To live a good life. To make honest money. To take care of myself and my family. Maybe find a good woman to take care of me!"

Roya gives him a look.

"Just kidding, just kidding. Relax!"

"No, I mean your special dream. The one that's just for you," she responds.

"Roya, it's different for me than for you. Everyone can dream, but some have the options to turn those goals into reality. It works differently in Iran. I don't have a talent like yours, and my parents are getting old. They rely on me."

"Ehhhh Omid, I didn't take you to be a hypocrite! Doesn't really fit your personality." She pauses and eases the volume of her voice. "I'm not going to pretend like I know your life, and I'm really not in the position to tell you how to live. But, I think you are the one now selling yourself short. Aren't you the one that just said dreams are a reason to live? You tell me I can do both, yet you talk as if it's impossible."

"Yeah, I sure did say those things." He says quietly looking away from Roya.

"Don't break my heart and tell me that was all empty words to make me feel better. I know you meant them. You also deserve a chance. You can't let all this wisdom go to waste now, right? You gotta show people how to really live!"

"Look who's coaching who now! The roles have really flipped, I see."

"*Merci, merci.*" Roya flips her hair to the side. "A good teacher is also a good student."

Omid laughs. "A few weeks in Iran, and you've turned into Rumi!"

Roya smiles. "I mean, I read something similar to that in some self-help book. It's so true, isn't it?"

"Indeed, Roya. Indeed."

"Well, we better get going. Speaking of flowers and bees, Khanoom Jaan is coming over. We are fixing up Mamani's garden. I've been watering all of Khanoom Jaan's plants. Now, she is teaching me how to properly tend to the soil."

Omid lifts an eyebrow.

"Oh c'mon! It's not as lame as it sounds."

"I just find it funny how much plant talk you've had lately. Now, if you apply that tending the soil to your music too, there could be some blooming potential. You see what I did there? I'm telling you!" Omid laughs.

"Yeah, yeah. Well, I can't magically find an orchestra right now, but I can pat down some mud on the ground for now. Let's start there."

Omid lifts his other eyebrow. "I won't even make a joke right now. But hey, are you still going to Sepideh's tomorrow? I told her you would be."

"Shit, yeah. I forgot I had promised. It's so early though!"

"A promise is a promise."

"I know." Roya sighs.

"So, I'll pick you up from there as planned. Sound good?"

"Yup! Shall we go now?"

"Let's. Wouldn't want you to miss the fertile soil tutorial."

****

She stretches her arms outward with her fingers pointing towards the sleeping city. The people of Tehran must be awakening soon to begin their day. Omid had suggested she join one of Sepideh's guided yoga meditations to clear her mind. Yet, Roya's imagination begins to wander. There's a thin layer of smog hovering over the city high rises. From where Roya is standing, the air feels open and clean. As she watches the pollution curl in-between the city landscape and mountains below, she thinks of the families in their homes. She tries to imagine herself as a young woman living in Iran instead of just vacationing. *How would my life be different? How would it be the same?* She thinks of her own family's past. What their lives must have been like before they had to leave everything and start over. The idea frightens and intrigues Roya. The chance to begin anew in a foreign land where the identity is still malleable and the past a thing to be mourned. *How much of their identity could my parents have chosen to create? How much became the product of their forced circumstances?*

Sepideh's voice plucks through Roya's continuous thoughts.

"Raise your hands like this, ladies." Sepideh looks over to make sure they are doing the position correctly. "This exercise does not mean anything unless you feel it in the right places. The way you stretch your hands, the way your feet push into the ground, they all determine your balance. Watch your breath, ladies! Today, we are going to learn how to breathe the right way."

Roya observes the way everyone is breathing. Her eyebrows bend into each other again. *Breathe the right way? What the hell. Have I been breathing wrong this whole time too?*

Sepideh looks as though her body was made to move with the flexibility and ease that yoga demands. She stretches her arms in front of her as if she's aiming for the apex of the mountains. She inhales deeply through her nose. Her feet press into the earth welcoming the dirt beneath the cushioned mats. As she exhales, her shoulders relax backwards. Her chest falls down. Everything about the way she moves seems fluid and comfortable.

Roya looks to her own feet to make sure they are positioned at the correct angle. Her legs are wobbling and her arms aching. Sepideh slowly gets up and walks behind Roya. Placing her hand on top of Roya's, she guides her arms just an inch upwards. "There, like that." She pulls her hip down by the waist just a bit. "Fall into yourself. Take it easy. Trust your feet to plant you in the ground."

*Trust my feet to plant me in the ground, right. Whatever that means.* Roya flattens her feet and tries to squat backwards so that her hips are lowered.

"You're trying too hard. Here, hold on. Lay flat on your stomach. Let's do this together. Step-by-step." Sepideh softens her voice as if she's putting Roya into a trance. "Alright, Roya. I want you to think of a place. It can be somewhere you have been before, somewhere you want to go, or even somewhere created in your own mind. Imagine all the details of this place. The colors, the textures, the temperature, the way it makes you feel. What are you doing there? Is there anyone around you? Are you alone? This place is where you feel the most peaceful."

*Hmm. Where would I go?* Roya's mind first goes to her home. *Everyone probably feels the most comfortable in their childhood home, right?* But, the image seems unnatural to her. She thinks back to the bright turquoise paint, the empty spaces on the walls, and all the people that would pass through those doors. She thinks back to Friday movie nights where her and Azadeh would squish in-between their parents and argue over which movie to watch.

*"Something romantic! No, something funny! A cartoon!"*

Eventually, they settle on something their father suggests.

*"Okay kids, let's just get along. How about we watch this one here? Does that look good to you two?"*

Roya and Azadeh give up. Eventually, they rest their cheek on either side of their father's chest as their mother extends an arm over them. It doesn't matter what they watch. They argue, because they can. Just as quickly, they forget. All they wanted was to spend time with their parents.

Those memories make Roya happy. But, then she thinks of the slamming doors, the nights of tossing and turning in bed, and the relief when she'd leave for college to get away from that house. Any reason to have her own space, so she could rid the clutter in her head.

"I want you to hold that image in your mind for a moment, okay?"

*Wait, no. Not that image.* Roya tries again to think of somewhere that brings her peace. She thinks of the ocean or the gazebo in her university's courtyard. None of the images feel right. She gives up and takes a deep breath with her eyes still closed. "Yeah, got it Sepideh."

"Okay, now I want you to focus on all those details. Feel yourself there."

Roya keeps breathing and hopes that Sepideh is convinced she's helping. After a few moments, she starts to imagine herself in a garden hidden in a forest. Roya doesn't recognize the place, but she feels at home. The trees are a deep, dark green. Light pink and purple flowers are blossoming close to the ground. A stream moves through a narrow opening. She follows the stream towards the sound of water splashing against rocks. She runs her hands against the bark of the tree trunks. The top coats are coarse. When she pushes down against the firmness, the bark softens. She continues following the stream up over the hills. The air is not too hot or cold. Finally, she reaches a fountain near a large waterfall. The fountain resembles the one from the park where her and Azadeh would make their wishes, but this is not their childhood park. She places her hand in the water and raises it over her head. The water drips from her palms onto her scalp and down her neck. She breathes in through her nose deeply as her chest rises. With the exhale through her mouth, her chest falls again. She's wearing a light garment that moves with the wind. Everything is quiet, except for the sound of water moving against the rocks and some birds in the distance.

"Very good, Roya. You're getting the hang of this breathing thing."

Roya had not even noticed that her breathing has changed. Her body feels both light and energized. She opens her eyes. Her pupils adjust to the orange rays of sunlight piercing through the sky, welcoming the morning in.

They complete their yoga session and walk over to the balcony table. The surrounding trees give them privacy. Roya is drenched in sweat, while the rest of the girls look as though they had just stepped out of a lifestyle magazine. Sepideh opens the sliding glass doors and walks into the apartment. Moments later, she comes out with a large, circular tray holding various small dishes. Cut cucumbers, cubes of feta cheese, bright red tomatoes, omelets sprinkled with saffron, a pile of toasted bread, and fig jam are neatly placed. Roya can feel her stomach speaking to her as she eagerly eyes the jam.

"One last touch!" Sepideh runs back into the apartment and returns with a vase of pink peonies. "Perfect."

"So Roya, what's going on with you and Omid?" Leila says abruptly as she smooths some honey on her slice of bread.

"What do you mean? We're friends."

"Hmm, friends that close? Didn't you two just meet this summer? You guys act like you've known each other for a long time." Leila is on a mission, subtly pushing for answers.

"I mean, yeah we are. It's how it is I guess. We just get each other."

"He's attractive. You're attractive. You two get each other. And you're telling me you two don't want to sleep with each other?" Leila now sticks her spoon in the fig jam.

Roya sips chai to wash down the bread stuck in her throat. "Umm, no? I don't. And I don't think he does either. We're just close friends. Yeah, it's a deep bond. That's just the kind of guy he is. He's easy to talk to."

"Deep? Omid is deep. Who would have known." Leila mumbles.

"Well, if you took turns listening and talked less about yourself, maybe you'd know too." Roya says in an irritated, yet even tone.

This time Leila's eyes look genuinely surprised by Roya's response. She begins to say something, but Sepideh speaks before she does.

"Ladies! There's no need for this. We just had a peaceful yoga session. Let's not ruin it now, okay?" She flashes a smile and looks over to Roya with apologetic eyes. "Roya, Omid mentioned you're working on some music. How's that going?"

"What? I'm not working on anything. I just have ideas. I know how I want it all to sound, but I'm having a hard time lately. The idea of people hearing it makes me nervous I guess."

"Ah, I see. You're holding back?" Sepideh passes Roya the fig jam.

"Yeah, and it's not working at all."

"That makes sense. Music has to be real." She pauses before continuing. "Why are you afraid of sharing how you really feel? I hear you have a gift for composition."

Roya suddenly feels shy. "Thanks, Sepideh. That's really nice of you to say. I think I'm just working through some complicated emotions right now."

"Alright. Well, I'm excited to hear what you come up with." Sepideh flashes Roya an understanding smile while Leila scrolls through her phone.

Roya appreciates Sepideh not pushing the subject. She glances at her own phone and sees two missed calls and a text from Omid. "Oh, shit!"

"What happened?" Sepideh asks concerned.

Before Roya can answer, Omid nonchalantly walks through the doors.

"I call both of you, and you just forget about me, huh?" He smiles as he pops a tomato slice in his mouth.

"Omid, how did you even get up here?" Sepideh giggles.

"Sepideh, all this time you live here, and you don't even know your own doorman well. Do you know what that round bellied man will do for *lavashak* from Agha Zeytoon's? I told him there was a sale, and he just ran! Fastest I've ever seen him go." He shoots his hands up into the air mimicking a departing flight.

Everyone is laughing now, and the awkward tension from before somehow disappears. Even Leila smiles and puts her phone down.

"Now, back to you two." He looks over at Roya and Sepideh. "I told you I was picking up Roya around this time. She has some work to do!"

"Wait, work? You never told me I had work. You just said to be ready." Roya looks over to Sepideh confused, but it's clear that Sepideh knows what's going on already.

"Oh, I wouldn't really call it work... but there is something you'll have to do." He puts his hands together like he is praying. "Just trust me, okay!"

"Sepideh, what's going on?"

"Let's just say he wanted to do something special for you."

Roya grabs her bag and walks to the restroom to change her clothes. She quickly puts a thin coat of blush and mascara before heading to the living room to meet Omid.

****

The taxi pulls up to a large, tan building crowded with young students walking around with bookbags. A modern coffee shop attaches to the side of the building and reminds Roya of her own campus café. Two of the baristas have those swoosh haircuts like the California boys back home. The girls sport tight jeans, vibrant *roosaris,* and converse sneakers.

"Welcome to the University of Tehran. One of the top academic institutions in Iran. This place only accepts the best of the best."

"Oh, cool. Why are we here?"

"Because I think you are one of the best of the best. There are some people I want you to meet."

"Is this your way of encouraging me to get more excited about med school?"

"If I wanted to do that, I would take you to a hospital where there's some real action. Not to a campus where they're all walking around like sleep deprived zombies. Med school is great, and you'd be the loveliest zombie. But, we're here for something different."

Students rush past them. There is a contagious curiosity in the air—laughter, youthful chatter, the sound of hundreds of voices sinking into one unified buzz. Omid leads Roya to a wide hall with a tall ceiling. They arrive at a set of double doors made of dark wood. He slowly turns the knob and opens the doors.

Roya's eyes widen like a child at Disney World.

"Isn't it a beautiful auditorium?"

Roya nods her head as she stares at the burgundy, velvet curtains framing the open stage. The building is old, but the walls appear newly renovated. Lights beaming on the center of the platform make the gold trimming of the stage shine.

"You said you had the idea, but you need people to play it. Right? Me and Sepideh got some friends together. You can use some of the resources here. Come on! I want to introduce you to your leading orchestra. They're willing to help, but they want to meet you first."

"Woah. This is, uh, incredible. Is this for real? I can't believe you and Sepideh set this up for me."

"First, you have to show them what you're working with! Impress them. And yeah, I told you Sepideh has a good heart underneath all the glam. We do what we can." He looks over and sees Roya crying. "Eh, eh! What are you doing?"

Roya jumps and squeezes Omid. "Thank you! The fact that you even thought of this... it's one of the kindest things anyone has done for me. This is so cool!"

They walk down the steps to the stage. Once they get closer, Roya sees three women and two men standing there.

"Roya, this is Amir, Payam, Farideh, Bahar, and Golnaz ––she goes by Naz. Amir is one of the best composers I know. He can help you write your notes. Payam and Farideh are the top chair violinists. Bahar is a badass on the cello, and Naz is the mastermind of the piano. They are here to help you, but you will need to lead."

Roya shakes everyone's hands. The chairs on the stage look like they have been left over from a performance ––strategically organized, but slightly disheveled. Amir grabs a few and positions them in a circle. They all take a seat.

"Roya, it's a pleasure to meet you. How are you liking Iran so far?" Amir begins.

"I love it. Still adjusting, but this place is beautiful. And thank you for taking the time to meet with me. All of you! I'm sure you're so busy."

"Downtime is incredibly rare these days, but there's always time to help out a friend. Omid's always been there for us. It's the least we could do." Naz replies warmly.

"Plus, it gives us a chance to have some creative fun! Get away from our studies a bit." Payam chimes in.

"Your uncle was a legend in the arts. His work is timeless. A real inspiration." Farideh leans forward and places her chin in her hands. "You must be a fan of his music, I'm sure?"

Roya's cheeks are warm with embarrassment now. "I actually

haven't heard much of his work. I wasn't really into Persian music growing up. I've been listening to it more once I got here."

"Oh, Roya! You absolutely must. Even if it is just meant for you to understand him better as an artist. My mother says that to experience someone's creation is to witness the chaos and bliss of their soul. The struggle and triumph."

"Yes. In fact, in my composition courses, we were taught to practice tapping into our deepest emotions and using them as our muse. To search for the truth in our wounds. Iranians can be, how do you say it, dramatic at times. But, it makes for good art!" Amir says enthusiastically.

"Oh, believe me. Don't I know it! Guess it's in our blood to feel life deeply. Good to know, I'm not crazy!"

Omid looks across the room at Roya when she says this and playfully motions to her that she's still crazy.

Roya rolls her eyes and turns her attention back to Amir. "How do we start this? I'm so excited and grateful you're all here."

"The rest of the crew has classes soon. For now, we just want an idea of what kind of mood you are trying to capture and what instruments you envision. We can assemble your full team later." Amir takes the pen that has been resting on his ear and opens his notebook to a blank page. His presence is calm, but he is focused like a seasoned professor on the first day of a new semester. "You and I can set a time later and work through the notes together. Sound good?"

"Yeah, of course. I mean, I don't know where to start. I always imagined violins, cellos, a piano. Omid's dad played us some beautiful songs on this wooden instrument. I forgot what it is called, but I was mesmerized by its sound. I think that is the missing piece I was looking for."

"*Tar!*" Omid adds.

"Yes, the *tar*! I really liked it. I guess the most important thing I want the audience to feel is a range of music. I want them to forget themselves in the movement of the sounds and to find themselves again by the end —a song that carries you a distance but returns you back to yourself. Does that make any sense? I feel like I'm talking all abstract now!"

"No, no. I understand perfectly." Bahar speaks for the first time. "You want a lyrical odyssey."

They all look at each other in silent agreement.

"Yes, exactly." Roya's heart feels extra full in that moment.

They rise from their seats and hug goodbye. As they exit the auditorium, Roya whispers to Omid. "I know these are your friends, but how is the school just letting me use their stuff? I'm not a student here."

"I think you should visit Azar. You might have been a bit unfair to her, no? She was able to get us access to the auditorium and instruments by having you declared as a visiting performer."

"Oh. Yeah, I know. I feel terrible about that whole situation. I overreacted. I'm not proud of it." Roya looks at her shoes as she speaks. "Wait, how did you know about that?"

"Your Mamani told me. Thought I could talk to you about it."

"I see. And how was Azar able to get the access?"

"Her father is the director of the music department. Dr. Arman."

Roya's heart dives into her stomach. "Oh."

# CHAPTER 12

A young woman hands Roya a sheet of paper and then rushes to pass it to a group walking by in the halls.

"Wait! Wait a minute, please!"

The girl looks over her shoulder with an *are you talking to me* expression on her face.

"Yes, you! Can you please come back for a moment? What is this?" Roya calls out.

The girl walks over with fierce determination in her eyes. "It's for the protest."

"What protest?"

"The students are protesting. We are raising our voices, not our fists. It's a peaceful protest for change."

"But, what are you protesting?"

"Look around you. Don't you get it? It's like you're not even from here."

The young woman's bluntness takes Roya aback.

"No, I'm not from here actually. I am visiting."

"Oh, so you are American? Your accent makes sense now."

"Well, yes. I am visiting for the summer."

"You should get it more than anyone else then. I love my country. I am a child of Iran. But, we want opportunities. To be a part of the global world. To share our minds, our talent, our hearts with the world. We want growth."

Mamani had told Roya to refrain from all political discussions. She lowers her voice to a hushed whisper. "I don't really know what's going on. But, are you sure this is the right way?"

"Why are you whispering? It's not a secret. We are not looking to fight. All we want is peace and prosperity."

"Isn't this dangerous?"

"This is a reality of life." The young woman flashes a smile tinted with judgment. "Would you not do this for your home? Stand for what is right?"

"Yes, of course. I mean, I would like to think I would at least."

The woman scans Roya up-and-down. "You seem like a genuine person. What's your name?"

"Roya."

"It suits you for how you see the world. Like it's some dream. I like your honesty though. Protect it." To Roya's surprise, she says this with sincerity.

"Oh, thank you." *What is that supposed to mean.* "And your name?"

"It doesn't matter. Enjoy your vacation." Before Roya can say anything else, the woman sets off with her stack of sheets resting in her arms like an infant.

Roya folds the paper and puts it in her purse. She wants to show it to Amir when she meets with him for rehearsal, but decides to wait for Omid.

****

"No, no, no. It doesn't feel right. It sounds unnatural." Amir tilts his head with dissatisfaction at Roya's performance. He stares across the room as if he is deep in thought.

"I don't understand what I'm supposed to do." Roya fidgets with her fingers.

"You shouldn't have to think about it."

*Alright, focus. Try again.* Roya presses her lips together and begins humming. She scribbles a few lyrics on her notepad and hands it to Amir.

"Still not working. The tune started well, but the lyrics don't fit. Something feels too stale. He jumps out of his seat and walks to the opposite side of the room. He grabs the chairs and organizes them into a circle like last time. "I can't see your vision for you, but I can tell when something doesn't feel real. Can you step inside that circle I just made?"

"Uhh, sure."

Roya lifts her legs over the chairs and steps into the circle. She waits for Amir to say something.

"Actually, wait! Can you step outside the circle for a minute?"

Roya steps outside the circle.

"Okay, so work with me on this idea. Think of everything that has hurt you, angered you, elated you, and appeased you. Relax and try not to resist any memories. You don't have to share them with me. This is for you. When you step inside that circle, I want you to let go of your need for self-control. Just go for it. Let the music move through you. Okay? Just sing to me whatever words and rhythm come through. What is it you really wish to say?"

Roya listens closely and tries to digest Amir's instructions. "Alright."

She steps into the circle, closes her eyes, and begins to breathe the way Sepideh had taught her. She stretches her hands in front of her and rests them back down to her side.

*"Where are you going?"* Roya sits on the kitchen floor and wraps her little arms around her father's legs.

Her father scoops her off the ground and kisses her cheek. *"We will be back soon, dokhtaram. Don't give Mamani a hard time, okay? And watch out for Azadeh. You are the big sis-*

*ter."*

*"Why do you always have to go?"* Roya now wraps her arms around her father's neck and rests her head on his chest. *"This Tuesday all the parents are invited for the 5ᵗʰ Grade Farewell Ceremony. We're doing a show, and they're giving out awards too!"*

*"Bah, bah. My intelligent daughter. I'm so proud of you. Do you know that?"*

*"I know. But Baba, I want you to be there. And Maman too."*

*"You go to school and make us proud. And we go to work and make you proud. Remember that purple bike you saw at Toys-R-Us? The one with the light blue ribbons?"*

*Roya nods her head.*

*"If me and Maman don't go to work, how can we get you the bike? We don't want to leave you, but this is life, azizam."* He puts his daughter down and kneels to meet her eyes. He holds her hands in his as he speaks.*"When we come back, let's go to Toys-R-Us together and get that bike? How does that sound?"*

*"Baba, I don't want the bike! I want you to stay. Pleaaaaase."* Roya rubs her eyes with her knuckles.

*"Kaveh, do you have the tickets? We need to head to the airport soon."* Roya's mom hurries into the kitchen rolling her carry-on.

*"Yes, my love. I have them in my briefcase."* He looks at Delband with guilt in his eyes.

Delband walks to her daughter and wraps her arms around her. Roya can smell her mother's perfume on her suede coat. The scent is musky and warm.

*"Maman, please. Don't go again. Everyone's parents will be at the ceremony. Our teachers said you will have a lot of fun!"*

Delband's eyes mirror Kaveh's guilt. *"Azizam, we will be back soon. Mamani will be there! And when we come back, you can tell us all about it. Sound good? I know you understand. Please look after Azadeh too."*

Roya breathes in and exhales out.

Her memories now fast forward to her senior year of high school. California had just experienced a forest fire several miles away from Roya's home. That Fall, her neighborhood invited the surrounding communities to participate in their annual Halloween block party. Roya had been in charge of organizing the candy into small goodie bags for the children.

*"Hey toga angel, can I get one too please?"* The young guy smiles and lifts his eyebrows. He points to the bag filled with Snickers and Hershey kisses. *"I thought I might be a little too old for trick-o-treating. This doesn't count, right?"* He winks the way teenage boys do --clumsily and endearingly.

*"Excuuuse me. Toga angel? I am Cupid. Can't you tell?"* Roya says with one hand on her waist while she holds out the bag of candy.

*"Oh, sorry."* He pretends to analyze her costume. *"Hmm, well I think the wings threw me off. But, now I see what you mean!"* He laughs nervously as he takes the bag from her. *"Where's your arrow? How else are you going to aim and get 'em?"*

Roya squints her eyes and gives him a piercing look. *"I just look straight through them like this, and they know."*

*"The way you're looking at me?"*

*"Yup, just like that."*

*"Okay, good."* He smiles.

Roya blushes. *"So, what are you supposed to be? You're just wearing black. Let me guess. You're too cool for a costume?"*

*"I'm the supermassive black hole."*

*"You're kidding me, right?"*

The guy laughs. *"Well, it sounded better than admitting I think I'm too cool to wear a costume. Didn't want to sound like an asshole."*

Now Roya laughs. *"What's your name?"*

*"Cyrus. My family just moved to San Diego from San Francisco a few months ago. And your name?"*

*"Roya. Welcome to San Diego then!"*

*"Thanks, Cupid. And thanks for the Kisses."*

*"There's Snickers in there too."*

*"I know, but I like the Kisses."* He smiles with his eyes this time. The way he looks at her gives Roya butterflies all of a sudden. *"See you hopefully later at the bonfire?"*

*"Hmm, I don't know. We will see. I'm on a mission here, you know. Cupid is very busy these days getting people to love each other. It's not easy in this world. It's a science really. You gotta get the right pair."*

*"Well, whenever Cupid decides to take a break, I'd like to get to know Roya. Maybe at the bonfire?"* He waves goodbye and walks away with his eyes still shining.

The memories fade right there. All Roya sees is black. The first sound is effortlessly released through her vocal chords as if she were on auto pilot. "I don't know." Her voice cuts through the silence. "I don't care." She breathes in and exhales out. "But, please don't go. I just feel so alone."

Amir jots down her words in absolute silence.

Roya continues. "My heart is here, and you are there. My love, why can't you speak? I have been feeling so weak." She opens her eyes and feels her heart contracting and releasing. "Nagoo ke, nemiyay. Nagoo, naro. Delam gerefte."

Amir writes faster.

"Nagoo ke, nemiyay. Nagoo, naro. Biya, hamishe to delam hasti."

Roya begins to hum and mimics the instruments she imagines playing the music. When she finishes, she steps outside the circle and parts the chairs with her hands.

She looks to Amir with a depth in her eyes that could swallow a volcano. "This is what I really wish to say."

Amir walks over and hands Roya his notepad. "That is exactly what I was waiting for. What you just did…wherever that music came from…this can really be something. I feel it."

"Really? You think so?"

Amir points to his uneven handwriting on the notepad.

> *I don't know. I don't care. But, please don't go.*
> *I just feel so alone.*
> *My heart is here, and you are there.*
> *My love, why can't you speak?*
> *I have been feeling so weak.*
>
> *Nagoo ke, nemiyay. Nagoo, naro.*
> *(Don't say you won't come. Don't say it. Don't go)*
> *Delam gerefte.*
> *(My heart aches)*
> *Nagoo ke, nemiyay. Nagoo, naro.*
> *(Don't say you won't come. Don't say it. Don't go)*
> *Biya, hamishe to delam hasti.*
> *(Come, you will forever be in my heart)*

"This is like musical prose. And I didn't expect you to sing in Farsi! You just need the right instruments to bring these words to life. You need the right players."

"These words are too simple."

"Exactly. Let the words guide the notes. The orchestra will carry the audience home."

****

Roya waits until the auditorium is empty before pulling out the pamphlet the girl from earlier had given her. "Someone gave me this today. What's going on?" She hands it over to Omid.

"What is this garbage? Here they go again. With the protests!"

Roya is surprised by Omid's reaction. "All she said is that they want to be heard. It's all peaceful."

"Oh, so they're going to make posters, walk the streets, and hold up peace signs? Because that's what was stopping change from happening this whole time?"

"I don't get why you are so defensive about this right now." A lightbulb clicks in her mind. "Omid, are you scared?"

"Scared? These things aren't a joke. They require sacrifice. Am I scared for myself? To tell you the truth, maybe! But, you know what I'm really scared of? I'm scared of things getting out of hand —for my family, my friends, for everyone." He crumbles the paper and throws it into the trash can. "Look. I know I try to sound so sure of myself, but that's because I need something to believe in. To hope for something better. Of course, I want growth for my country and people. I don't know what is the right or wrong way." He softens his tone. "I do know you shouldn't worry about these things right now. You have a few days left here. Just try to enjoy it."

"Why does everyone keep treating me like I can't handle these conversations? You think that way too? I thought you'd be different. Everyone just avoids this subject every time I bring it up."

"Roya, it's not like that. You just don't understand."

"I am trying to."

"But, you won't."

"I want to! I want to try to understand. I'm not an idiot, Omid. I keep hearing pieces of conversations. I see things with my eyes. I can sense something."

"Yeah and what is that, Roya? What do you think it is that you are hearing?"

Roya is hesitant, unsure how to speak the forbidden words. *Revolution.* "That there is something brewing that has yet to reach the surface. People are tired of what has been."

"So? Then what? Say it, Roya. Say it."

Roya is silent. Omid looks away, but she can tell his eyes are wet. His body is hunched over in frustration. He finally turns his head, sits down, and looks straight into her eyes.

"You can't say it, can you? Do you see why I feel this way? This isn't a game. Everyone is trying to protect you. We are trying to live our lives and hope for the best. The change these protestors want to see happen, you think we don't want that too? You think we want to live with these limitations? No, of course not. Look around you. The Iranian people are some of the most liberal. We are not what they portray us to be on the news. But, what is the cost of change? When is potential gain worth the worst that can happen? Protests are not an inconvenience. People can die. People have died in the past. We can lose everything. Sure, we don't have as much freedom as we would like. But, we finally have been moving forward. We are at least safe. Our country is still functioning. I worry about my elders who have already been through so much. I worry about the kids whose entire futures depend on some stability. I worry about everything unraveling from what began with good intentions. And then I fight with myself. This feeling of my insides turning so much. I don't know if I'm anxious or sick. Because I know our country can be more. We can do better. We can have real freedom. I just don't know. What begins in a straight line can turn into a circle."

Omid dries his eyes with his t-shirt. Roya stands next to him and gently touches his arm. She knows nothing she says can mend how he feels.

"Omid, I know I am not in your shoes. I don't understand this the way you do. But, I am not a child either. Why didn't you talk about these things with me?"

"Because you are leaving soon. You go home back to your life. Iran will be a distant memory. For us, this is our reality. There is so much beauty here too. You've seen it. So much good. Why ruin that for you? Aren't we demonized enough? I wanted you to experience the side of Iran you'd be proud of. These other talks are things that even we must be careful discussing. It is not safe."

"Every country has its flaws. There is right and wrong everywhere. I didn't come to see the worst or best of Iran. I came here to experience the real Iran —to understand the layers of contradictions and rich history that make this country what it is. I don't want to pretend anything is perfect. I know better. I want the truth. I'm sick of people pretending all the time about everything. Not just here, but everywhere."

"Let's say you look for that truth. Do you think you will ever find it? What if you did? What then? You think you can change the world, Roya? How does one go about changing the world?"

"I know you have more faith than that. I'm not here to change the world. I'm here to do all that I can to just be better and do better. It's not about fixing the world's problems. It's about balancing out the wrong by trying to do right."

"And what is right?"

"I honestly don't know. But, I know if you act from a place of love, you can't go wrong. I'm not saying that in some hippy bullshit way. Faith is love. Courage is love. To forgive is love. To dream is love. You know that more than anyone. You have taught me that. I know the world can be messed up, and I don't know what the right answers are. I do know that even when the future is uncertain, we are not alone. Who knows if these protests will actually do more good or not. All I am saying is we can't avoid what is happening either. Whether you agree or not, there is tension in the air. The world needs people who can be peacemakers. It needs the believers, the ones who will carry the torch of light to guide the way without setting everything in their path ablaze. Does what I'm saying make sense?"

"Yes."

"Omid, what's your dream?"

"I already told you. I don't have dreams. I don't even know what's going to happen tomorrow. You want me to dream for what? Just to get my hopes up?"

"No, Omid. Not to get your hopes up. I want you to keep the hope alive. I know you will find a way. That's who you are."

"How do you know who I am?"

"Because I can see it in your eyes. I believe in what you can become."

"And what do my eyes say?" He now stands up tall with his shoulders pushed back.

Roya smiles. "They say come close, seek refuge. I am home to those searching for home. I am the shade of an Oak Tree in the summer and the bearer of light at dawn."

He eases into an innocent laughter. "You now speak like a poet." He checks the time. "Oh, man. It's getting late. We should head back to Khanoom Jaan's. Your Mamani will be waiting for us there."

"Can we stop by Azar's before we go back?"

"Why?"

Roya looks to the ground and back up. "I have some mending to take care of." She quietly wraps her arms around Omid with her head against his chest. She holds him for a few seconds and releases."

"What was that for?"

"Just because."

# CHAPTER 13

The daisies decorating the entrance to Azar's home look thirsty, but they are still intact. They hang from their stems loosely towards the sun. Roya pushes through the iron gate and pauses when she reaches the door. Her finger hovers over the buzzer. She turns to look at Omid waiting for her in the car just outside the gate. He gives her a soft smile of encouragement. Roya turns back to face the door. *Oh, God. This is so awkward. Where do I even start.* She takes a deep breath and presses the buzzer. *Please don't be home. Please don't be home. Maybe I should come back tomorrow when I've prepared something to say.* Azar's voice trails closer to the door. *Oh shit, she's home.* Roya wiggles her body and shifts from one foot to the other and takes another deep breath. *Exhale, Roya. Exhale. Just say what you wanted to say.* She slowly releases the breath. The door swings open.

"Roya jaan, *salam*. What a surprise! I didn't expect to see you here. Come in."

Azar's eyes are empathetic. They take Roya by surprise. Not that she expected hostility, but she didn't expect them to be so gentle either. Not after the other day.

"Hi. I, umm, just wanted to say a few words to you. I can just tell you here. I didn't mean to show up so randomly. Maybe I should have called. I shouldn't, umm, keep you."

"Don't be silly. I am happy you came by. Let's have some chai, perhaps?"

Roya feels shy and humbled by Azar's grace. "Oh, sure. That would be really nice. Thank you."

Azar leads her down the narrow hallway they had walked through the week before.

"Please, make yourself comfortable! I'll go get us some tea." Azar points to the living room sofa.

"Can I help with the tea?"

"No, no. You are my guest."

Roya insists. "Please? I'd like to help. It's the least I can do."

"Why don't you join me in the kitchen then? Do you know how to make tea the traditional way?"

"You just put the tea leaves through the filter, right?"

Azar smiles again. She is always smiling. "Let's give it a try."

The kitchen is compact, except for the sink. The sink is wide and accompanies a window facing a gap between the two neighboring apartments. Azar pours some tea leaves into a filter.

"You know what is the trick to making some authentic Iranian tea?" She sits the steaming pot on the stove and hands the filter to Roya. "Grab this by the handle for a moment."

Roya holds onto the filter.

"You must take the time to separate each leaf before placing it into the *samovar*. Shake it like this gently side-to-side. You want to make sure each leaf is whole and fresh. Pick out any particles that don't belong."

Roya wiggles the filter side-by-side from a distance.

"Hold it closer." Azar suggests. "Use your hands. Feel the leaves. Look closely."

Roya washes her hands and separates the pieces until they are scattered. One-by-one she removes any random bits. Raising the filter to her nose, she smells the fresh aroma of the ancient herbs ––hints of cardamom and Ceylon.

"Doesn't it smell wonderful?"

"Yeah, I never really noticed it before. I usually just stick a tea bag into a cup and pour some hot water over it." Roya admits.

"Ah, I see. We have that as well. But, I think this way is worth the extra few minutes. I enjoy it more."

Roya places the filter inside the kettle boiling with water. They wait as the tea leaves soak and their flavors release into the bubbling liquid.

"Azar, I have something to say to you. A lot actually. I've had so much on my mind. I feel like you'd understand. More so than myself. I guess I'll start by saying I am really sorry for my outburst the other day. I, I just, honestly, don't know what happened. I feel terrible and ashamed that I reacted that way with you. With anyone really. But, especially you."

Azar is quiet and attentive. She is about to say something, but pauses, knowing Roya has more to say.

Roya continues. "I thought about it a lot afterwards. That's why it took me so long. I really had to think about it, because I can't believe I acted like that. At first, I felt so angry. I wasn't sure if it was at you or my mom or myself. I just felt this heat inside of me rushing from the pits of my stomach to the tips of my fingers and flooding into my cheeks. The heat was so unbearable, it made me want to cry. Not tears of sadness or frustration. It was like these tears of desperation. It was beyond feeling bad. It felt like this intense pain and sorrow inside of me. And I had to ask myself, where was this all coming from? This isn't the kind of person I am. It's not who I want to be at least. So, I really thought about it."

Roya's eyes are filled with tears. She stares at the boiling tea kettle.

"I realize that I have been so scared. The fear has crippled me. And this sadness has been brewing in me for a long time, but it never boiled. It just became a part of me. This hidden side of me. Underneath my numbness, there was this pressing need to break out of my own mind. That day when you showed me the letter, I saw what I feared most staring me in the face. On a piece of paper, weathered with time and loss and regret. A piece of paper written by someone who I mirror in so many ways. Someone whose approval I yearn for no matter how much I tell myself I don't. Have you ever loved someone and somehow resented them at the same time? I can't believe I am saying this. But, I have to share it with someone."

Azar's presence is like a soft embrace cocooning Roya from her own vulnerability. "Roya, I didn't mean to cause you this pain. I am so sorry. I didn't think showing you the letter would make you feel this way."

"No, please don't be sorry. I am glad that you showed me. I needed to see the truth ––that no one is perfect, not even our idols. It's strange. As a kid, you look at your parents and think they have all the answers. You expect them to have done everything right, like a coloring book filled perfectly with your favorite shades. One day, you just look at them. You see all the blotches and scribbles. And before you realize, you're the one standing in front of a blank canvas praying you don't screw up. For the longest time, I couldn't understand my mother as a human. I just absorbed her fears and sadness, as if they were a disease. This whole time I couldn't see that maybe she was happy. That she found her peace. And that it might just look different for me. Maybe I ran away from everything she is just so I could have something that belonged to me."

Azar turns the kettle's knob and tilts it at an angle to pour herself and Roya tea. The steam swirls into the air as the deep burgundy chai fills the hollow space of the petite glasses. She hands Roya her cup and responds after a thoughtful pause.

"When my father used to share his stories, especially those of him and Delband, I'd be so fixated on my mother's expression. She'd gaze at him as he brought his memories to life. It was as if she relished his experiences even more than him. I asked her once why she enjoyed his stories so much. You know what she told me? *'Look at how much joy it brings him! His face is the most handsome when he is telling his stories with laughter.'* Can you imagine that? I hated it. I thought she was so weak for loving him so completely while he was still thinking of his time with another woman."

Roya is quiet. She feels like an invisible thread is holding her and Azar just a few feet off the ground. Like they are feathers relieved from the weight of their shared emotions.

"The day my mother died changed everything for me. It's odd how moments of pain can bring such startling and unapologetic clarity. It was in our home. Did you know that? My father had turned one of the rooms into a replica of a hospital minus the stale smell and blandness. Oh, no! It looked like it belonged in a medical facility, but it was vibrant and textured and just how my mother wanted it. I never even thought he noticed all her small wantings. How she preferred her water with just a couple cubes of ice. Or, how she enjoyed waking up with the sunrise only to fall asleep shortly after. She never wanted to miss a sunrise, because she wanted to rise with the light so that her and the sun were one. Doctors would come and go. Nurses were around at all times to monitor her, but also to take her out into nature. That way she could be in the peace of her own home, yet free to go out in the world. My father would stop by her room every morning before work and give her a kiss on the forehead, then her cheek, then her lips. If she was asleep, he'd leave her a note with just a couple of words. Mostly, a single *asheghetam*.

The day she passed away, I remember first hearing the sound. It was terrible. The steady *beep, beep, beep* would keep me awake all those nights. But that day, it was this screeching, agitated, singular note — the sound of machinery alerting the loss of a heartbeat. I thought hearing that noise would be the last sound seared into my mind from that day, but I was wrong. It was my father's muffled wails as he pressed his face against my mother's hand on her bedside. He got up and sat down several times before he finally sat still. But, he never let go of her hand. The nurses came to pull him away. He begged them to leave. *'I want to be alone with my wife for just a moment longer.'* I watched from a distance. He spoke to her gently. A few words here and there between his cries.

I couldn't hear everything. I was in shock myself. I just lost the most beautiful woman, the most important woman in my life. So, I stared for a long time. I'll never forget the way my father looked at her. In that moment, I truly understood the depth of his love for her. You cannot sugarcoat death. Even the most peaceful passing hits the ones it leaves behind like a hailstorm made from cement. But, my father held onto my mother's hand as if he were the one protecting her. As if he wanted to turn his love into a vacuum in which she could forever exist, suspended gracefully in time."

"Wow." Those are the only words to leave Roya's lips. She, too, feels lost in Azar's poignant memory.

"Yeah, truly wow. It took me a lot of time to process the power of what I felt that day. It's an image I always carry. I asked my father several years afterwards why he would talk about Delband as often as he did in those early years. Why wasn't what he had with my mother enough for him? He said to me, '*One road leads to another. There are no dead-ends in life. Even in death, there is a road. Delband lead me to your mother. She will always be a part of my life. She is the history that has created the man you see. But, your mother was my life. She is the woman I had to first become man enough for so that I could be capable of giving the kind of love she was ready to give. And to receive hers when she did.*'"

Azar lightly touches Roya's hand. "I didn't think you would react that way, but I understand why. For a moment, I forgot my own feelings. After all this time, I have finally come to see that love is so vast that it can swallow you, heal you, move you. If you allow, it can even destroy you. But, it can also create you if you let it. Some say you're lucky if you fall in love once and it stays. There is no separation filled with what ifs. But, I'm not so sure if those are the lucky ones. It depends on the person I think. For some, the real gift is in the heartbreak. When you fall in love again, it's like a miracle isn't it? It's nothing short of courage. Maybe even a touch of the divine if you want to look at it that way. To lose yourself deeply and to become new. To be reborn in that way.

The day my mother died, a part of my father did too. He poured that grief into his work. He would rise early in the morning and return late at night. Never stopped for a moment. Except for every anniversary of her passing, he visits her grave with flowers. He never speaks, just remains silent. I asked him once, *'Baba, why don't you try talking to her when you go? She is still there you know.'* He held my hand the way he held hers that day and said, *'No, my dear, she is not there. She is everywhere. Your maman will always be everywhere.'* I know that should make me sad, but it doesn't. It makes me hopeful, because my father had two great loves. One who taught him how and the other who showed him you can love again."

Roya wants to say something comforting, but *I'm sorry for your loss* seems unnatural. So, she holds onto the curving spine of the glass with her tea untouched. The way the handle bends reminds her of Cyrus when he'd lean over to tie his shoes.

*"Ah, dammit. I'm going to be late for class!"*

His bare back is the color of olives. Not actually green, but in the way people give abstract names to describe things. He is an olive-skinned guy, as they'd say. It never made sense to Roya. To her his back is like the bronze orange of Sahara's sand dunes once the sunlight hits. He knots the last shoelace and scurries across the room searching around the shelves with his hands. His hands are always soft, except for his knuckles. And warm. Always warm. When the temperature would drop and the San Diego winds took over the night, he used to hold her two hands and stick them in his jacket.

*"There it is!"* He slips on his watch and adjusts its band. *"Hey Roya!"*

*"What?"* Roya rests her head on the pillow and notices the faint, happy trail leading from his belly button to the edge of his boxers.

Cyrus smiles at her. *"You know what's my favorite Roya?"*

*"Hmm, no. Tell me."*

*"Morning Roya."*

*"What? Ew. I look like a mess. I haven't even washed my face yet."*

*"I know."* He walks over and touches her lips with his. *"I kind of dig this smeared mascara look you got going on. Just a bit*

*under the eyes like that. It's real. And I get to wake up and look at you. That's how I get to start my day. With something real."*

Roya's body feels like she's sitting on one of those massage chairs with the rolling compression, except for the sensation is moving inside her chest. She lacks the words to express her love, so she just looks at him before raising her head from the pillow. Running her fingers through his hair, she pulls him closer with her other hand embracing his neck. She returns the touch on his lips with hers. Their kiss is like continuously sharing one, joint breath.

*"You better hurry to class! I love you."*

Cyrus gets up, pulls his sweater over his head, and opens the door to leave. *"By the way..."*

*"Yes?"*

*"Check beside the table on the floor."*

Roya sees a cardboard cup from Coffee Bean.

*"When did you get that?"*

*"When you were sleeping. Matcha tea, extra matcha. Just how you like it."* He winks at her before closing the door behind him.

"Your tea is getting cold, huh!" Azar's voice returns Roya to the present.

"Azar, if love is enough, why do some things end?"

"I wonder the same thing. I don't know."

"Well, how do you know if Shayan is the right one for you?"

"Hmm. I suppose because I don't find myself asking why I am in love with him. I just am. Of course, there are many things I love about him, but those are not why I love him. Does that make sense?"

"I believe so. Sort of."

"You never mentioned what happened with your ex. Do you think he was the right one?"

"I thought I did. I'm not so sure anymore."

"Why is that?"

"I'm still figuring that out. Something just changed."

"Stories without conclusions are like open wounds —sensitive to the touch and easily infected with assumptions. I know it hurts, but try not to wait for answers. The only way to find them is by pursuing life itself. I know it all sounds terribly cliché, but there is some truth in these repetitions."

"You are right. Mamani said the same thing. It makes sense."

"And what about Omid?"

"Omid?" Roya is taken by surprise. "What about Omid?"

"You two seem to have become very close."

"Are you trying to say it looks like we are romantic?"

Azar laughs. "Not at all. Just close. There is more than one way to love someone. It is not always romantic. Sometimes, it's just a bond between two people who help each other see themselves a little more clearly."

"Yeah, it is kind of strange how we are. I don't feel that romantic chemistry. You know? That thing that has to exist. But, there is a closeness like I've never felt before. Like we've shared some past together. Speaking of him, he should be back any minute now. I should head out soon."

"You never had your tea."

"Oh, right. I got distracted."

"Shall we chug it?"

"Chug tea?"

"Sure, why not! Let's make a toast."

"Okay. What should we toast to?"

"To the shadows, shade, and sunlight!"

"To the shadows, shade, and sunlight!"

They clink their tea glasses gently and down the cooled liquid in two gulps.

"Cooled cardamom kind of tastes like cinnamon." Roya sets down the glass. "I'm really happy I met you, Azar. Thank you for hearing me out. And for sharing your story. I don't have the right words to say, but I want you to know it means a lot that you told me."

"Anytime, Roya jaan. After all, we too, share a history. I will see you in a few days at your show, no? How exciting!"

"You'd really come?"

"I wouldn't miss it."

# CHAPTER 14

"Tonight, we have a special performance in store for you. All the way from the United States." The MC is a young woman with a fierce, spunky energy. She holds the microphone like a rockstar, riling up a crowd. "Please show some love and put your hands together for Ms. Roya."

The audience claps politely. Roya walks into the spotlight.

"*Salam* ladies and gentlemen. I am thankful to have the opportunity to perform my piece in tonight's show. Thank you to my incredible team for inviting me into your hearts. I was a stranger to you, but you treated me as a friend. This piece could be many things ––a creative outlet, entertainment, or simply another sum of instruments that you will listen to before the show moves on. But for me, this piece is a love letter to my past, my release. It is the reckoning of my dormant dreams. When I first arrived in Tehran, I saw this as a few short weeks where I could escape myself. Halfway into the trip, I felt like maybe I was starting to discover who I am. Now, as I near the end of my trip, I realize I am left with many more questions than answers. Perhaps, that is what I was seeking all along ––the right questions. I have come to learn that the languages we speak and the syllables on our tongues are the windows to how we see the world. Yet, we are more than the sum of what we do and where we are from. We are the sum of all that we have opened our minds to and the people whom we have sheltered in our hearts. This composition is the shadows that I have carried brought into the light. Sharing this with you now is my victory."

The audience is silent with anticipation.

Roya inhales through her nostrils the way Sepideh had shown her. She slowly exhales through her mouth. She looks over to Amir. His hands are raised in the air with the elegance of a *parastoo* in flight. He smiles with his eyes, giving her that *are you ready, let's do this* look. Roya feels the heat of the stage lights. Her hands are clammy like the residue of Spring showers in Shomal. Her heart is beating fast ––fast like the motion of cars on Tehran's highways. She stands tall ––tall like the remnants of Persepolis, the statues of half-beheaded lions where once an empire stood. She searches for lion-hearted strength within her as she looks to the crowd. Their faces are a blur. Tens of heads filling the auditorium now look at her.

*Let the orchestra carry the audience home.* Amir's advice rings in her ears. She scans the audience. She sees Mamani, Khanoom Jaan, Azar, and Sepideh. No Omid. She searches the other side of the room. Still no sight of him. She looks to Amir again and takes one more breath. Just as she is about to give him the nod to begin, she hears footsteps. The shadow of a blob appears below the stage.

"Roya, psssst." Omid waves his hands in the air trying to get her attention.

Roya freezes. All eyes are on her. She looks down without saying a word. Omid silently slips her a folded paper and scurries to an empty seat next to Sepideh.

> *I know this is last minute. Hope this doesn't embarrass you.*
> *I just want to remind you to remember this moment. Okay? Re-*
> *member how you feel ––every nerve bouncing in that brain of*
> *yours just before you begin. Take in all that is around you. You*
> *will never have this exact first again. I know your heart must be*
> *dancing in loops right now. Roya, this is the beginning of every-*
> *thing for you. Everything you have wanted starts now. Boro*
> *digeh! Give them a show. ––Your First Fan, Omid*

Roya sets the letter on the stand beside her notes. She pushes her shoulders back and holds her head up. She smiles at Omid before turning to face Amir with a nod.

*Let's begin.*

Amir's hands motion up, down, across, and back as if he were untying a ribbon in the air. The sound of the solo violin is the first to cut through the hushed room. Farideh's chin rests on the edge of her instrument as her worn bow cajoles the strings awake.

"*I love you.*"

"*You love me?*"

"*Yes.*"

Roya laughs. "*Do you even know what that means?*"

"*Not exactly. I just know what I am feeling with you I have never felt before. I want to talk with you more and more. And see you again and again. Enough is never enough.*"

"*And that is love?*"

Cyrus holds her closer and kisses her completely. "*You're asking me too many questions. All I know is I'm really happy right now. Here with you. You make me feel something. And that says a lot.*"

"*Men really are the true romantics, they say!*"

Cyrus smiles. "*Definitely. We won't admit it to the boys, but yeah. We are all secretly little Romeos.*" He holds his heart like he is in a Shakespearean play. "*Just don't break my heart, okay?*"

Roya kisses him on the cheek. "*Look, I will put your heart next to mine. I'll guard them both with my life. Deal?*"

"*Nahhh, that's not how love works. I give you my heart, and you give me yours. That's how it goes.*"

"*And how do I know you won't break mine?*"

"*You don't. Aren't you the artist? That's the thing. You never know what's going to happen! You just choose who is worth that chance.*"

Roya watches the way his boyish grin causes the sides of his eye to slightly crease. *"Hmm, well I think I love you too."*

*"You finally said it! Now Ms. Roya, you tell me. What does love mean to you?"*

Roya bites her lower lip nervously and looks into his eyes as if she is trying to search for the future. *"I don't know. I'm scared out of my mind. Here I am, knowing neither of us knows anything about love, but I don't even care. Crazy, right? I just want you."*

Roya leans into the microphone, closes her eyes, and begins.

"I don't know. I don't care. But, please don't go. I just feel so alone."

The rest of the string orchestra now follows. The depth of the cello and discipline of the bass produce a comforting rhythm before the violin breaks through again with its cries.

*"It's over?"* Cyrus puts his face in his hands.

*"Yes."* Roya stares at the ground. *"I guess it is."*

Both of them speak through muffled sentences.

*"Let's just talk about everything. Like old times."*

*"Like old times? Now you want to talk about things? Do you know how many times I tried to talk to you about everything?"*

*"So, this is what you want? Are you serious?"*

*"No. This obviously isn't what I want. I wanted us to be happy. Not all this bullshit. I can't do this anymore. Do you even know how stupid I feel?"*

*"Roya, I can change."*

*"You already have. We both have. That's the sad part."*

"My heart is here, and you are there. My love, why can't you speak? I have been feeling so weak."

The tar and piano join in. Their combination is like the past and future walking hand-in-hand. The tar sings from a place of nostalgia, the piano with longing for what could have been.

*"Maman? Will you always be here?"*

*"What do you mean, azizam?"*

A twelve-year-old Roya clings to her mother's side and reaches for her father. *"You too, Baba. Will you always be in my life? Forever?"*

Her father holds her little hand in his own. *"We are forever with you. But, one day me and your Maman will be long gone. That's how life works, my dear. We all get old, and one day we pass."*

*"No! I want to go before you do. I love you both so much. I don't want to ever live in this world without you."*

*"Ehh, God forbid!"* Roya's mother holds her daughter tightly. *"Don't talk like that, Roya. This is life. We all come and go. That's the beauty of it. We are together now."*

*"Well, I never want to grow up then! I want to stay right here."*

*"Oh, is that right? If you never grow up, how are you going to be a famous musician one day? Inspire the world?"* Her father tickles her chin before giving her a light kiss on the head.

*"Or, a doctor! To help everyone. Remember?"* Her mother hopes her words will sink in for the future.

"Nagoo ke, nemiyay. Nagoo, naro. Delam gerefte. Nagoo ke, nemiyay. Nagoo, naro."

*"You know, Roya jaan. I think you are something special."*

*"Me? Why me?"*

*"There are many creative people, but a true artist is a translator. They feel the world so deeply, and it is their duty to translate those feelings for others to understand. They create what there are no words for. They make others feel whole by sharing pieces of themselves in everything they touch. That, my dear, is something honest. That takes courage."*

*"Khanoom Jaan, I really appreciate that. But, I don't think I'm as courageous as you think. Look at me. If I was so brave, I wouldn't be feeling all that I am. I wouldn't be where I am in my*

*life."*

Khanoom Jaan smiles tenderly. *"It is the feeling that takes courage. Do not be mistaken."*

"Biya, hamishe to delam hasti."

Roya is now silent. The entire orchestra has officially awakened. The instruments carry her notes across the room like a tidal wave. The final note belongs again to the solo violinist. The lights dim. The spotlight is on her as her bow takes its final dip before shooting up into the air. The room is completely still. Roya's heart still beats fast, but now feels light. The crowd remains quiet until Amir has placed his hands to his side. He nods his head subtly to Roya once more.

*"Pain is the drug of all poetic souls, Roya. The moment pain becomes beautiful, you must turn it into art and move on."*

Roya searches for Mamani's eyes beyond the stage.

****

The crowd makes music with the bare flesh of hands —the ripples of applause. The orchestra stands in unison holding their instruments in front of them like badges of honor. They wait for the composer's signal before bowing. The applause echoes, but the noise sounds distorted to Roya.

Her memories play before her eyes like a movie trailer on fast forward. For a fleeting moment, she remembers the sensation in those nights crouched in the shower with her arms wrapped around her legs, folding into herself. The memory disappears abruptly, replaced by a euphoric pulse reaching into her fingertips. Then, a completely foreign feeling —absolute harmony.

She stands on the stage until she feels an arm on her shoulder.

"Roya!" Omid stands next to her with one arm around her back. "That was incredible. The crowd loved it. You almost got a tear out of me. Almost!" He points to his heart while hiding his other hand behind him. "My eyes did get wet. Just a bit."

Roya smiles still processing everything. She's surging with energy.

"Still can't believe it, huh? You did it Roya!"

"Yeah, it feels so surreal. Like, what! All that stuff I had written down just came to life. Omid, we did it! I couldn't have done this without your help."

"Na, that was all you. Don't give me credit I don't deserve. It goes to my ego. You know how I get." He grins without revealing his hand. "Too bad your parents couldn't be here to see what you're capable of! I think they'd be really proud of you."

Suddenly, Roya's eyes glaze with a look of sadness. "Yeah, too bad. I would have loved for them to be here."

Omid's eyes widen as they do when he is proud of his own meddling behavior. "Hold on, hold on." He pulls out his hand and places the iPhone in front of Roya's face. "Sorry the quality isn't the best. The reception is a bit unpredictable in here."

Baba and Azadeh wave from the screen with their faces huddled close. Her father has tears in his eyes. Roya can't remember the last time she saw her father cry. The camera shakes as Azadeh jumps uncontrollably holding the phone.

Roya waves back in disbelief. "Omid, how…"

"Sometimes, being nosy does some good. I asked your Mamani for your sister's contact info. She told your parents, and we set this up!" He turns the camera to face himself, waves hello, and hands the phone to Roya. "I figured you would want them to be a part of this, even when you pretend it doesn't matter."

Roya tightly embraces Omid and holds the phone back in front of her face. "Hi Baba! Hi Azadeh! Ahhhhh, can you believe that just happened?!" Both screens shake as her and Azadeh jump. "What time is it there? I can't believe you watched it live."

Baba wipes his eyes and takes the camera from Azadeh. "Ah, here we go. Let's hold this still for a moment, so we can see you. We wouldn't want to miss this. It has been so long since I have seen you so joyful. That's my girl."

Roya smiles, but her eyes are searching. "What about Maman? I understand if she was busy or something... it happens."

Azadeh turns the camera to her mother squinting at her computer on the floor. "Oh, no worries. She saw the whole thing. She is currently trying to figure out how to save the recording."

"She recorded it?"

"Obviously! I came home to find her trying to hook up the phone to the TV too, so we can see you up close. All by herself. It was hilarious." Azadeh turns the camera back, so that her and Baba's faces are on the screen. "I know she doesn't always talk about your music, but she's been so excited for you. One sec, let me go get her."

A few seconds later, Maman's face pops up on the screen. Before Roya can speak, her mother begins. "Roya jaan." Her voice is shaking. "My little girl. What a young woman you've become. I am so proud of you. Seeing you up on that stage."

Roya holds the phone with both hands now. "Maman, you have no idea how good it feels to hear you say that. I love you." Roya looks around the room and pauses. "Would you like to say hello to someone? Someone I think you know well." She tries to scan her mother's face for a reaction.

"It has been many years." Maman's smile consents as if she already knew.

She runs off the stage holding the phone behind her like Omid had. There is a man saying farewell to someone with his back to Roya. She waits until he is alone and taps him on the shoulder. "Excuse me, Dr. Arman?"

The man turns to face Roya, and their eyes meet for the first time—an encounter bridging two distant worlds. His eyes are a deep brown with swirls of hazel around the edges. His thinly framed rectangular glasses sit on the tip of his nose. She had expected his features to look softer, but his face is stern. Until he smiles that is. When he smiles, his face relaxes. His eyes become welcoming.

"Roya jaan, hello. We meet at last. Azar has spoken so highly of you. Your performance was wonderful."

"*Merci*. I just want to thank you for everything. For letting me use this auditorium and the instruments. This means so much to me. You have no idea."

"Please don't thank me. That is what this space is for. For you students to imagine, to play with your own curiosity, to inspire. I am glad it could be of service to you."

"I have something for you too. Someone who would like to say hello." She pulls the phone out and hands it to Arman. Never had she seen the pure look of awe on an old man's face.

"*Salam*, Arman." Delband smiles.

"*Salam*, Delband."

"Thank you for making this possible for Roya. From my heart to yours."

"The road of love––" Arman begins.

"––always remains open." Delband completes. "I remember. I wish all joys are yours––"

"––and that all the stars align for you." Arman nods his head. "I, too, remember. It is good to see you, my old friend. You sound just the same."

"As do you. Take care, Arman."

"Same to you, Delband."

He hands the phone back to Roya, begins to walk away, then turns back. "*Merci*, Roya jaan. For returning to me a part of my youth. Continue what you are doing. You have her essence, yet a life all your own. What a gift. Do not take lightly what God has given you. This desire in you, it is fighting to be heard. Listen to it."

He walks away slowly and embraces his daughter. They wave to Roya from afar. Azar signals that she will find her later. Hugging her father around the waist, she walks him outside the auditorium and into the open streets. The doors close behind them, and they are gone.

Roya turns around to find Mamani and Khanoom Jaan standing behind her. She walks into her grandmother's arms and places her cheek on her shoulder. "Mamani, is this all a dream?"

"All of life is a dream, remember?" Mamani kisses her on the head. "But, sometimes, it can feel very real. And when it does, it seems as if it were too good. That's when we know we are doing something right. Don't question it so much. Good things happen, eh!"

Roya turns to Khanoom Jaan and holds her hands. "That day when you said a flower cut from its stem dries out more quickly. I understand now."

Khanoom Jaan squeezes Roya's hand. "And you've developed quite the green thumb too." She winks at her and gives her one last hug.

Omid hurries to them. "We should leave soon. The late night chantings are beginning. With the protests going on this week, we don't want to be out too late. Just in case. I can give you all a ride home."

****

Roya expects the streets to be buzzing like usual, but tonight's traffic is sparse. The changing colors of the streetlamps decorate the pavement —blue, red, green, purple, and blue again. She rolls down the windows in the backseat and lets the wind graze her cheeks as the car turns into a narrow alley near Mamani's condo.

"Why are we not going on the main road?" Roya puts her head back inside the car and raises the window halfway up.

"Better to go this way." Omid says whistling.

"The streets are really quiet today. The loud kind of quiet."

"Yes, I know what you mean." Omid changes the topic. "How are you feeling about leaving tomorrow? You ready?"

Roya faces the window and watches the neon lights of the closed shops blur. The curves of the Farsi signs look once again like dancing, rainbow swirls.

"I am going to miss it here." She finally replies.

Mamani looks at her from the rearview mirror. "Someone had a change of heart, I see. Don't be sad. We will be back."

"Yeah and look on the bright side. Now you won't be coming to a sea of strangers. You will have friends waiting for you. By then, I will have thought of new ways to annoy you. It will be just like before."

"No, it won't. Things always change." Roya remains staring out the window.

"That's true, but some things don't." Omid looks at her from his mirror too. "Even if they do, who says it won't be better?"

They pull up to the condo. The voices echo from one rooftop to another and create a bouncing effect as if the protestors were speaking to each other with their unified chants.

"I'll let you two have a moment. Omid dear, you shouldn't stay long. Roya, I will wait for you inside." Mamani leaves the door cracked open.

Roya jumps into the front seat. "Hey Omid, can I see you in the morning before I leave? I was thinking we could stop by that one place overlooking the city where the waterfall is. I want us to have a proper goodbye."

"I'm taking you to the airport. You know that, right?"

"Yes, but still. It won't be the same."

"Alright then. Pick you up at 9:00am?"

"Perfect." Roya gives him a kiss on the cheek before leaving the car. "*Merci.*"

*What do we want?*
*Freedom!*
*What do we want?*
*Freedom!*
*What of the chains?*
*Break them!*
*What of the shame?*
*Absolve it!*
*In the name of Liberty and Love,*
*Raise your voice to the sound of*
*Freedom.*

The trail of voices march through the night.

# CHAPTER 15

Roya wakes up before her alarm. There is no chanting. Tehran's streets continue their usual honking and chatter. People are rising to the shifting colors of the morning sky, pigments of light blue mixed with a clementine orange. She walks over to the mirror and runs her hands through her hair. She examines her face once more. Her face has gained some color since she first arrived. The edges of her nose have begun to softly peel and look slightly pink. Once more, she presses on her suitcases with her knees to close the zippers shut. *I come with one, and I leave with two. Typical.* She rolls them to the door and returns to check for any forgotten items. The doll with the painted rosy cheeks and exaggerated eyes is still where she first found it. *Great, now my cheeks look like yours. Rosy little thing.* Twisting the top off, she opens the doll once more. And opens again. And again, until she has reached the last carved work of art. She arranges the pieces across the table from largest to smallest. *There, that's better.*

The condo is quiet. She tiptoes to the kitchen. Mamani walks down the stairs to a table covered with fresh bread, raspberry fig jam, cream, and honey.

"Finally, I wake up first! I made you breakfast." Roya wipes her hands on a rag and pours Mamani a cup of chai. "I'm going out for a moment with Omid. I will be back soon. Is that alright?"

"Yes, but please don't be late. I want to arrive early for our flight."

"It won't be long." She kisses her grandmother on the cheek and runs out the door as Omid pulls up to the gate's entrance.

"Ready?"

"Yup!"

The Peugeot winds around the shoulders of the Alborz mountains.

"Music?" Omid taps on the steering wheel with the palms of his hand.

"Can we just listen to Tehran? I want to take it all in." The smooth pavement turns into delicate gravel the higher up they go. Roya can hear the tires crushing the stones and the engine rattling as the elevation rises.

"As you wish."

When they arrive at the top, they park the car near a bench overlooking the landscape. Smoke is rising from the tall buildings. Smoke is always rising in the city.

"This view reminds me of my hiking trips in San Diego. I used to love standing so high. Just me, some chunks of rocks that look like castles, probably some animals hiding somewhere. Other hikers too. But for the most part, I am alone. It was the best feeling. Then, I stopped going. I felt too lonely. I think when I get back, I'm going to go for another one of my solo hikes. Like before."

"Is that why you wanted to come up here?"

"No. I mean, the view is great, but that's not why." She pauses. "Omid, you make me feel important. You helped me see myself. Like I don't have to run anymore. I can just be here and that's enough. I wanted to come here, because I want you to remember this moment. Me and you standing here, knowing we are so small, yet feeling so grand. I don't know where life is going to take us, how many times we will come close to the edge, skimming life's unknown. But, I don't want to just skim. I want us both to dive into it all. Like you said, make hope our wings. As great as standing here feels, true living is in the valleys ––in the lush, vibrant, tangled in-betweens. Before we go out into the world and do all that we dreamed, I want you to know that this Omid was always more than enough for me."

She hands Omid a large envelope.

"What is this?"

"Don't be upset, okay?"

"Yeah?"

"Well, you're always talking about the meaning of life like you're Plato or something. It was kind of annoying at first, but then it was sort of charming. Anyway, well, Azar mentioned that one of her father's colleagues was looking for an assistant teacher at Sharif."

"Sharif!"

"I know, I know. Azar told me it's also one of the best. And I think you're one of the best. So, I mentioned it to her, and we submitted an application for you."

"I can't believe this."

"Like I said, don't be upset! But, yeah. Open the envelope."

Omid lifts the flap, pulls the piece of paper out, and stares.

"You're officially Assistant Lecturer Omid. More like an internship, but I heard the mentor you're working with is a big deal or something." Roya's eyes sparkle.

"Do you know who this is? This is Dr. Farahmand. He is one of the leading scholars in the Department of Philosophy and Metaphysical Ethics."

"I told you he sounded like a big deal." Roya laughs eagerly. "He is your new boss."

"Royaaaa! You have outdone yourself."

"Oh, hold on! One more thing. Two more actually." She takes a medium sized envelope from her purse and hands it to him. "*Allegory of the Cave.* Figured a Plato wannabe should have a copy of his work. I had to really hunt that one down though. You were right. That was harder to find than some *aragh* on a Friday night. Ready for the last one now?" She pulls out a small envelope sealed with a sticker. "This one is actually a bit of a teaser. I don't want you to open it yet. Save it for a day when you need to hear something nice. Something that will remind you of how powerful and brilliant you are. No matter what happens with all this stuff going on here. You can be anything. I won't know, obviously, if you really will wait to read it. But, I think it would add that extra *oomph* if you did."

"Roya, can I hold you?"

"Umm, duhh! I'm a hugger, remember?"

"No. I mean hold you."

"Only if you take a selfie with me afterwards." She laughs. "One day I'll show it to someone and ask them what they think the story is."

He wraps his arms around her shoulders in absolute silence. He lingers before releasing and kisses her forehead. "I know I goof around a lot, but I mean it when I say I will forever remember this moment. *Merci.*"

"See, doesn't the view make this extra special?"

Omid looks into her eyes. "Yeah, you're right. It does."

Roya didn't even notice her *roosari* has fallen off. "We should head back." She adjusts it, but her hair still peeks out from underneath.

"All this time, yet you still struggle with that thing!"

Roya shrugs. "Maybe I like it peeking out!"

They get back in the car. The windows are down. The roads are open.

****

Mamani is waiting for them when they arrive and so is a large van the size of a mini bus.

"Looks like we have some company to the airport." Mamani points to the faces sticking out the window.

Bijan, Asal, Sepideh, Roozbeh, Khanoom Jaan, and Azar.

"Did you expect anything less? Let's make it a party!"

*Oh, there it is. The woman with the booming voice. She's here too.*

The booming voice lady sticks her head out from the front seat window. "Hurry up! You don't want to be late! Omid, you too. We will all ride together."

They load the suitcases into the car and take their seats.

"I'm convinced that's the only volume of speaking Parvaneh knows." Omid whispers to Roya.

"Who?"

"Your grandma's cousin? The one with the loud voice. Her name is Parvaneh. Oh c'mon, Roya. You didn't know that by now?" He laughs.

*Ohhh, that is her name.* She simply shrugs.

Parvaneh yells Roya's name. "Since you are the guest of honor, what music shall we play? Some rap? I know you young people like that Persian rap!" She starts wiggling in her seat.

Roya smiles back. "Hmm, how about some Mansour."

Everyone looks at Roya at once.

"Mansour, huh?" Omid winks.

"You heard her, people. Mansour, it is!" Parvaneh wiggles again.

"Since when do you listen to Iranian pop from the early 2000s?" Omid looks amused.

"Since I guessed Parvaneh would love it. That way she won't talk to us the whole ride."

"Clever. Quite clever."

"Here. I think you will like this song." She hands him her spare headphone as she plugs the other side in her own ear. "'Buildings and Mountains' by The Republic Tigers, one of my favorites."

They rest their heads against one another and listen —savoring the moment.

# SUNLIGHT

# CHAPTER 16

The car pulls into the cobbled driveway lined with tall, bending palm trees. Maman holds Mamani's hand and walks her to the door. Baba grabs the bags from the trunk. The sky is a highlighter blue.

"Here Baba, let me help you." She grabs her other suitcase. Together, her and Azadeh lift it up the steps.

Roya first notices the home's signature scent ––a lingering mixture of hardwood, a trail of Baba's cologne, and a smell Roya can't describe. One that has always just been there. Next, she notices the vase sitting on the shelf by the dining room. *Did Maman get a new vase? Has that always been there?* She circles the living room before returning to the kitchen.

"Hey Azadeh, do you want to go for a quick drive?" She grabs a notebook and some pens. "Do you have the stuff I asked you to get?"

"Yup! Right here."

Roya grabs the small bag from the counter. "Maman! Baba! Me and Azadeh are going for a drive. We will be back soon!"

"A drive? You just got here." Baba looks up.

"It will be quick. I promise."

"Where are we going?" Azadeh follows her sister.

"You'll see. Not far. I have an idea."

****

Roya parks the car and leads Azadeh to the fountain --their wishing fountain. The "Under Construction" sign has yet to be removed. The weeds have outgrown their decorated trimmings. She peers inside the fountain.

"At least the water is back! Here, take these." She hands some paper and a pen to her sister. "I was thinking we both write down a wish. Something short. We can give each other the note to hold onto, and throw a penny in like old times. We won't read it, of course. What do you say?"

"We haven't done that together in forever."

"I know."

"Okay, sure. I guess!" She grabs the materials from her sister.

"Let's sit here." Roya sits on the ground with her back against the fountain.

"On the dirt? Who are you? What did you do with my sister?"

"Oh, c'mon. You're overexaggerating." Roya theatrically pats the empty lot of dirt next to her. "This is 5-star soil, Azadeh."

"Fine. Let's do this."

A few minutes pass. They ink the paper with their words, fold them over, and hand them to each other before picking up a penny. They close their eyes. Roya breathes in heavily and releases through her mouth making the *shuuuu* noise.

Azadeh opens her eyes. "Why are you breathing like that?"

"Like what? I'm just breathing. Actually breathing. Taking it all in."

"Oh. Okay." Azadeh closes her eyes again.

They toss the pennies over their heads and open their eyes.

"So, what now? Is it all over? Do you feel better now?" Azadeh says with an inquisitive innocence.

Roya smiles as she takes the sunflower seeds out of the little bag.

She runs her fingers through each seed and places them in the ground. "Sort of. It's more like another beginning." She pats the dry dirt firmly over the seeds and smooths it over with her hands. Her eyes concentrate on the ground. Her lips stretch into an upward curve. "Azadeh, do you think it's possible to be born twice in a lifetime? As if one day you wake up to find that everything before that moment was a dream. Let's say, a practice run for the real thing? As if all your hopes and fears played before your eyes to prepare you."

"You mean, like, being given a second chance?"

"Sort of. I mean… more like being given your first real chance." Roya uses the empty bag to gather water from the fountain and pours some on top of the dirt. She waits for it to sink in and then pours some more water.

"Hmm. I'm not sure I understand what you're saying. Sounds like a bunch of hippy talk." Azadeh playfully gives her sister the *I'm totally judging you* look. "You sure you didn't smoke something while you were in Iran? I hear they can throw some crazy parties."

Roya smiles. "I can't really explain it. I have yet to understand it myself or find the words for it. But, I feel different Azadeh ––like that emptiness inside of me before I left has stretched and expanded beyond itself. Like I've been turned into a human vessel, and it's up to me to fill it. I feel more curious than ever. I want to learn. I'm hungry for growth. I want to see this world. I want to feel alive."

"What do you mean?"

"I told you. I don't know how to explain it. Honestly. I'll just have to show you."

"How?"

"By creating. By giving something back to this world and letting it move me in return. By choosing who I wish to become."

"Opraaaah, here she comes! Don't forget us when you're sitting on that couch giving your motivational speeches, okay?" Azadeh holds onto her sister's arm.

"Forget about you? Umm… you're coming with me! Front row, baby.

It's me and you for life, remember?" Roya holds her sister close. The warmth of their bodies is comforting in the crisp evening air of San Diego. She can't remember the last time they shared a moment like this. "Azadeh, thank you."

"For what?"

"Well, for many things. But, someone I recently met, someone wise told me: *'We make up our mind, and then make a road when there is nothing but gravel. Sometimes, we have to create ships with bare hands to travel the seas and climb mountains on bare feet. When we've done all that we can, we bow our heads, touch the ground, kiss the Earth, and raise our hands to the sky. Then, we trust. We trust with our entire heart. We make hope our wings and give ourselves at least the chance to soar — a chance, however small, to be what we want to be.'* Before hope became my wings, there was you. You have always been by my side, even if it were in silence."

"Is that new somebody you met that cutie Omid? I see you!" Azadeh nudges her sister.

"Yes. But, it's not like that! Not what you're thinking at least." She nudges her back.

"On a serious note, I always wanted you to feel free, Roya. I want that for you."

"I know. And now I want you to dream too, Azadeh. I want that for you. Maybe we can sit on Oprah's couch together, huh?" Roya rests her cheek on her sister's soft hair.

"Oh, God. We hug for two minutes, and now you want me everywhere." Azadeh laughs. "I need to get used to this new Roya, but I kind of like her more already."

When they return home, Mamani is resting on the *takhteh* in the backyard. Their parents sit next to each other on the patio couches. They are each reading a book, but Maman has her hand placed in Baba's. The sunset has begun to gently fade, but the sun still peeks from behind the clouds. Roya looks up and sees the moon has already come out. Its light is faint among the daylight, but they are both present and beautiful as ever.

The telephone rings. Mamani answers. A few minutes later, she hangs up. "Roya jaan." She calls out just as Roya is about to go upstairs. "That was Khanoom Jaan asking if we made it back safely. She wanted me to tell you she says hello."

"Khanoom Jaan! Miss her already. The next time you speak with her *salam beresoon* please."

"I will. One more thing. She asked me to remind you that if it doesn't rain, don't forget to water the seeds yourself. California can get too dry at times. She said you'd understand."

****

Roya opens her journal, its new pages crisp and untouched. She reaches for her favorite pen, its grip hugging her fingers. She jots down a quick note.

> *We often chase the things we are afraid to lose. We run away from the things we fear hold the greatest potential. Like the sun and moon's love affair, we find ourselves at odds. Yet, sometimes these worlds collide. When the timing is ripe, all is one. Our hopes and fears. Our joy and pain. Our mind and heart. All is right. And in such moments, we feel what it means to be whole so that we carry on —vast in heart, limitless in soul, and resilient in mind. The stars align for those who believe in the strength of a dream.*

## About the Author

Elnaz Moghangard is making her novel debut with *Roya*. As an Iranian-American woman, she sees the merging of these two identities as one of her greatest strengths. She believes storytelling is more than an art form; it is a way to bridge worlds.

She has a background in International Relations, Journalism, and Business Law from the University of Miami, as well as a Juris Doctor from George Washington Law School. She is also the Founder of Millennial Nomaad —a creative empowerment movement capturing the voice of the "wandering generation."

### Instagram:

@roya.the.novel

@millennialnomaad

### Website:

www.millennialnomaad.com

### Twitter:

@elnaz_mogh

Made in the USA
San Bernardino, CA
09 March 2020